Tell-Tale Bones

ALSO BY CAROLYN HAINES

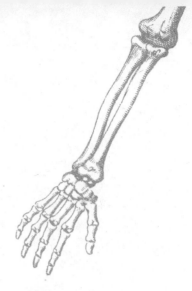

Tell-Tale Bones

A Sarah Booth Delaney Mystery

CAROLYN HAINES

MINOTAUR BOOKS
NEW YORK

First published in the United States by Minotaur Books, an imprint of St. Martin's Publishing Group

TELL-TALE BONES. Copyright © 2023 by Carolyn Haines. All rights reserved. Printed in the United States of America. For information, address St. Martin's Publishing Group, 120 Broadway, New York, NY 10271.

www.minotaurbooks.com

The Library of Congress Cataloging-in-Publication Data is available upon request.

ISBN 978-1-250-88585-2 (hardcover)
ISBN 978-1-250-88586-9 (ebook)

Our books may be purchased in bulk for promotional, educational, or business use. Please contact your local bookseller or the Macmillan Corporate and Premium Sales Department at 1-800-221-7945, extension 5442, or by email at MacmillanSpecialMarkets@macmillan.com.

First Edition: 2023

1   3   5   7   9   10   8   6   4   2

For Jennifer Haines Welch, who keeps her eye on the goal

Tell-Tale Bones

1

The January sun warms my shoulders and arms as I haul the wheelbarrow of old hay out to the compost area and dump it. The weather has been cold and rainy for most of the month, but this day is a harbinger of spring. I love nothing better than being in the barn working, unless it's riding horses with Coleman, wild and free, across the cotton fields. Today, though, is a workday. Musty old hay out—clean space for the bales of the first spring cutting.

I'm humming "Wayfaring Stranger" as I work. My mind slips away to one of my great aunts on the Baker side, Nellie Calhoun. She loved my mama more than life itself, and when my mother was killed, it took the life out of Nellie, too. She was an exemplary person and a great lover of spirituals. She'd taught me the words to "Wayfaring Stranger."

I let my mind wander the corridors of memory. There are many ghosts at Dahlia House. Mostly good, but a few ringers. I can see Nellie standing on the backdoor steps, waving me to come inside as she used to do whenever she visited. I wave back at her, just to be sociable.

"She cuts a fine figure of a woman."

The male voice so close to me it almost gives me whiplash as I whirl to see who's talking. The dark-haired gentleman is not of my reality. He wears a black frock coat, broadcloth in fabric, and a stock. His dark, fine hair is in need of a cut. Wide, expressive eyes, beneath a broad forehead, study me with keen interest. He is a handsome man possessed of elegant bearing, though he is slight in stature.

"You can see Aunt Nellie?" I ask. Not an unreasonable question.

"Those who dream by day are cognizant of many things which escape those who dream only by night."

I am no literature whiz, but I recognize the Poe quote. He was a favorite of Aunt Nellie, and she would often perform a rendition of "Annabel Lee" for me, creating a delicious ambience of horror. She loved the minor key of life and had given me the same taste for it. Mama had often teased me about singing dirges that Aunt Nellie taught me, not to mention my penchant for ghost stories. Which was a good thing since I now live with my very own haint, who is in the middle of deviling me right this red-hot minute.

"Jitty, why are you pretending to be Edgar Allan Poe?"

"Your great-aunt Nellie sure loved that man."

"So you can see her?"

"Sure. She and Uncle Lyle Crabtree are here quite often. They look out for you. Aunt Loulane, too. Though most of the time you give her the vapors by your conduct."

I open my mouth to object, but then Aunt Nellie waves again and I wave back. She's gone in a blink.

I check out Jitty's natty attire—from the frock coat and silk vest to the silk ascot. She appears as a young man, before the blue tinge of death has touched him. Romanticism almost leaks from his pores.

"Nice outfit. Can't wait to see you swelter in the summer heat." I can't help myself. Jitty brings out the brat in me.

". . . But why will you say that I am mad?" she asks, and it's a line I can't place. Yet.

"If you wear all those hot clothes in August, you'll be barking mad."

She gives a playful "ruff-ruff" and turns to walk away.

"Don't leave angry," I tell her, amazed that I've managed to get one over on her. In fact, I want her to stay. The barn is clean, the horses graze at the back end of the far field, and I'm in the mood for some company. Coleman is in Jackson at a sheriff's convention. "Hey, Jitty," I call after her, revealing how much I want her company.

She whips around and her Poe smile, though melancholy, is a joy to behold. "What conversational topics strike your fancy?"

"How about the dangers of being haunted?" Poe is probably the best writer I can ask that question. "Am I courting madness because I talk with you?"

"I don't advise talking with all spirits. Unrelenting melancholy can destroy any chance of happiness."

"Edgar, may I call you that?"

Jitty nods.

"What did you really die of?" Poe's cause of death has been hotly debated for decades. He was a young man when he died, only forty. Some thought he'd been bitten by a rabid cat or fox, poisoned, or that his fondness for drink and drugs killed him. The list of possibilities was long.

Poe smiles. "Bad company. The source of many a young man's death."

I won't argue with a writer I so greatly admire. "I wish you'd written more."

"Thank you." He performs a courtly little bow, and when he stands upright he transforms again into Jitty. The face softens and rounds; the eyes shift from nearly black to amber brown, the smile is now full and generous.

"If you're going to hang out with me, lend a hand with that manure fork," I say, motioning to her to spread the hay over the compost.

"You're full of sh—"

I stop her with a "Hush. Proper ladies don't use those words." I turn away to keep from laughing.

"No proper lady would be caught dead with you for company. Libby raised a heathen child. Aunt Loulane did her best to tame you, but she was outgunned in the stubborn department."

"How did this devolve into a criticism of my character?" I ask. Somehow Jitty always switches it around so I'm the one in the wrong.

"I'm just talented that way." Jitty smirks, spouts a line of iambic pentameter, and flashes into nothingness. I am alone, standing beside the compost with the manure fork in my hand, wondering what just happened.

My muscles moaned a little as I settled on the front porch with a Lynchburg Lemonade to close out the evening. The lovely winter weather had seduced me into work that would leave me sore for a couple of days, but a deep sense of satisfaction at my accomplishments filled me.

I recognized the big silver car that rolled slowly down my driveway. Tammy Odom, known professionally as Madame Tomeeka, drove the Lincoln land cruiser because she said it was the last luxury sedan made in America—a 2011 model. The car was old, but she was always quick to point out that though her mpg was ghastly, she wasn't behind the wheel very often.

Tammy, a high school chum from back in the day, parked at the front steps and got out. I could tell she was agitato as she came up the steps.

"What's wrong?" I asked. Tammy had the gift of second sight and a lot of other sixth-sense abilities. When she spoke, I paid attention.

"My dreams are driving me crazy, Sarah Booth. I need help."

"Sure." I didn't know what I could do about dreams, but I was willing to try. "Have a seat and I'll get you a lemonade with a little kick to it." I put words to action and hurried to the kitchen. I returned a moment later with her drink. She took it and gulped a swallow.

"Tell me the dream," I suggested.

Tammy bit her lip and frowned. "It's awful. I am sound asleep in my bed in my house, and I begin to hear this steady pounding. Thud, thud, thud. Like a ticking clock, but only not as crisp. More . . . internal." She looked down the driveway to collect herself. "I know I'm dreaming, so I wake up and I'm still hearing it. It's terrifying. It's coming from somewhere inside my home."

I could see that noises would be disconcerting, but "terrifying" sounded a little too dramatic, and Tammy was never overly dramatic. "You're hearing a thudding sound. Like someone hammering?"

She shook her head.

"Like equipment working?"

Again, she shook her head, her expression even more concerned.

"Like the wind banging a shutter?"

She caught my gaze and held it with hers. "Like the deep, steady beat of a heart. It gets louder and louder and I feel it in my chest and my bones and the bottoms of my feet when I stand up. It's the sound of a human heart beating and begging to be heard."

Pluto jumped on the porch and landed with a thud. Tammy and I both lurched forward in our chairs. I almost spilled my drink. "Dang it!" I looked at the black cat and pointed my finger. "Enough of that!"

Pluto sauntered past me to hop in Tammy's lap. Cats don't take correction well at all. Mostly, they ignore any attempt to massage their behavior.

"Leave the cat be," Tammy said. She had a soft spot for Pluto and the rest of the Dahlia House critters, including Coleman.

"What else happens in the dream?" Tammy's dreams, or visions, were multilayered and open to numerous interpretations. Almost without exception they were precognitive warnings of something to come.

"I can feel the beating under the house, and blood begins to seep up between the floorboards. It rises past my ankles, then up to my knees. The redness of it vibrates with the thud of the heartbeat. I go to the bathroom and the tub is overflowing with blood."

It was a frightening dream, I had to agree. "What does it mean, Tammy?"

"Something bad is coming."

"Can you be a little more specific?"

She drained her glass and set it on the wicker table between us. "I don't know any more than that. It scares me. Normally the dreams scare me for others, but this time . . . it just seems to be a message for me or someone I hold very dear."

"How's Dahlia doing?" I asked. Tammy named her daughter after my family home, and I loved her girl like the godmother I was.

"She's fine. Loving life on the road with her husband's band. They're playin' in Texas now but will swing back through here next month."

"She's a fine person." Tammy had been so young when her daughter was born. Too young. And the conception hadn't been voluntary, but Tammy had never considered not having her baby. As young and terrified as she'd been, she'd held on to the knowledge that she could love and support her baby without a partner. Because Tammy had love and support, she'd turned a crime into a gift, and Dahlia was her reward. I was glad to know her daughter—and precious granddaughter—would soon be on the scene. That always perked Tammy right up.

"Tammy, what do you think your dream means?" She was always better at interpretation than I was.

"I don't know. I can only tell you that I haven't often been as disturbed by a dream as I was by this one."

Jitty's words came back to me. "Those who dream by day . . ." I had to ask. "Did you dream this last night?"

"No, I took a nap late this morning and that's when I had the dream." Tammy looked a little bit unsettled.

"I may have a lead on looking into this." It was a long shot, but I knew what I had to do.

"Tell me and I'll help."

I put a hand on her shoulder. "This one is on me, Tammy. Let me do some legwork and I'll call you. I promise."

She touched the corner of my smile with a finger. "You are up to something."

"No." I denied it with a shake of my head. "I just may have some information that will explain this dream. That's all. But I want to check before I send you down the wrong path."

"You're being mighty cagey about all of this."

I was tempted to tell her my sudden inspiration, but I didn't. I'd learned, from Coleman, that verification was the calling card of the true professional. "I'll be in touch. Would you like another libation?"

"I need to finish up some chores, so I'll pass on the drink." She stood up from the rocking chair and walked to the edge of the porch. "This is such a beautiful place, Sarah Booth. After Aunt Loulane died, it was so sad. You were in New York City and no one was here to love the house. It was almost as if it was mourning, too. Now you're here and life is coming back."

"You have a fanciful imagination."

"Do I?" She smiled that secret smile that had drawn me to her when we were schoolkids. Tammy always seemed to know things.

"You do. And I revel in it. You're a special friend."

I walked beside her and put my arm around her shoulders. She was shorter, and she leaned in to me. We'd both traveled some hard roads.

"Have that baby, Sarah Booth. Before it's too late. You'll never regret it."

"In case you've forgotten, Tammy, it takes two to tango."

"You're just scared. Loving anyone is dangerous, but you've opened your heart to Coleman. And look at Tinkie. Have you ever seen her so joyful and happy?"

"No." But Tinkie was made of sterner stuff. She hadn't lost what I'd lost, and she was unafraid to put her heart on the line. She loved Maylin with every fiber of her being—the only way she knew to love her child.

"It's a gamble. I won't deny it. But think about it. And if you decide no, then you have plenty of friends who will share their grands with you. You'll never go without children in your life. I'm hoping Dahlia will move here with her family. Her husband is going to talk to Scott about some work."

Scott Hampton owned Playin' the Bones, the hottest blues joint in the Delta, and he would recognize the value of a gifted musician in town. "I hope that works out."

"I hear Scott has a steady girl now."

I was happy for him. "He deserves a good partner."

"Everyone is settling down, Sarah Booth. It's a new stage of life. An exciting one."

"Even Harold. He's still in touch with Janet Malone down on the coast. I think she may be the one. He's smitten with her and she seems to care for him, too." All of my Sunflower County friends were building extraordinary lives.

"Call me when you have some answers," Tammy said as she walked down the steps to her car. When she was driving away, she lifted a hand in farewell. I hurried inside to shower and get ready for some sleuthing.

2

Since Zinnia didn't have a bookstore, my first stop was the library. I was tempted to call Tinkie to meet me there with Maylin, but I resisted the impulse. I'd tell her all about it later. It didn't take me twenty minutes to find an anthology of Edgar Allan Poe's short stories and to open it to "The Tell-Tale Heart." I'd remembered the visceral power of reading the story in high school and the chilling effect of the beating heart. The guilt—or insanity—of the narrator. How the heart, buried beneath the floorboards, made them tremble.

It was as though Tammy had shared the dream of a murderer with a long-dead writer.

Tammy was incapable of any unkindness, especially

murder. But if my hunch was correct, then she'd dreamt a portion of Poe's chilling short story. But why? Of all the people I knew, Tammy had no reason to carry guilt, and she certainly was sane. Why was she dreaming of the beating heart of a murder victim?

And why had she chosen to tell me about it?

When I stepped out of the library, steeped and marinating in the power of Poe, I called Cece. She'd been quite the reader in high school and she had an enviable library in her house now. For someone who wrote facts, she adored fiction. She liked to walk on the dark side, too.

"What do you know about Poe's 'The Tell-Tale Heart'?" I asked when she answered. In the background I could hear Ed Oakes, editor at the *Zinnia Dispatch,* issuing orders like a field commander. It was morning deadline and I wished I'd thought to consider that before I called. Still, Cece greeted me with a droll hello.

"The short story was a masterpiece of an unreliable narrator drawing the reader into the mind of a person who is insane. The heart itself symbolizes what the narrator can never have—humanity and compassion. What else do you want to know?"

"How'd you get to be so smart?" Cece had a wide breadth of knowledge that I truly did admire. She was a terrific journalist.

"Born lucky," she said. "Books were my safe place. I could hide there from the disappointment my parents never tried to conceal from me or the contempt the other boys felt for me. Reading was always a haven and a place to learn more about who I was."

"You never disappointed me or your friends."

"Thanks, Sarah Booth. I know that. My friends made life tolerable. Only someone who has been on the outside can truly comprehend that gift of being accepted."

"We don't just accept you. We love you." It was merely the truth. "I'm heading over to Tinkie's. When your deadline is over maybe we can meet for lunch?"

"Sounds like a plan. Why're you asking about Poe?"

"Tammy had a nightmare about a beating heart. Something reminded me of the story. I wasn't a reader like you, but I loved Poe's work."

"Must have been a helluva dream to remind you of that short story. I can still hear the pounding of that heart when I think about it."

"I'll see if Tammy can meet us for lunch."

"Any excuse for Millie's cooking is a good excuse. Hey, I hear Scott Hampton has a serious girl."

"So I've heard. I'm happy for him." Scott was a great guy, but Coleman was the man for me.

"He wants to have a celebration at the Club very soon. Will you attend?"

"A pack of raving politicians couldn't keep me away."

Cece laughed. "Well put. I'll see you at noon at Millie's."

In another five minutes I was knocking at Tinkie's back door. When I opened it, she was cradling Maylin in her arms. I took the baby as soon as I was inside and held her high up in the air to make her giggle. Maylin was an extraordinary baby. She was bold and courageous and filled with joy.

"You are smitten," Tinkie diagnosed me.

"I am."

"What's up?"

She took Maylin and fed her while I told her about Tammy, the dream, and the short story.

"All fascinating, but what we really need is a case," Tinkie said. "We can sit around and analyze Tammy's dreams for the next month, but we need an assignment."

She was right about that. We'd worked through the Christmas holidays on an interesting case, but we'd been without work for more than two weeks now. It was time to be gainfully employed once again.

We packed up all the baby crapola—traveling with Maylin was almost like loading the Ringling Bros.—and headed to Millie's Café. Millie was the best cook in the Delta, hands down, and she was one of our closest friends. She'd have something to say about the hideous heartbeat. Millie was also one of the hottest columnists in the county with the Sunday column she wrote with Cece for the *Zinnia Dispatch* called "The Truth Is Out There," featuring everything from alien abductions to the ghost of Elvis. In fact, the beating heart of a murder victim was right up her alley.

Millie's Café was packed to the gills with local businessmen and farmers, drawn there by the wonderful food and social interaction. Millie found a table in the back corner that would accommodate the wagonload of people and baby accoutrements. We'd just gotten our sweet iced teas when Cece arrived. She had news—it was all over her face. "I have some hot gossip about the legal shenanigans Tope Maxwell has been up to."

Before Cece could begin, Tammy Odom joined us. She was smiling but the tinge of melancholy still clung to her. I had the honor of holding Maylin but offered her to Tammy to cheer her up—and it worked. The tension dropped from her shoulders, and she blew a kiss at me.

"I think your dream relates to an Edgar Allan Poe short story," I told her. She didn't look surprised. At all.

"I remember that story. They made a horror movie out of it way back in the '60s. I remember that hideous heartbeat." She nodded. "That must have been in the back of my mind. Thank you, Sarah Booth. You've put my thoughts to rest."

I had a sudden cold feeling that being on guard might be better than at ease. I pointed to Cece. "Tell us your news about Tope."

Cece took my iced tea and sipped, holding us in rapt attention. She had the timing of a professional raconteur.

"Spill it," Millie said to Cece as she came over. "I'm busy, so start talking. You're going to pop if you don't."

"Tope Maxwell filed papers to declare Lydia Maxwell legally dead."

"What?" Tinkie said. "She's not dead. Her body has never been found."

"Tope's got a new woman in his life and rumor is that he's wanting to marry her. Lydia's been missing a long time. I honestly thought he would have taken this action sooner."

"Lydia Redd, correct?" I asked. She hadn't been in our class—she'd been a few years older, so I didn't have solid memories of her, only that she was an extremely wealthy woman who'd become something of an activist during her college years. Tope Maxwell had been the quarterback standout at Ole Miss while he was in college. The two had seemed the perfect match, but after marriage, instead of leading the Daddy's Girl calendar of events, Lydia had virtually disappeared from the Delta scene. She and Tope would attend the de rigueur events, like holiday fetes, but after the first months of marriage, they stopped hosting parties and then Lydia stopped going out altogether. The change had been gradual and without controversy, and because I wasn't part of that world, I'd barely noticed—until Tinkie pointed it out.

"Tope is seen in town all the time; running his high-end real estate development business," Tinkie noted. "He's at the Club in the evenings a lot. Oscar has commented on it. Lydia was never with him, and then suddenly she was gone. That was years ago."

Tope's real estate reach extended from Memphis down to the Gulf Coast, and it was rumored that he had part interest in several of the most popular casinos on the Mississippi coast. "I just assumed she was at the beach or some other property until her mother filed that missing persons report several years ago," I said.

"Why didn't Tope file the report?" Millie asked.

"There were rumors," Cece said. "Abuse. Common talk was that Tope had a violent temper and didn't hold back when it came to his wife."

"I can't believe that Elisa Redd would tolerate any mistreatment of her daughter," Tammy said. "Ms. Elisa is a client of mine sometimes. She likes to have a tarot reading, get a little psychic work done. She never asks about Lydia, but she always asks if there's a message from the other side. One time I asked her who she hoped to hear from and she only said, 'No one. I hope not to hear from anyone.' It was so strange."

"Elisa hired a Memphis private investigator to dig into Tope, but from the gossip I heard, the PI didn't turn up anything," Cece said. "The Maxwell family hushed it right up. You know they're all lawyers. Even Tope. He just doesn't practice law because he's in real estate."

Tinkie nodded. "I heard there was a fight in a downtown restaurant, in the ladies' room. Lydia came out with a bloody nose and a black eye—after Tope went to the bathroom, too—but Lydia refused to even talk to the police. She said nothing had happened. That she had tripped and fallen into the edge of the stall door. Elisa couldn't find the evidence she needed without Lydia supporting her, so the police chief had no option but to ignore the bruises. Tope wasn't charged or even investigated." Tinkie had more facts than I knew.

"I can't imagine a mother having to endure that." To me, a black eye and bloody nose equaled the need for a beating with a cast-iron skillet if the man ever fell asleep near me.

"Broken bones, bruises. She had to have 'sinus surgery.' Or that was the official story. I always assumed he'd broken bones in her face that required a plastic surgeon. She went to New Orleans to have it done. Shortly after that, she was just gone." Cece looked grim. "They weren't married even a year. He was a brute."

"Elisa is her only close relative? No brothers?" I asked. I knew Dalton Redd, her father, had died when Lydia was a child. "No able-bodied relatives to beat the tar out of him?" Sometimes justice didn't come from a judge. A man who abused women deserved whatever he got.

"She is an only child. Or was," Cece confirmed. "When I first started on the society page, I dealt with her a little for the newspaper. She was super nice. Not like some of the high-society dames."

"What was her friend's name? The one she was always seen with?" Millie asked. "They would come in the café, whispering and plotting about politics. Access to birth control, equal education, financial rights for women."

"She was Bethany Carter," Tinkie supplied. "She was a powerhouse. I remember hearing some of her speeches about the rights of women when I was in college. She had a martial arts studio in Jackson for a while, teaching self-defense. She was passionate. I always admired her."

During my time in New York City, I'd missed a lot of local happenings. Thank goodness for my friends, who could catch me up. "Where is Bethany?"

Tinkie nodded. "She disappeared the same time Lydia did. She told everyone she was going to Afghanistan to help the women there. Then she was just gone."

"Did anyone report her missing?" I asked.

"Even when she was thick with Lydia, she never attended any of the Delta social events. She made it pretty clear she thought they were classist and an affront to women."

"She could be abrasive," Millie said. "But she was really Lydia's only good friend."

"Lifestyles of the rich and famous. I think it would be hard to know who is truly a friend when you have a lot of money." Maylin started to fuss and I reached over and jiggled her plump little leg. "Now this princess will never doubt how much her mama's friends love her."

"Gossip time is over, let's have your orders," Millie said, pad at the ready.

3

Stuffed to the gills, Tinkie and I took Maylin for a stroll in the beautiful park that Harold Erkwell had provided for area residents. The day was incredible, and we took full advantage. Tinkie sat in a swing holding Maylin and I pushed them. There would still be bitter cold days to come, possibly even snow, but today screamed, "Spring is coming!"

"I wish I'd brought Sweetie Pie and Pluto," I said. "How's Chablis taking the new baby?"

Tinkie bit her bottom lip. "To be honest, it's been hard on her. Oscar and I both make an effort to include her in everything, but Maylin has a lot of needs. I'm afraid Chablis sometimes feels left out."

"I'll call DeWayne and see if he has time to pick up the

dogs and bring them to the sheriff's office. We can get them from there and I'll walk them while you push the stroller."

"Do it!" Tinkie said, grinning. "I should have thought of it, but I still have pregnancy brain fog. Tammy assures me it will pass, but it is taking forever."

Tinkie was sharp as a tack, whether she knew it or not. I made the call to DeWayne Dattilo, Coleman's right-hand man, and we ambled toward the courthouse. The pedestal where the Johnny Reb statue had stood for decades was still bare, and I wondered what the city officials intended to put there, if anything. Honoring the past was all well and good, but when a symbol became too painful, what was the point? Historical perspective had given the Confederate statuary an unhealthy tarnish. Best to move it all to a place where it could be put into educational context and find common ground so all citizens could appreciate the artistry of public statuary. Figures of treason didn't deserve to be displayed before public buildings.

"Maybe they'll put up a statue of Eudora Welty or William Faulkner," I said.

"What about Beth Henley?" Tinkie said. "She was born in Jackson, and she really captured Mississippi in her plays. Faulkner and Welty have a lot of honors."

"Yes! *Crimes of the Heart* is one whale of a play." Black comedy was my favorite, and the conversation brought me back to Poe. "I'm still troubled about Madame's dream."

"Yeah, it's . . . macabre. Have you connected it to anything?"

"No, and, to be honest, I'm not eager to make a connection. It's been heaven not to work all the time." Even as I talked, I realized I wasn't being totally honest. It didn't matter that I hadn't been hired for a case, I was still caught up in Tammy's dream. And the short story involved a murder. The murder of a man with a blue eye—a vulture's eye, as Poe called it. I couldn't get those images out of my head.

Tinkie bent down to put the pacifier in Maylin's mouth. "Do you think DeWayne has the dogs inside the sheriff's office yet?"

"Let's check." I was always eager to see Coleman, so I helped pick up the baby stroller to navigate the steps and led Tinkie inside the lovely old building. There had been talk of building a county complex on the highway leading out of town, but so far the Save Zinnia Committee had held that off. The courthouse was not modern, but there was such character in it.

We arrived at the sheriff's office to find Sweetie Pie already asleep under Coleman's desk. Chablis was pacing up and down the counter. Tinkie scooped her into her arms and gave her a big smooch. "Thank you, DeWayne."

Sweetie gave her famous yodel of greeting and came to sniff my pants legs, no doubt picking up the delicious odors of Millie's Café. She put her famous sad hound-dog look on me. Her mournful eyes spoke clearly of her disappointment that I hadn't brought her a treat from Millie's. She could smell my crime all over me. She gave a weak and desperate-sounding huff. Tail between her legs, she went back to Coleman's desk and collapsed.

"Now I feel like a heel," I said. DeWayne and Coleman were laughing.

"That dog knows how to work you," DeWayne said. "I stopped by the chicken place and got both of them a couple of fried tenders. They aren't hungry, but they're sure good at acting. I think you could get them a job in Hollywood."

He spoke the truth, and I gave Sweetie Pie a baleful look to let her know I was onto her. She stood up, circled a few times, and collapsed again, this time with her back to me.

I picked up the leashes and the jangle of the clips had Sweetie on her feet, tail wagging, ready for a walk. Chablis, too. "We'll be over at the park," I told Coleman.

As I stepped toward the door, it flew open, and none other than Elisa Redd swept into the room. Almost as suddenly, she started in on Coleman and DeWayne. "You must reopen the missing persons case of my daughter, Lydia. And her friend, Bethany Carter. That abuser Tope Maxwell is trying to get Lydia declared dead so he can take her inheritance." Elisa was a beautiful woman, even in her mature years, but today her face was pale, her voice trembling.

Coleman came to the counter and nodded. "Elisa, have you heard anything from Lydia recently?"

She swallowed, her eyes misting before she blinked the tears away. "I have not, but that doesn't mean she's dead. She fled an abusive marriage. She hasn't resurfaced because she's afraid of Tope and the entire Maxwell family."

Coleman's voice was gentle. "I'm happy to help you, but your daughter has been gone for what, over six years? The last time she was seen she was reportedly leaving for Afghanistan with her friend. Both of them dropped out of sight."

"Out of sight, yes, but not dead. No bodies have ever been found. No death certification." She was adamant.

"I'll do everything I can, Elisa, but it's within Tope's right to ask for this. When I was first elected, I did run some queries. Neither woman has filed tax returns, insurance has lapsed, there's no record of their existence."

"What if they're in Afghanistan living the life they want?

You know Tope beat Lydia. Everyone knows it but I was a coward and didn't pursue charges against him. I was afraid he would kill her if I took any action. She was afraid he'd kill me if I stirred up trouble. You know that's true. I should have hired a hit man and had him put in the ground."

Coleman ignored her obvious frustration and the threat it spawned. "I do know how much this hurts you, Elisa. And I tried to help Lydia. She refused to press charges with the police chief. She denied the abuse when she was questioned. I warned her that Tope would escalate, because that's what the statistics show, but she wouldn't help me help her."

"You're right, but we can't give up. You sound like you believe it's all her fault!" Her face was white with anger.

"I didn't say that. I'm only telling you how the law works. I think Tope is a mean bastard who hurt your daughter. But Lydia wouldn't do the necessary things to bring the law into the picture. She always lied in his defense. At the hospital, in the police department, here. Whenever she was interviewed by city or county officers, she always said that she fell, or had a bicycle wreck, or tripped. The law's hands were tied."

Elisa took a deep breath and leaned against the counter. "I know you're right, but it galls me. If Lydia is dead, he killed her. Now he's going to take her birthright. Lydia is hardheaded. I told her to make a prenup. I begged her to leave Tope. I offered to give her money to run away. I didn't care for myself, I only wanted her safe. I just couldn't make her do it. Neither could you. It isn't your fault."

She lowered her head a moment to compose herself and I saw the pain on Coleman's face. For all of his physical toughness, he had a truly tender heart.

"Can you reopen her missing persons case?" Elisa asked, unable to meet Coleman's gaze.

"Do you have anything new?" he asked her.

"Like someone has seen her?" Elisa asked.

"Something like that. Or new evidence. Or anything that would give me a reason."

"The only definite thing I have is Tope turning in the paperwork to the court to ask that she be declared legally dead. I knew he'd do it one day. I just didn't know when."

"Have you had any indication she's alive?" Coleman asked gently.

Elisa shook her head. "I can't lie. I don't have any concrete proof, but I got a hit on the tip line I have on the internet. Last week a caller said he'd seen her, and he has photographic proof. So far, the tipster won't identify themselves."

Tinkie, the dogs, and I had tried to make ourselves tiny in a corner of the room, but Coleman's gaze fell on us. "Have you ever hired a private investigator to look for her?" he asked Elisa.

"When she first disappeared. I hired a man out of Memphis. He tracked her to the Memphis airport with Bethany. They both had tickets for Afghanistan. That was a special interest of Bethany's, to try to teach the Afghan women about their human rights, to provide a basic education. She was very passionate about it. After that the trail went cold."

I couldn't imagine the horror of waiting and watching for six years, afraid my loved one was in a country ripped apart by turmoil. If Lydia and Bethany had gone to Afghanistan and acted against the Taliban's laws, they might very well be dead. I kept my lips zipped, though. No one needed to hear my morose conjectures.

"Do you think they actually went to Afghanistan?" Coleman didn't have to say that he thought such an action was dubious and dangerous. This was old ground for us. Coleman hated rash actions taken by anyone because he generally ended up cleaning up the resulting mess.

"I don't know." Elisa's voice was threaded with stress. "When they first disappeared, I thought no. That they'd concocted a cover story to get Lydia away from Tope. But now . . . It's been such a long time. Surely if she was around here, she'd give me a sign."

"Would Lydia be prepared to take on such a challenge?" I asked. "Did she want to teach?"

"I don't know." Elisa's voice cracked. "She wanted to make a difference in the world. She and Bethany both. But why didn't they find a way to let me know?"

I had no answers for Elisa.

Coleman put a hand on her shoulder. "Elisa, do you know Sarah Booth Delaney and Tinkie Richmond?" He drew us into the conversation. I wasn't sure if I was glad or not.

"The private investigators." She nodded. "Synchronicity at work, don't you think, Sheriff?"

"Maybe, but they may have some ideas for you. I can re-open Lydia's case if I have even the smallest reason to do so. Maybe they could help you find something, like the tipster who called your line."

Elisa stepped toward us. "Of course I know Mrs. Richmond, and Sarah Booth's mother and father were always helping people." She stared directly into my eyes. "Would you consider helping me?"

Tinkie put a hand on my lower arm. "Let us discuss it, Mrs. Redd. I've just had a baby, and we've worked steadily for the past two years. We were looking forward to a break." Tinkie was giving us the cover space we needed to talk it over.

"Certainly." She pulled a card from her pocketbook. "Call me when you've decided. I do feel that it was destiny that brought us together. You may be the only people who can help me bring my daughter home. Alive."

It was a mighty high mountain she'd shoved in front of us, but I didn't say a thing. Elisa thanked the sheriff and left.

"I hope you're okay with that," Coleman said. "I can't burn more resources looking for a woman who hasn't been seen in the county in years and who was last known to be headed into a war-torn country."

"Coleman, I'm not certain we can help her," I admitted. "This case sounds like it needs someone with official clout. No one in Afghanistan will take a call from me or Tinkie." I was pointing out the obvious. "I don't want to get her hopes up and lead her on."

"I can help with information in that regard. In fact, I'll get with some friends who know their way around the federal and international bureaucracy and get the ball rolling. If we can even get validation that they flew to Afghanistan, that's a place to start."

I looked at Tinkie. "What's your take?"

"If anything happened to Maylin, I'd do everything in my power to bring her home. I say we take the case but tell her we are uncertain of how effective we can be. We can't go overseas to look. We'll have to rely on records and law enforcement."

I was still uncertain, but my emotions had been engaged by Lydia's awful situation and Elisa's grief. The least we could do was try. "We won't take any money until we have some results," I said. "I don't think this is smart, but it may be the right thing to do. Besides, we don't have another case, so we aren't really losing out on anything."

"It's settled, then." Tinkie smiled. Maylin, who'd been snoozing in the warm office, awakened and cooed at me.

"I'm taking that as a sign," I told Tinkie. "Let's head to the park for a stroll with the dogs, and you call Elisa and tell her we'll try to find Lydia."

4

Because we had all of Maylin's many necessities already in the car, after our walk we drove right to Dahlia House to work. Tinkie did her thing on the computer while I made some calls to airlines and some government agencies to see what I could find on either woman. My quest resulted in nothing useful. Tinkie had better success.

"Both women were issued passports seven years ago," Tinkie said. "They're still valid."

"How did you find that?" I asked.

She held up her hands and wiggled her fingers. "Magic digits."

"Really." I wasn't amused.

"Harold has a friend in the agency that issues passports. He asked for me. But he couldn't get anything else. That was it. He didn't know where or if the passports had been used. Neither Lydia nor Bethany has an active bank account in Sunflower County. Bethany never had one, but Lydia did and it was closed over six years ago, right after she disappeared. I'm presuming Tope closed it and took all the cash."

Tinkie had Tope pegged for the skunk I also viewed him as. "I'll put on a pot of coffee." It was going to be a long afternoon of tedious record searching.

"Can you check the overseas flight records?" Tinkie asked.

"I can't but maybe Coleman can. He did offer to help since he threw this case in our laps." Once the water was heating for coffee, I called Coleman and told him what we needed.

"I'll do what I can," he said. "I told you I would. I'm glad someone is trying to help Elisa. She looked pretty worn down."

"She did." I couldn't imagine living the last six years without knowing if my child was dead or alive. "The worry and grief must be horrific."

"I don't have a good feeling about this case," Coleman said. "I'm going to pay a visit to Tope Maxwell and see if I can find the reason he's filing for a declaration of death at this particular time."

"He has a new girlfriend. Rumor is he wants to marry," I said. "State law says seven years. We're almost at the time period."

"Good enough. I want him to say it. I'll let you know how it goes."

We hung up and I reported in with Tinkie, who'd unearthed Lydia's reputed wealth.

"She's a millionaire. Land holdings. Stock investments," Tinkie said. "No will was ever filed in her case. If she left one, Tope hasn't told anyone. Also, Tope had access to their joint accounts, which he has cleaned out. Without a will, once she is declared dead, Tope will get everything."

A husband inheriting was normal, but we both disliked Tope so it sounded sinister to us. "Elisa can't stop him? They weren't even married a year before she disappeared. And he abused Lydia."

Tinkie shook her head. "If there really wasn't a will and there are no children, then all of the assets will go to Tope. There's no legal complaint of abuse. No indication of foul play. Tope comes out the winner."

"Her mom gets nothing? I mean, it was her money to begin with."

"That's not how the law works. But I can't imagine that Lydia didn't have a will. She's an heiress. Surely Elisa would have made sure she had one."

"You would think." Which led me down another long train of thought with unflattering views of Tope. "Do you think he destroyed Lydia's will?"

"Yes." Tinkie didn't hesitate. "I think that's exactly what he's done. It probably took him six years to find it, which is why he's waited until now."

That was a distinct possibility. Tope was a snake, and that was insulting to slithering reptiles. "Can we throw up any roadblocks to slow this down?"

"I'll check. Oscar knows some pretty smart estate lawyers who might have some suggestions, but it will only slow this, not stop it. Remember, Tope has a law degree and a family law practice to fall back on."

"A little time is better than nothing. We'll get busy."

"Ten-four. Now I'm taking Chablis and Maylin home. Pauline will be glad to see this little bundle of joy and she can put her down for a nap. Then I'll be ready to sleuth."

In the two months since Pauline moved in to be Maylin's nanny, she'd become a vital part of the household.

Coleman stopped by Dahlia House shortly after he finished talking to Tope, who he found on the golf course at the Club. Coleman's face was set in grim lines when he came into my office and sat on the corner of the desk. "Tope is a piece of work," he said. "When I asked him about the injuries Lydia sustained when she was with him, he said she was ungainly and clumsy. That she was always hurting herself. And then he laughed, saying that all of the dance lessons Elisa had paid for were worthless."

Steam was almost coming out of Coleman's ears. "Remember what you told Elisa," I said. "There was nothing you could have done. You weren't even sheriff then. And even if you were, until Lydia was ready to file charges, your hands were tied." He knew that, but sometimes it helped to hear it.

"Tope's best days are behind him. He's squandered his inheritance from the Maxwell family, and they had plenty. Now he's after the Redd fortune. If he gets his hands on Lydia's money, it'll be gone in under ten years."

"I'm sure you're right about that. But unless we can prove Lydia is alive, there's not much we can do. If she is alive, she should have known this would happen eventually. If she's dead . . ." I shrugged. "We can't change the laws."

"Tope is still handsome, but he was a god in high school. He's buried a lot of good farmland under concrete with his developments, and he hasn't really contributed anything to society. He golfs and drinks and counts his money. Judging from his red face, he's a heart attack waiting to happen."

"I remember him. He was the big quarterback on the football team when I was in middle school. Popular, handsome, charming, worthless, and cruel." I had a yearbook open on the desk in front of me. I'd backtracked Tope to his glory days. He hadn't been a nice kid in school, and he wasn't a nice man now. Why had Lydia ever married him?

"I went to Tope's house before I found him at the Club. His new girlfriend was upstairs and wouldn't come down to talk. The maid said she had a migraine, and I had no way to force her to talk to me. Maybe you and Tinkie could stop by and put your eyes on her. I'm a little worried. Tope was brutal to Lydia. He'll be the same or worse with this young woman, who doesn't bring a dowry with her. He knows more about Lydia's disappearance than he's letting on. Maybe this new potential wife will let something slip."

"Will do." I wanted to talk to the big man himself. And I wanted a gander at his new girl. If he was already brutalizing her, she might need my help. I called Tinkie and told her I would pick her up.

On the way to get Tinkie, I reviewed what I knew about Tope and his development deals. The modern home he'd built "for Lydia" was set on two hundred of the Redd family acres. There was a cross-country jumping course for equestrian events, tennis courts, an Olympic-size pool, and plenty of luxury. It killed me to think that if Lydia was dead he'd take over the land. Money could be replaced. Land couldn't. The Redd family were fifth-generation Mississippi farmers. It was bitter irony that Lydia married a developer, a man with no regard for the land and what the rich, alluvial soil could produce. Tope was happy to see it popping up subdivisions, roads, and other modern horrors. I'd seen his handiwork on some of the county areas that had once boasted forests and natural water sources. They'd been brutally bulldozed and copycat houses had been built side by side. My aunt Loulane had loathed that practice. "You can't spit out the window without hitting your neighbor," was the way she'd described it.

The new homeowners were stranded in the middle of a brutally hot field with no trees for shade and lawns that turned into marshes after every rain. There was nothing quite like the "gumbo" soil in a cotton field when it rained.

I grew madder and madder as I drove to pick up Tinkie. When she was in the car, she put a hand on mine, which was gripping the steering wheel. "I feel the same way, but we can't show it if we hope to get anything out of Tope or his girlfriend. By the way, her name is Vivian Dantzler. Cece looked it up for me. You know she has her finger on the pulse of Delta society."

She was right. I relaxed my shoulders and hands and inhaled. "I don't like it."

"When this is all said and done, maybe we can just beat him half to death."

"Why only half?" I asked.

"We can save half of him until Easter is over. I can give up wine for Lent if I think I'm going to have Tope to beat on."

Tinkie wasn't politically correct, but she sure made me laugh.

We examined the house before we got out of the Roadster.

It was three stories, with Juliet balconies at the front windows on every floor. A widow's walk topped it. The house was symmetrical and balanced. It followed a traditional design, but the building materials had baffled some of the locals. Giant cement blocks centered with rebar and filled with more cement. Tope had boasted that it could withstand hurricane- or tornado-strength winds. There was something formidable about the house, I had to agree. It would be standing long after I was gone. I could only hope someone nicer than Tope would live there.

"Do you think Lydia is alive?" Tinkie asked.

I thought again of Tammy's dream. "I don't know. I am inclined to think not."

"Why?"

"Once she escaped Tope's clutches she could have filed for divorce in any state at any time. I think she would have done that if she'd been alive."

"Good point." Tinkie opened the door and got out. In a moment we were walking to the front door.

Tope was still on the golf course but it was the girlfriend, Vivian, who we most wanted to meet, as Coleman had requested. I wanted a conversation with Tope, but it could wait, and we calculated that Vivian would be more forthcoming alone.

We knocked at the door. Five minutes passed with no response. We rang the doorbell several times. Still, no answer. Determined, we walked around to the back. We found a slender young woman in a large garden hat working in a flower bed, planting bulbs.

"Ms. Dantzler?" Tinkie said.

The young woman stifled a gasp and stood up. She wore jeans and a long-sleeved knit top that revealed her figure.

Huge sunglasses hid her eyes. "Who are you? What do you want?"

"We're looking for Vivian Dantzler," I said. "We rang the bell, but no one answered."

"What do you want?" She backed up a few steps, obviously in flight mode. I thought of a deer, poised to jump and run at the first hint of danger. No matter how rich or handsome Tope might be, I didn't want the life Vivian was leading.

"We aren't going to hurt you," Tinkie said soothingly. "Honest, we're trying to find some leads on Tope's wife, Lydia. Her mother has hired us to find her. If we find out she's dead, it will only help Tope to resolve his marriage issues and the estate."

"She's not here and hasn't been in years." Vivian dropped the trowel she held and her hands were shaking. "Please leave. I can't tell you anything. I only met Tope about six months back. I never met his ex-wife, and I don't know anything about her. Everyone says she's dead."

"Technically, a body hasn't been found, so he's still married to her," I said casually. "He is moving to declare her legally dead, I think so he can marry you." She wasn't wearing gardening gloves and I pointed to the big diamond on her finger. "Looks like he's serious."

"It's true. Tope did ask me to marry him. The declaration of death is just a legal formality, he said. He said Lydia has been dead a long time. I'm not poaching another woman's husband and I'm not a home-wrecker. Tope will be free of his marriage. It's just a technicality."

Vivian was young. Probably mid-twenties. And she was naïve—a deadly combination with a man like Tope Maxwell. I took it all in—the house, the grounds, the ring—it was like a fairy tale come to life. I'm sure Lydia had felt the same way, initially. I had a strong urge to warn Vivian of what she was getting into, but I held my tongue. She wouldn't believe me, and if I was lucky, I'd soon have the evidence that Tope was an abuser to show her.

"A word of advice," Tinkie said. "You might want to ask around town about Tope. He has something of a . . . reputation."

"What are you implying?" Vivian clenched her fists at her sides. She was in deep. She really loved the guy.

"That you need to be careful," Tinkie said calmly. "Things aren't always what they seem to be on the surface." She looked at me and shrugged. "I had to give her a heads-up."

I didn't disagree. I just knew Vivian was now even more devoted to defending Tope. She was in thrall to him and nothing short of a near-death experience would wake her up.

"You need to leave before I have to call for help. My husband has men who work here to keep me safe. That wouldn't end well for you."

It was good to know that there was some security at the mansion. It might factor into our future plans. "Thanks for talking with us. I don't suppose you'd let us look around Lydia's old room?"

"You must be nuts. If I let you inside, Tope would . . ."

"I understand," I said. She stopped herself. Had she been about to say that he'd likely beat her?

Tinkie suddenly stepped forward and extended her hand. "It was a pleasure to meet you."

Vivian grasped her hand and Tinkie lifted her other hand and pulled Vivian's sunglasses off, revealing a blue, purple, and green shiner. Instead of getting angry. Vivian covered her eye with her hand and jerked backward. "I slipped in the shower and hit a towel rack."

"Cold compresses will help," Tinkie said. She was distressed and angry. "Look, Vivian, you don't have to put up with that."

Vivian stiffened. "Mind your own business and get off this property."

Tinkie started to balk, but I touched her arm. "We should leave."

She followed me but turned around. "Vivian, Tope is dangerous. If Lydia is dead, it's probably because he killed her. You don't have to live this way."

Tears trickled down Vivian's cheeks but she dashed them away and picked up her sunglasses. She knelt and resumed her gardening. My heart weighed heavy as we left. We hadn't helped her.

5

We swung by Dahlia House to pick up Sweetie Pie and Pluto and then I drove to Hilltop. We could work at Tinkie's house as easily as mine and we'd be in close proximity to Maylin. That little girl was becoming the focus of my day. Tinkie and Oscar lived by her whim, and it was a beautiful thing to watch. To see my society friends dealing with diapers, drool, and baby tantrums was unbelievable. Maylin had bent them to her will in record time.

When we arrived at Tinkie's home, Chablis was delighted to see her furry friends and they took off into the backyard to explore. Tinkie's cat, Gumbo, joined in. We went to the office Oscar had set up for us and I held Maylin while she looked out the window, gurgling at the critters' antics in the warm January sunshine. It was a day filled with simple joys.

"I found a great photo of Lydia on the internet. Bethany, too." Tinkie handed me some pages she'd printed and I stared at the lovely young woman with striking amber eyes.

"She's a beauty." I looked at the other page. Bethany Carter stared directly at me. She was a handsome woman. Strong features. Even in a photograph she exuded strength. She was a woman who knew her own value and didn't suffer fools. "Bethany is a friend I'd want."

Tinkie tapped away on her computer. "Listen to this. Bethany was expelled from Ole Miss for protesting a speaker on campus."

"What? Why would they expel her for protesting?" That sounded a little harsh to me.

"The speaker was a prominent political figure with some very misogynistic views. She and her group pelted him with rotten tomatoes."

I had to laugh. "Isn't tomato tossing a form of free speech?"

"Apparently not." Tinkie was also amused. "There's a bit of info on Bethany in this article. She opened a martial arts studio and taught classes to college coeds for free. She's founded soup kitchens, held fundraisers for animals, heckled numerous political speakers pointing out the plight of children waiting for adoption or even foster care. Goodness, she's videotaped mistreatment at nursing homes. Bethany has never met a cause she didn't take to."

I liked her instantly. She didn't just talk the talk, she took action. As far as I was concerned, the world needed a lot more people like Bethany.

"Does it say anything about her friendship with Lydia?"

"Not in this article, but I found a news story where Lydia funded a weeklong seminar on the divine feminine at the

Shack Up Inn. I kind of love the juxtaposition of place and topic." Tinkie grinned big.

"Lydia paid for it?"

"Yeah. She rented the place so attendees could stay for free. The teachers were also paid by Lydia so it was all free for the women who attended. They had classes on all kinds of issues. I would have loved to have attended," Tinkie said.

The Shack Up Inn was located outside of Clarksdale and consisted of cabins that were outfitted for vacation accommodations. It was an unusual place to vacation and there was always live music and something happening. Often the Shack Up Inn featured famous blues performers who taught seminars, classes, and gave fabulous performances.

"Me, too. To be honest, I really wasn't aware of Bethany." I'd been in New York for a lot of that time, and prior to that I'd had my eyes set firmly on Broadway. My entire world was composed of plays and movies, my theater friends, learning to act onstage and in front of a camera. I had dared to dream big, though it hadn't worked out for me. "I feel like I missed someone important to Mississippi."

"She was a voice for women's rights at a time when a lot of women wouldn't speak out. And she was fearless. I guess that's the thing I remember," Tinkie said. "Women, and Southern women in particular, are raised to make everyone else comfortable. From what I know about Bethany, she didn't buy into that for a hot minute. What I don't understand is that if Bethany knew Tope was abusing Lydia, why didn't she take action? My understanding of her is that Bethany would have beat the stew out of Tope."

"Interfering in another person's marriage is dangerous for all involved." I didn't have personal experience, but I'd heard plenty of stories at my kitchen table when my mother was alive. People came to her for help, and they told of their hardships. I'd sneak under the table and stay very still, eavesdropping. I learned a lot of hard truths there. Plenty of times a brutal man was at the root of a woman's troubles. My mother offered advice, resources, engineered a getaway, and helped with pets and children. But she didn't step into another's marriage. "'For any change to stick, the woman has to take those steps,'" Mama had always said. "'I'll help all I can, but I can't take them for her.'"

I cleared my throat. "Remember that it was Bethany who talked Lydia into going to Afghanistan."

"Do we know that's even true?" Tinkie asked. "Did they really go?"

"I hope Coleman can find that out."

"And Elisa said someone had claimed to see Lydia in the flesh. We need to check that out, too. In fact, that probably should be our priority. Proving she's alive will solve all the inheritance issues."

As usual, Tinkie was right. "Call Elisa and put her on speaker," I suggested.

Tinkie dialed the number and we sat across from each other, waiting for Elisa to answer. "I hate that Elisa is going through this all alone," I said.

"It's tough." Tinkie held up a hand as Elisa answered. Tinkie let her know she was on speaker and told her what we needed.

"We're ready to get busy," I told her. "We've talked to Vivian, the new girlfriend. She's sporting a black eye."

"Tope is up to his old tricks," Elisa said. "I'm not surprised. One of my friends said her daughter dated Tope a few times until he grabbed her too rough. She took a job in Los Angeles to put him in her rearview."

"If Lydia is alive, we'll do our best to find her. What was the evidence that came in on your tip line? Who called, the number, tell us everything."

Ten minutes later we had heard the message Elisa had been smart enough to save, and we had the number that showed up for the caller. It was a Mississippi number, so at least we had some help in tracking the person down. Budgie, Coleman's deputy, was excellent at those things.

"We'll let you know if we find anything," I told her. "Did you ever call the tipster back?"

"I tried, but he never answered," she said. "I left messages saying I had the reward money ready to give him."

"Reward?" I asked.

"Yes, ten grand for information leading to Lydia's return."

She was assuming Lydia would return and that a caller wanting reward money would be honest about what he'd seen. My hopes fell.

"I know tipsters aren't reliable," she said, "but there's as good a chance he's being honest as there is that he's trying to scam me."

I wouldn't argue with that because she needed to hold on to hope. "We'll check it out. If he can be found, we'll have a face-to-face with him."

"Thank you. I know this is a cold case and there's not a lot of reason to expect a miracle, but for some reason I trust you two."

"We'll do our best," Tinkie promised.

An hour later, I'd wrangled Budgie into checking the number for us. Tinkie and I both called and we each left a message. Tinkie mentioned the ten-grand reward and how much we'd like to pay it, but I played it a little tougher, saying I was an insurance investigator. Neither of our efforts netted a response. When we were about to give up, Budgie called. "I tracked the number from the tipster. It's a Greenwood, Mississippi, landline. Who has a landline these days?"

"Who uses it to call tip lines?" Tinkie followed up.

"I'm driving," I said. "What's the address, Budgie?"

He texted it to me so I could put it in the GPS and Tinkie called Elisa to get photos of Lydia and Bethany sent to her. I could take the phone to a printshop and get some posters made to put up in Greenwood. It was days like today that I missed the national printshop chain, Kinko's. In high school I'd had a flirtation with the very handsome Rick Ralston, who'd worked there. I'd finally learned to use all of their machines when the company disappeared.

Tink's phone pinged and she showed me the photos. Lydia was a beautiful woman. Every photo flattered her. Her smile was radiant, and the fun in her eyes was compelling. We flipped through the photos to one of Lydia in her wedding gown. She did look like a princess about to step into her happily ever after. Only we knew how that had ended.

There were only three photos of Bethany. In one she wore a martial arts suit with a black belt. In another she was in jeans and a halter top, sitting on the tailgate of a truck, and in the last she was with Lydia, their arms linked together, laughing. It was the happiest photo of Lydia. Whatever had happened to the missing heiress, I didn't think Bethany had played a role in it. My best guess was that Bethany shared Lydia's fate, whatever it was. But we had photos that would reprint just fine to make our posters.

The address for the tipster that Budgie sent was in one of the older residential areas in Greenwood. It was a bit over an hour's drive, but we got there with plenty of daylight.

The tree-lined street was quiet, the yards well maintained. It reminded me of Zinnia, where I'd ridden my bicycle around town, fearless of any danger, welcome wherever I stopped.

One of my closest college friends, also studying theater, had hailed from Greenwood. She'd opted for Hollywood, where she had steady work on comedies and dramas. I was thinking of Pattie as I let the GPS direct me to a two-story white home on a spacious lawn.

"This is weird," Tinkie said. "Why would someone living here call a tip line?"

"Good Samaritan?"

She looked at me over her sunglasses. "Right. Because there are so many of those."

We went to the front door and knocked. A stylish woman in her sixties opened the door. "May I help you?"

We made the introductions and showed her the photos.

"Why would I know these women?" she asked.

"Someone here called a tip line saying they'd recently seen one of them. They've been missing for a long time. People are eager to find them."

She shook her head. "I didn't call anyone. I wish I could help, but I have no idea what you're talking about." She inhaled dramatically. "Except that maybe I do. It's Gavin, perhaps."

"Gavin?" Tinkie asked. "Who is he?"

"Gavin Jerome, the young man who rents the apartment above the garage. He's a nice guy. A little . . . different."

"Is he home?" I asked.

"Check for yourself." She pointed at a walkway that led around the house to an apartment over a four-car garage.

6

Tinkie climbed the stairs and knocked. In a moment a middle-aged man came to the door. He explained to Tinkie that Gavin wasn't in but that the telephone number from the tip line was indeed the landline to the apartment. He refused to tell us where Gavin was or when he'd be back, and we had no legal authority to make him talk. He also denied having made any calls but said he'd have Gavin get back with us. I doubted that would happen but at least we knew where to find the would-be reward collector. We also made it clear that Mrs. Redd was happy and eager to pay for any tips that panned out.

We drove to downtown Greenwood, once the cotton capital of the South back in the day. It was a small city with a lot of money and a lot of poverty, like most of the Delta.

I loved the brick roads and the old bridges that spanned the rivers that were so important to the shipment of cotton. The Yazoo, which was formed where the Tallahatchie and Yalobusha Rivers joined, was a vital waterway during the development of the state. Grand Boulevard, lined with oak trees the city had been wise enough to protect, was named one of the ten most beautiful streets in the nation. In the 1990s, the downtown had seen a surge of renovations and more preservation efforts for some of the fine old homes.

Print That, a local shop, offered the services we needed to make our posters about Lydia and Bethany. Tinkie was pretty good at designing flyers. Before the hour was up we had two small bundles of flyers to staple to telephone posts and to hand out. If Gavin wanted to collect ten grand, we'd give him every bit of help we could to claim that money.

We set about our work, stopping pedestrians to give them a flyer and ask if they'd ever seen either woman. We didn't get any hits, but we were awakening the populace to the big reward. If either woman showed up in the Greenwood area, I felt we might get a call. We considered checking in with local law enforcement, but we decided Coleman could better handle that. He'd know how much to tell about Lydia's past and marriage.

On our way home, we had an appointment to talk with Nettie Adams, one of the Greenwood society grande dames that Tinkie knew. She'd been Lydia's friend in college and her maid of honor at her wedding. She'd married another Delta rich boy and lived the life Tinkie had been trained for. Unlike Tinkie, who had a solid marriage, Nettie had gone through an unexpected divorce, then another. Now she worked as a horticulturist for Mississippi State University. Folks said her thumb was so green she could bring dead plants back to life. She'd found her passion.

Nettie met us at the front drive. She'd been in the back working with spring plants while the weather was so nice. She took off her gloves and dropped them at the front door, along with her muck boots, and ushered us inside. "Let me put on some tea," she said, "or would you prefer coffee?"

"Coffee, please." I'd never taken to the hot-tea habit.

"Make yourselves comfortable. The bathroom is just down the hall. Would you like some homemade cookies? Chocolate chip and pecan."

"Yes," Tinkie said immediately. She threw a look at me. "I'm still eating for two," she said with a sly smile. That would be her excuse to eat sweets for the rest of her life— not that she needed one. The truth was, I could use a cookie or two myself. Chocolate chip and pecan was my favorite. I'd once dreamt that Aunt Loulane might marry Famous Amos, the cookie maker, and that I would become a master cookie baker. That was before I realized how much trouble it was to cook.

When the coffee had brewed, Nettie brought a tray with brimming cups and a plate of cookies. "I'm not doing the formal coffee service thing," she explained to Tinkie. "Too much effort. I hate to see all the lovely manners and traditions disappear, but I work an eighty-hour week most of the time. A lot of niceties have slipped from my grasp." She gave a self-deprecating laugh. "My mother would be so disturbed."

"Different generation, different times," I said.

"Too true." She checked her watch. "What can I tell you about Lydia and Tope?"

She got down to business, which I found refreshing. "Was Lydia happy in her marriage?" I asked.

"No. Never. Well, maybe that week of their honeymoon. She had such . . . expectations of what her life with Tope would be like. I will never forget the shell of the woman who came back from that honeymoon. She had a broken wrist and a black eye. She said she fell off her surfboard. I knew better but couldn't stop it. I had to watch her slowly shrivel. The reality of what Tope truly was—and that she was legally bound to him—nearly broke her."

"We heard he was abusive."

"Yes, he took every disappointment or difficulty out on Lydia. He wasn't just abusive, he was cruel. He enjoyed hurting her and watching her spirit break in front of him." She looked out the window for a moment. "I was going to give Lydia a dog. She always loved animals and I knew how lonely she was in her marriage. She wouldn't take the dog. She said Tope would hurt it in front of her. He was that kind of cruel. She was terrified she'd get pregnant because she feared Tope would abuse the child. But why are you asking about this now? Lydia has been gone for years."

"Tope is planning to remarry and he wants Lydia declared dead so he can take over her holdings from the Redd family inheritance."

Nettie paled, then shook her head. "I knew this would happen eventually. Tope married Lydia for her money and for arm candy. He's never cared about anyone but himself. When she started trying to thwart him, I worried for her. He was banned from the stables on the property. He didn't care about riding horses but the fact Lydia hired protection for the horses sent him over the deep end. They weren't living there six months before she gave her horses away one weekend when he was at his hunting camp. She helped load them up, crying so hard she couldn't breathe. And then they were gone, safe from him. I tried to talk her into running away, but she was stubborn. Then that kung fu woman befriended her and *poof,* she was gone."

"Do you think she left on her own?"

Nettie sipped her coffee. "I've given that question a lot of thought. She had enough money to escape, if she wanted. I heard Bethany Carter took her to Afghanistan to work with the educational system for women there." She paused. "To be honest, I never believed that. I knew Lydia pretty well. She was athletic, but not outdoorsy. She played a mean game of tennis, and she could ride a horse like she was born in the saddle. She loved hiking and swimming. But to live in a tent in the desert? I just don't see it." She gave a sad smile. "If she could see me now, she'd be worried about me because I spend most days digging in the dirt. She wouldn't see that as enjoyable."

That was an interesting take on the Afghanistan angle. I could see the appeal of helping women, but I also understood Nettie's disbelief. I loved camping—for two nights. After that I wanted a hot shower and clean sheets. Roughing it was not high on my list of things to do.

"Did you know Bethany well?" I asked.

"No. I liked what I knew, but she wasn't a Delta girl. None of the polish and no ambition to marry well. Or perhaps to marry at all. Bethany was physically, financially, and emotionally self-sufficient. I think all the mama's boys and buddy clubbers she'd had to deal with had left a bad taste in her mouth for the local males."

I liked that Nettie could mock herself and the culture that was so ingrained in certain places of the South. By her definition, I wasn't part of the DG circle, either. My mama would heartily approve that I was not.

"How did she come to befriend Lydia?"

"They met in a college sociology class and found they shared the same ideas and values. I don't think Lydia had ever imagined what life would be like with Bethany's courage and conviction. Lydia was well loved by her parents, but she was raised with certain expectations. Marriage, acquiring more money, preservation of beauty and culture. Certainly not that tough independence Bethany had. When she saw it, she wanted that, too. It was like she was reborn."

"And yet she married Tope," Tinkie said.

"She did. I suspect that marriage had been in the works for a decade or so. Tope was handsome, from a wealthy family, popular in school. And he treated Lydia like a princess. We were all pea green with envy. I remember that. What a shock it was the first time I saw her with a black eye and that broken wrist."

"You're positive she didn't injure herself as she said?"

"The ink had barely dried on the marriage license. It wasn't two months after they got back from their honeymoon that I saw her in the grocery store with big sunglasses and a scarf tied around her head, shielding her ears. The cast had just been cut off her arm."

"That's horrific," Tinkie said. I could tell by the flush in her cheeks that she was very angry. Tope better not cross her path or she'd light into him.

"Yeah. He blackened her eye and cut her ear. She had stitches and her short, sassy hairstyle didn't cover her injuries.

That's when she started letting her hair grow out. Tope preferred it long. And it also hid some of the bruises and scars."

"Her mother didn't step in?"

"Elisa was traveling in Europe. She wasn't told until the truth became too obvious. Lydia did everything to hide the truth from her mother. Like it was Lydia's fault that Tope was a monster. That's what's so infuriating. He made her feel guilty, like she deserved to be hurt."

"Tope is a real gem," I said with venom. "Why didn't Lydia just leave?" I wasn't asking Nettie; I was just pondering. We all knew the answer—at first it was love and the belief that she could change him, make him a better person. Every woman I knew had traveled this road at least once. Lydia had gone from that to being paralyzed and then believing she deserved bad treatment. Thank heavens Bethany had helped her.

"Tope says he has evidence that Lydia is dead." Tinkie bluffed.

"What evidence?" Nettie asked. "We searched high and low for her. Not just the authorities but her friends. We figured Tope had killed her and had weighted the body down in the Mississippi River. We hired rescue patrols and searchers to comb the riverbanks. We looked in the Yazoo in some of the deep holes. We honestly did search for her."

"And found nothing," Tinkie said sadly. "But you looked. I remember, Oscar and I donated to some of the funds. Did Tope even look for her?"

"No. It was as if he knew she would never come back. His dream had come true." She was bitter and I didn't blame her.

"Do you believe Lydia is alive?" I asked.

"On days when I'm optimistic, I know she is. I think I can sense her, just in the distance. I believe she escaped her hellish marriage and is living a good life somewhere. On the dark days, I believe he killed her. I vacillate." She sighed. "What evidence would prove that she's dead?"

"A body."

"Other than a body?" Nettie pressed. "I mean Tope can't manufacture a body if there isn't one, but he could create other evidence, like a suicide note he suddenly finds or some document that shows she intended to commit suicide."

Nettie knew Tope well. "Excellent points. The Sunflower County sheriff is going to talk to Tope and see what he has."

"Whatever it is, don't believe it. Promise me. And please let me know."

"Will do," I agreed.

We rose. We had to get back to Sunflower County. Tinkie had gone too long without Maylin in her arms. As we walked to the car, I put my arm around her shoulders. "You've been lucky in marriage."

"I know. I love Oscar and he loves me. Now we have Maylin. She completes us. You'll find out," she said slyly.

"I already know, just by watching you."

7

The next morning, Coleman and I were up before dawn. The mild weather held, and we wanted to take advantage with a horseback ride. We finished our coffee and went out to saddle up just as the sun peeked over the horizon. The fallow cotton fields glowed in the beautiful light.

We walked, side by side, warming up the horses and ourselves. I'd already told Coleman my impression of Vivian, Tope's current main squeeze.

"Do you think he'll really marry her or is this just an excuse to push for the legal declaration of death on Lydia?" he asked.

"The latter. If he's already hitting Vivian, he won't marry her. He doesn't have to. She's hooked already and he's getting everything he wants from her."

Coleman cast a look at me. "Harsh, some?"

"Nope." I rocked along with Ms. Scrapiron, loving the cold morning but the warm sun, the way the horse's hips moved mine in a gentle motion. The best activity ever to loosen up my cold back. "Tope is a predator. The hunt is everything to him. The bringing the game down and feeling that sense of power in taking the life of another creature. He isn't legally killing Vivian, but he actually is. Each time he hits her, he takes a little bit more of her spirit. It's a slow and brutal death and one he loves to dole out. But he won't marry her. He had to marry Lydia. Probably first off for the money, but she would never have submitted to his abuse without that legal tie. Once she was married, she couldn't just walk away. She was bound to him and extricating herself would be difficult. I'm sure he terrorized her."

"You make sense, unfortunately." Coleman put a hand on my thigh. "So many people suffer so much in life. Loss is unavoidable, but cruelty is inexcusable. Tope will eventually get what's coming to him."

"Hopefully sooner rather than later." I remembered an old Dixie Chicks song, "Goodbye Earl." "I wish Bethany would put him in the trunk. Like Earl."

Coleman laughed. "I don't want to hear that you and Tinkie are planning on camping by a lake."

We laughed together and asked the horses for a trot, then a canter. I was too busy riding the buck out of Ms. Scrapiron to worry about Earl or Tope. Karma had a way of working her charms on everyone. When the horses dropped back to an extended trot, we posted with them until they settled to a walk. We made the loop and headed home. My day had gotten off to the best start possible.

"What are you doing today?" Coleman asked.

"I want to talk to Tope. Alone. Tinkie can take a swing at him later if she wants. She has the advantage of class, and I worry Tope will hold back in front of her. I want to see the real Tope. After that, we need to check back in Greenwood to see if that tipster will talk to us. I hate backtracking, but that's where we are. If Budgie gets a hit on any flights to Afghanistan or anything else about the women's potential travels, let me know."

"Will do."

We were in the barnyard and Coleman slid to the ground. He handed me Reveler's reins and I took the horses into the barn to unsaddle while he headed off to work. We had developed a daily rhythm that gave us both a lot of pleasure. It wasn't the relationship that my parents had had—my mother and father had embraced romanticism. They lit candles and danced to the record player. Coleman and I were caught in the more practical aspects of living, but it was equally fulfilling. Dancing was good, though. I made a note to put more dancing in our schedule.

It was still very early. After I showered, I took Sweetie Pie and Pluto with me to the mansion on the Redd property where Tope lived. I meant to catch him before he left the house. He would not welcome me, but I felt he'd let me inside to talk.

I knocked on the door and a maid answered, doubt clear on her face. "Mr. Tope should be down for breakfast soon. Ms. Vivian may be later." Her face revealed her worry. I suspected there'd been an argument between Tope and his fiancée. Ms. Vivian likely wouldn't be down at all if she was trying to hide signs of her being abused.

The maid ushered me into the dining room, where a

breakfast buffet had been set up. "Please, help yourself. I'll let Mr. Tope know you're here."

I didn't intend to eat, but the biscuits were so light and flaky, plus I figured it would get under Tope's skin, so I loaded up a plate with eggs, grits, bacon, biscuits, and what had to be homemade dewberry jam. Someone in Tope's kitchen still practiced the fine art of jelly and jam making.

I was shoveling it in when Tope came into the room, his brow furrowed with displeasure. "What are you doing here?" His lean, athletic good looks had run to not exactly fat but an unhealthy beefy look. With the lock of hair on his forehead, he looked like a prime Hereford headed to the sale. The glower he shot at me held real dislike, not just annoyance at being disturbed.

I swallowed the bite of biscuit with a gulp and introduced myself. "I came to talk to you about something important. Elisa Redd has hired my PI agency to find her daughter, dead or alive. Since you've filed to have Lydia declared dead, I figured this could work in your favor, too. Or at least there's a fifty-fifty chance it will benefit you—if I find a body."

"Or he's lying. There's nothing I know that can help you." His hand swept up and pointed to the door. "You should leave."

"Would it be possible for me to examine her room or any of her belongings you might have kept? There could be some clues to her intentions or possible destination. If we can strike a trail, we stand a better chance of finding her. Dead or alive."

I could see the calculation pass across his face. A dead Lydia would be an ironclad case for taking over her inheritance. He didn't seem to think she was alive, but if he had killed her and knew where the body was, it would benefit him for me to find it—as long as it didn't result in him being charged with murder.

"I don't want you or anyone else poking around my house."

"Finding her would resolve all of this so much more easily." This was how I hoped he'd view my investigation. If he'd killed her, after six years he might feel safe enough.

Seemingly not. "Her room has been totally cleared and redecorated." He rang a silver bell on the buffet and when the maid appeared, staring at the floor instead of him, he told her, "Tell Chuck to get in here. I want him to escort Ms. Delaney to her car. Now." He looked at his watch to make a point.

"Yes, sir." She was gone.

He poured himself a cup of coffee and sat at the end of the table. "Do you have any leads on where Lydia might have gone?"

"Not yet. Do you?" I countered.

"I believe she's dead in Afghanistan along with that awful friend of hers, Bethany Carter. Lydia and I had a great marriage until Bethany started putting strange ideas in her head. Talking about the dire need of education for Afghan women, of how it was the responsibility of Americans to fix things around the world. America isn't big daddy to the world or to the people here too lazy to stand up and grab the American dream."

Born into money, privileged, Tope had grown into the asshat that his high school behavior toward smaller, weaker kids had foreshadowed. "You and Lydia weren't married long, but long enough. Did you ever think of having a child?"

"What's your point?" He was cool, but fire crackled in his eyes. "Lydia wasn't pregnant, if that's what you're implying."

"I just wondered if the marriage was business or romanticism. Two powerful Delta families marrying—that's generally a bond sealed by children to inherit." I was pushing my luck, but he wouldn't dare hit me. I hoped to see how hot his temper really was, but not to suffer too much in the process.

"Lydia was unfit to be a mother. I had no interest in having a child with her."

"I hope Vivian proves more to your . . . liking. She's a lovely young woman. You might want to childproof the house now, since she's a little accident prone."

"What are you trying to say?"

"Me, nothing. Children can be such rascals, getting into everything. Tinkie is learning all about that right now with little Maylin."

"Yes, Mrs. Richmond, your partner. You're quite successful with your detective work." He wiped his mouth with a linen napkin and pushed his coffee cup away.

"We have been, and I'm hoping we can bring a final determination to Lydia's fate. Elisa needs closure, and so do you."

"Good luck with that."

A young man came to the door. "You needed me, Mr. Maxwell?" He cast a curious gaze at me and then focused totally on Tope.

"Yes. Ms. Delaney was just leaving. Make sure she gets to her car safely." He looked at me. "Anything else I can do for you?"

"When was the last time you spoke to Lydia?"

He tossed his napkin on the table and stood up. "I don't recall."

"Did Lydia have her own credit cards or were they in your name?"

He hesitated. "My name."

"She had no access to any of her money? The Redd family money that was hers?"

"We were married. Her money was mine and mine was hers. The Maxwell family has been affluent for decades."

"Yes, but I heard you'd taken some losses on a few developments." It sure was handy having Tinkie and her banking knowledge as a partner.

"I don't care for this line of questioning. You're trying to make trouble for me."

"Sorry, I don't mean to be offensive. I'm just doing my job. So the last time you talked to Lydia, did you fight over money?" It was a wild guess on my part.

"I've pushed that whole distressful situation from my memory. Lydia couldn't balance a checkbook or use a credit card responsibly. I did what any good husband would do to protect her assets." He put his hands on the table and leaned toward me. "To be abandoned by one's wife is a public humiliation. I trained myself not to think about it. Or her. I hope she's dead. Now please leave."

On that I stood up and followed Chuck out of the room to the front. Tope had put a chill through my body. He was surely capable of killing Lydia—or, seemingly, any woman—and feeling not a shred of remorse. Was the term "sociopath"? "Narcissist"? I wasn't able to give a clinical diagnosis, so I would have to settle for Aunt Loulane's definition. The man was pure evil.

8

Tinkie and Chablis were ready when I stopped in front of Hilltop. Tinkie wasn't even miffed that I had gone to see Tope without her. We'd agreed on the phone that later on, if necessary, she could track him down at the Club and grill him in front of his peers. Tinkie could do it with charm, and Tope was too socially conscious to show his anger.

"We could concentrate on Tope, but talking to this Gavin fellow is more important," I said. "We won't call and alert him we're coming. Let's catch him by surprise."

Tinkie was good with the plan, and she chatted about Maylin's extraordinary intelligence as I unloaded Sweetie Pie and Pluto at her place. They would have more fun at Hilltop than waiting in the car.

When we pulled up on the beautiful Greenwood street

a block from our destination, Tinkie and I slipped around the big house to the garage apartment where we believed Gavin lived. As we climbed the stairs to the second floor, we could hear two men arguing.

"Those women will be back. If you have information about that missing woman, you'd better tell them. She's from a prominent Delta family. They can make life hell for both of us if they choose to."

"Just ignore them if they call. They'll get tired and go away."

"I don't think so."

"Well, I do. So let's not argue. Let's go get something to eat."

Perfect. All we had to do was stand on the landing and wait for the door to open. When it did, the look on the two men's faces was priceless. The one man we recognized from our last visit, but Gavin Jerome was a handsome man with a carefully manicured scruff, jeans slung low to reveal an admirable set of hip bones, and a T-shirt so white it was almost blinding.

"Hi, Gavin," Tinkie said, sticking out a hand that he had no option but to take. "We need a word with you. You may be in line for a chunk of change! Wouldn't that be wonderful?"

"I told you this would happen." The other man slipped past us down the stairs. I was happy to see him go because my business was with Gavin and he would be easier to work alone.

"I'm sorry, ladies, but I have an appointment," Gavin said, trying to follow his friend, but Tinkie and I closed ranks and stopped him.

"We'll only need a few minutes of your time," Tinkie said,

bulldozing her way forward and forcing him back. I was hot on her heels. When we had him inside, I closed the door and locked it.

"What are you doing?" He looked a bit furtive.

"We don't want to be disturbed," I said. "This won't take long, and as my partner noted, you stand to gain ten grand for information."

"It's about that missing heiress, isn't it?" He sat on the arm of a sofa. "I'm sorry I ever made that call."

"Why? Tinkie asked. "Her mother is desperate to see her. She's very loved. Why wouldn't you want to help her get home?"

"Because when someone wants to go home, they do. When they stay away, they generally have a good reason. Any money that comes from this will be tainted and bad luck."

"No, I can assure you Lydia's mother loves her and the reason she ran away, well, that man's life might not be as peachy as he believes it will be. He's earning his karma and it's going to make him very unhappy." Tinkie nodded. "Just tell us if you saw her or not."

"I can't be certain."

"Tell us what you saw." This was getting ridiculous. "If you saw her, great. If it wasn't her, you're not liable for anything. No one is trying to trick you. We only want information and to give you money if it pans out."

He looked at the door as if he hoped help would come, but then he sighed. "Okay, a week ago she was at a garden center at the edge of town. I could have sworn it was that woman you said, Lydia Maxwell. Same hair, those piercing eyes, and when she realized I was staring at her, she dropped her purchases and left in an old pickup truck."

"Was she alone?"

"There was another woman driving the truck."

I pulled up the photo of Bethany Carter I had on my phone and showed him. She would have blond hair now. "Is this her?"

"Yeah. Yeah, it is. Who is she?"

"A family friend."

"So the Lydia chick isn't in any trouble?"

"None at all, and neither are you. Do you know where they were headed?" I asked.

He shook his head. "The truck had an Adams County tag. It was an older vehicle. Two-door red Ford, maybe a 2010 model."

"Thanks, Gavin. If we find Lydia or Bethany based on this tip, I'm positive Mrs. Redd will give you the reward. And, trust me, the reward isn't tainted. You've done a good thing."

He smiled. "Thanks. The women looked okay. Just a little spooked at me staring at them. But they didn't look hurt."

"Do you remember what they were buying?" I asked.

"Some herbs and flowers. Some vegetables. They left them all, though, and took off."

"Thanks. You've been a big help."

As soon as Tinkie and I were in the car, she gave one of her best sorority girl squeals. "I think Lydia is alive!" she said.

"I sure hope so."

"What?" she asked. "You don't believe Gavin?"

"It's the timing. Tope announces he's taking legal action to declare Lydia dead and suddenly she's spotted. After six years."

Tinkie bit her bottom lip for a few seconds. "You think Elisa paid him to say that?"

"Maybe. Or someone else paid him."

"It is very convenient." She looked like someone had let the air out of her.

"But it's equally possible that he did see both women, just as he said."

"He noticed the truck tag. Who does that other than law officers and us?"

She was making a list of reasons not to believe him. "Coleman can call the Adams County sheriff's office and ask. It's easy enough to check, but let's not get Elisa all hopeful until we catch sight of the women. I think tomorrow we may need to take a drive to Adams County."

"The women were sighted in Greenwood driving a vehicle with a tag from Natchez, Adams County." That was a good three hours away. Or over two if I was driving. Surely there was a produce stand closer to home for the women. Then again, who knew where they had come from or where they were going.

My cell phone rang and Tinkie answered it since I was driving. Her gasp made me look at her. Tears welled in her eyes but she didn't cry. "I'll tell her. We're on the way home," she said.

When she lowered the phone, she put her hand on my arm. "Vivian Dantzler is dead. It seems she jumped off a third-floor balcony at Tope's house."

I knew Tope was dangerous, but I didn't think he was stupid. Had he actually thrown his fiancée to her death? Or had she jumped in despair of what she'd learned about him?

Were Tinkie and I responsible?

The shock was like a punch to my solar plexus. Tinkie groaned softly. "Did we do this?"

"No." I said it firmly, though I, too, was feeling the guilt. "No. If anyone did anything it was Tope."

"That was Coleman who called. He's working the case. He didn't give any details. He just said he'd see you at the sheriff's office in a little while. We should go there and wait."

That was exactly what we *should* do. Instead, I turned the car toward the Maxwell house. Tope was standing beside a sheriff's cruiser when we arrived and when he saw the Roadster, he started over and I knew he had every intention of punching me in the face. Tinkie, too.

"You did this," he bellowed. "You told her a pack of lies and made her doubt everything. She threw the engagement ring at me and the next thing I knew, she'd jumped to her death. There was nothing I could do! Now you're going to pay."

I got out of the car and met him head-on. He drew back, but before he could deliver the punch, DeWayne had handcuffs on him.

"Cool off, Mr. Maxwell," DeWayne warned him.

"She's responsible. Running her mouth like all the women in the Delta do. Starting trouble, poking into things that aren't their business." He tried to lurch free, but DeWayne held him and moved him toward the backseat of the cruiser.

"Don't make it worse for yourself, Maxwell," DeWayne said as he helped him into the backseat.

"You can lay down for the sheriff's side piece to walk on you, but I don't have to do it and I won't. She's the one who told Vivian all kinds of things about me. Lies. It pushed Vivian over the edge. She went crazy. She threw herself off that balcony."

The more he talked the less I believed him. I kept my piehole shut, though. Provoking him wouldn't help anything, only put DeWayne in jeopardy of either getting hurt or hurting Tope. The satisfaction of hearing him howl wasn't worth the risk.

Tinkie and I walked toward the house, where the coroner's hearse waited with the motor running as two attendants wheeled a sheet-draped body into the back of the vehicle. Doc Sawyer would perform an autopsy. What I wanted to see was the balcony she'd "jumped" from.

We entered the house to find the maid talking with Budgie. She sobbed as she recounted how she'd heard an argument and then Tope had come running down the stairs and out the front door, yelling for her to call 911 and an ambulance.

"That poor girl was dead. I hope she didn't suffer, but . . ." She broke down sobbing.

While the maid was preoccupied, Tinkie and I slipped up the stairs. The entire third floor of the house was a ballroom, with a section walled off to use as an attic. We entered the big, empty room and saw the broken window instantly. The house had been built with walk-in windows that led to the small Juliet balconies. Vivian had either crashed through one of the windows or, more likely, been thrown through it. Tinkie and I were careful not to walk in the glass or otherwise disturb anything that the law officers might need to document.

We eased toward the balcony and Tinkie took photos as I stepped through the opening and looked down onto the lawn. Vivian had hit the cement apron of the pool. I hoped her death had been instantaneous.

"We should have dragged her out of here," Tinkie said, feeling exactly the remorse that was eating at me.

"It wouldn't have done any good. She would have come back. You know that. You can't help a person until they're ready."

"That sounds logical and like common sense, but why do I feel so guilty?"

I put my arm around Tinkie's shoulders. "Because we would have changed this if we could have."

Tinkie straightened her back and looked down. The paramedics were finishing up, and Budgie and DeWayne were helping Coleman collect evidence and mark shoe prints and pieces of the balcony railing that Vivian had taken down with her when she died.

"I don't believe she jumped," Tinkie said.

"Nor do I."

"Tope is a cold-blooded killer."

"I suspect he was angry when he did this. I wonder what Vivian did to make him so mad."

Tinkie sighed. "You know as well as I do that the woman doesn't have to do anything. The fact she's there, breathing and convenient to abuse, is the only justification a man like Tope needs."

We backed away from the balcony and stepped around the broken glass and wood. We had the photos we needed but not the definitive proof to put Tope behind bars. This would chafe at Coleman and the deputies. A lot. I had faith in them, though. If the evidence to prove Tope had killed this woman was there, they would find it. A jail term for Tope wouldn't bring Lydia home, but it would dang sure get the wife abuser out of the way.

While we were upstairs, Tinkie and I decided to poke around a bit. We probably wouldn't have another opportunity. The ballroom—the hardwood floor immaculately waxed and polished as if a dance would be held any minute—was empty except for an enormous fireplace. The door that led to the storage area of the attic wasn't locked, so we began our search there. Dome-topped trunks filled with incredible clothes from the last two hundred years made me almost breathless with desire. I had no use for the clothes but they were exquisite, and they made the lost years of history real.

"Lydia was active in the historical society," Tinkie said. "She lent these family clothes for exhibits."

We found furniture, lamps, kitchen gadgets—plenty of items once very expensive and valued but whose day had come and gone. We could have spent a week up there, but I hustled Tinkie along. We hadn't found anything of Lydia's that I could identify. On the second floor maybe we'd have better luck.

The master bedroom was a terrible mess, and I noted a small pool of blood in the bathroom sink. Budgie was taking samples. Vivian's clothes were out of the closet and thrown about the room that also contained several open suitcases. It looked as if Vivian might have been packing to leave.

Tope wasn't the kind of man who let a woman walk away until he was ready to tell her to go.

"Do you still think Lydia may be alive?" Tinkie asked.

Seeing the consequences of life with Tope had really shaken Tinkie. And me, too. "I don't know. We should tell Elisa that Vivian is dead right away. But let's leave out the details."

"Agreed," Tinkie said.

We hurried forward with our search and were rewarded just as we were about to give up. A doorway that blended in with the hall paneling caught Tinkie's eye. She motioned me to come with her as she pressed on the paneling until we figured it was a pocket door that slid into the wall, revealing a tiny foyer and an ornate door. Tinkie tried it, but it was locked.

"We need to see what's back there." She reached into her backpack—a fashion accoutrement I never dreamt I'd see her use—and brought out a lock pick set. "A Christmas present from Harold."

He'd given me a nifty pen that was also a recording device. I watched as Tinkie moved the tumblers in the door and opened it quietly. "These older doors are easier," she said.

We stepped into a bedroom that sent chills down my spine. The photos of Lydia on the wall and on the bedside table made it clear this had been her room. A nightgown was laid out on the bed with slippers on the floor. A wedding gown was thrown over the back of a vanity chair.

"Damn," Tinkie said. "This looks like she's going to walk right back into this room from the shower or something." She bit her bottom lip. "And marry Tope again."

Definitely creepy, especially since Tope was now wanting to declare Lydia dead. "Are you certain this is her stuff?"

Tinkie went to the closet and searched through the clothes hanging there. "I'm positive these are her clothes. I remember some of them because they fit her so exquisitely. That coral silk suit was a showstopper at the Club." She checked through the drawers of the bureau. "I can't identify anything else, but I'm pretty sure this room is meant as a . . . tribute or honor to her."

"Or a prison." I pointed to the door. There was no handle on the inside to open it.

"Good heavens." Tinkie put a hand to her mouth.

I snapped photos of everything, and then we left. I didn't know if Coleman had arrested Tope, but if he hadn't, Tope was likely to come walking up the stairs at any minute. He would be furious at us for poking around his house. Tinkie had the same idea and we hotfooted it down to the first floor, and just in time. Tope walked back and forth in the foyer, anger sparking in his eyes.

"Get out of my house."

Tinkie stopped to say something, but I grabbed her wrist and we both shot out the front door. "No good will come of talking to him. Let's get out of here."

I found Coleman standing at the side of my car, and I told him about what had to be Lydia's room.

"It's definitely creepy," Tinkie said. "If he honestly believes she's dead, why does he have her clothes laid out for her? It's like one of those old Vincent Price movies."

"Tope's a creepy kind of guy," Coleman said, giving me a kiss on the cheek. "Now both of you skedaddle before you get charged with trespassing."

"Are you charging Tope?" I asked.

"Not yet. I need evidence he pushed Vivian out the window."

"That's not going to be easy to find." I had seen a lot of physical evidence but none that positively tied Tope to a murder. Unless Doc Sawyer could prove that Vivian had been hit in the head or heaved over the railing, I didn't know how anyone would find evidence beyond a reasonable doubt in a broken window and a woman dead from a three-story fall. Yet I couldn't believe that Vivian had jumped. Proving it enough to get Tope charged was the challenge. He wouldn't lack for legal representation. Coleman would have to have rock-solid evidence to bring murder charges against him.

I drew Tinkie around to the back of the property. I wanted to examine the place where Vivian had fallen. The evidence techs were excellent, but I wanted to look, and photograph, for myself. Coleman was always generous in sharing information, but other law enforcement agencies would be involved and it was best for us to have our own photos and experiences.

"Stay back," I warned Tinkie. She wasn't squeamish or too delicate to see a crime scene, but there wasn't a good reason for her to witness the results of a bad fall. She didn't argue, and I photographed the blood and chalk marks where Vivian had met the cement. No one would pick that death even if they were suicidal.

We heard voices approaching from the rear and we stepped into the shrubbery, slowly making our way to the front of the house. It was time to go. We had other leads to follow.

Just as we were about to step out of the shrubs and onto the driveway to run to the car, I heard Tope talking. I put out a hand to slow Tinkie and we crouched lower to eavesdrop.

"You better dry up those tears, Ruth Ann. And keep your mouth shut."

"Yes, sir."

I recognized the maid's voice.

"Did you let those two private investigators into the house to snoop around?"

"No, sir. I didn't realize they had gone upstairs."

"They are never to enter my home. Or any of my property. Tell Chuck and the other staff."

"Yes, sir."

"Now wipe your face and get to work. You barely knew Vivian. Tears for her aren't necessary."

"Yes, sir." The maid walked right past the bush we were behind but she didn't look. She was too busy wiping the tears from her face.

Tope turned on his heel and went in the front, slamming the door hard. Tinkie and I popped out of the bush and raced down the driveway. Luckily, we'd parked a little distance from the hubbub. Coleman and the other law officers and ambulance were already gone.

9

We drove straight to Elisa Redd's house, a beautiful ante-bellum home set with an avenue of oaks in the Old South tradition. A maid led us to the sitting room, where Elisa joined us. She looked tired and worn.

"We wanted to tell you that Tope's fiancée, Vivian Dantzler, is dead." Tinkie matter-of-factly delivered the shocking news.

"How? What happened?" Elisa sat down.

"She fell from a third-floor balcony, but all of the details aren't known. The sheriff is investigating."

"Tope did this." Elisa had no doubts. "I know he did. He's a murdering brute." She looked at me, stricken. "If he killed this woman, it's likely that he also killed Lydia and Bethany."

"There's no evidence of that." I had to get her back on the main track or she'd send herself into mental anguish. It looked bad, but there was no evidence. I had to hit that again and again until she heard me.

Tinkie went in search of the maid and ordered some calming tea for Elisa, and I held her hands and talked to her. "We found the man who said he saw Lydia and Bethany at a roadside market." I told her what we'd learned and how I'd stressed to Gavin that he should call and collect his reward. It took a while, but I got her calmed down.

"You talked to Tope. What did he say?" she asked as Tinkie brought the teacups in and served us.

"He denied everything. He said Bethany was at fault and had caused Lydia to leave him. He says he hasn't had contact of any kind with her—with either of them—in the last six years."

"Why didn't this Gavin person call and claim the reward money?" she asked.

A very good question. "I suspect he thought it was a trap. Two missing women. Someone who has seen them. Maybe he was afraid he'd be accused of harming them. Since we talked with him, I'm hoping he'll come forward."

That seemed to make her feel better. "Elisa, do you have any other people we can talk to about Lydia or Bethany? Someone who may have known of her plans?"

She shook her head slowly.

"When she disappeared, did Tope talk to you? Can you tell me the sequence of events?" Tinkie asked.

"When she didn't call me back after I left her several messages, I drove over to see if she was sick. Tope wouldn't let me in. He said she'd left him. He waved a typewritten note in front of me but wouldn't give me a chance to read

it. Then he told me to clear off his property. *His* property."
For the first time a hint of bitterness registered in her voice.
"In Mississippi, a person only has to be missing seven years
before the paperwork to declare them dead can be filed.
We're almost at that deadline. Tope is just getting a jump
on the filing deadline. He means to have everything that
was Lydia's."

The Maxwell family was reportedly rich, but Tope had
been spending their money like a wild hog in a berry patch.
Had he run through his inheritance and now needed Lydia's? Coleman seemed to think so. "How long were Tope
and Lydia married? Before she went missing."

Elisa closed her eyes to concentrate. "Nine months. She
put up with it a lot longer than I would have. I begged her
to run away. I would have given her money, help, whatever
she needed."

"I'm sorry she didn't take advantage of your help."

"It whipped me raw every day to wonder if she was still
alive when I woke up, to drive by the house too afraid to take
any action because he would hurt her if I became a nuisance.
When she told me about Bethany and her mission to help
the women of Afghanistan, I begged her to go. I felt she was
safer in a war-torn country than in her home." She sniffled.
"Did I send my daughter to her death in a foreign country?"

"No!" Tinkie sat beside her and put an arm around her
shoulder, hugging her close. "You did everything a mother
could do. Lydia married Tope. She knew she had help if she
wanted to leave him. The decisions she made . . . you can't
be responsible for them."

"I don't think Lydia had trouble in Afghanistan." I said
it assertively. I couldn't produce Lydia but I could help alle-
viate Elisa's guilt.

"Why do you say that?" she asked.

"Coleman has friends and he's had them checking for Lydia entering or leaving the country. So far, nothing. And if an American citizen—two, if Bethany was with her—were kidnapped or in trouble in a country where we had a military presence, someone would have known about it. The nomad tribes of Afghanistan are more often peaceful. They might not appreciate women trying to change their culture, but they wouldn't harm them." I said it all with total conviction, though I was talking through my hat. Elisa had a lot of guilt. That wouldn't help us or her.

Tinkie gave me a quizzical look. "How do you know so much?"

I rolled my eyes. "Internet. It's a remarkable tool."

Tinkie threw a pillow at me, and we had Elisa laughing.

"Thank you," she said. "Thank you for the visit and the laugh. I know you'll find Lydia. I feel it in my bones."

"Was Lydia a fan of literature?" I asked.

"That's an odd question. She loved to read. When she was a young girl, she fell in love with Edgar Allan Poe's work. She thought he was a visionary. A man who clearly saw the darkness and knew how powerful it was."

I kept the smile pasted to my face. I'd had a premonition, but Elisa confirmed it. Lydia and Poe were irrevocably intertwined in my mind now, given Tammy's Poe-inspired dream.

"Lydia was really smart," Tinkie said. "She was good at finance and literature. I remember she won an award in English at Ole Miss, didn't she?"

Elisa smiled. "She did. She was a well-rounded young woman. She excelled scholastically and was a dancer on the cheer team for two years. She fell hard for Tope. It galls me to admit it, but I did, too. He was so charming and had such good manners. They'd flirted in high school, but Tope went off to college. Lydia followed and they reconnected somewhere down the line. They dated for over two years. When Tope proposed, I honestly thought I could relax, that Lydia would be happy for the rest of her life."

"How could you know?" Tinkie said. "Abusers are clever at hiding their evil and they terrify the people they abuse, making them afraid to even ask for help."

"Do you remember anything that might have triggered Tope? Did he want children? Was he opposed to Lydia's friendship with Bethany?" I was trying to find something I might be able to use if I ever had Tope alone for an interview. Something that would rattle his brain and maybe unhinge his tongue.

"When we were planning the wedding, Lydia told me that Tope wasn't ready for children yet, but they had decided on having a boy and a girl. I told her that couldn't be counted on and she said they would 'keep trying.' She was so excited for the future. They had the house plans drawn up and the house built before they married. All of their furnishings were in place, so they moved in the day they returned from their honeymoon." She blinked away tears. "Lydia left for that trip a bride thrilled with life and her future and returned a shadow of herself. From there it only got worse."

Lydia and Tope had been a couple that had the world by its tail. And Tope had destroyed it all with his need for cruelty and brutality. "I'm so sorry."

"Now a young woman is dead at his hands. I'm positive of it," Elisa said.

I agreed, but I had no evidence to support my opinion.

"Coleman will do everything in his power to put Tope away."

"Coleman Peters is a good man. Decent and honest. I know he will. Tope is just clever, and he knows the law as good as any law officer or judge. He knows how to avoid prosecution. That's something Lydia told me when I tried to get her to press charges. She said Tope knew how to avoid paying for his actions and that if she filed charges and they didn't stick, he would make her suffer even more."

It made my blood boil that Tope would use his connections, money, and education to avoid paying the price for his actions. While Coleman would never let a man's position or wealth interfere with his application of the law, not everyone was so honest. The jails were full of poor people without influence while wealthy criminals often avoided incarceration. That reality had particularly irked my father, who'd been a local lawyer and circuit court judge.

"We'll do what we can," Tinkie told her, holding her hand. "And let's just hope that Gavin Jerome in Greenwood is correct, and Lydia and Bethany are alive. We're tracking that down."

"Thank you. And I'm sorry about Ms. Dantzler. I wish I could have talked to her, warned her."

"Sometimes a warning falls on deaf ears," I said. "We'll get back in touch if we learn anything new."

We were almost out the door when Elisa's phone rang, and then mine. We both checked our screens and I saw the same unknown number. Elisa looked at me. "Someone sent a photo."

"Me, too." It was strange enough that we both stopped and opened the message. I showed the image to Tinkie.

"That's Lydia, isn't it?" Tinkie asked.

"It is," Elisa answered. "It's my daughter. Alive and at an airport. Look, it's a recent photo. I'm certain. Lydia has aged, but she is alive! Lydia is alive and now I have proof."

Tinkie and I glanced at each other. It might be proof. Or it might be a cruel, cruel trick. Photographs could be manipulated. "I'll send this to Budgie and see if he can find any details for us," I told Elisa. "We have to know who took it and where for it to be real evidence to stop Tope's legal maneuvers."

"Yes." She couldn't stop smiling. "But why hasn't Lydia gotten in touch with me? There are many, many questions to be answered. But as long as she's alive, everything else will fall into place."

While I was standing in the foyer, I forwarded the photo to Budgie with my questions about it. Budgie had more training in technology than anyone else I knew. When Coleman hired him, he got a bargain—a man who knew the law and how to apply it and a techno-nerd who could find the answer to a billion questions.

"I'll call as soon as I hear anything. You should send that to your lawyer and start the process of fighting Tope right away," I said. "We may not be able to prove the photo is legit yet, but Tope can't prove it isn't, either."

It was good for a stalling device, at least. Tinkie and I took off, headed to the office at Dahlia House to make some calls and do a little research of our own.

10

Coleman arrived home just as I was putting a chicken pot-pie into the oven. It was one of the few dishes I'd mastered, and he loved it, so I made it often. Sweetie Pie and Pluto snoozed on the kitchen floor in front of the warm oven, but they moved to the den when Coleman lit a fire that crackled and sparked merrily. We sat down with a glass of wine each to wait for dinner to cook.

"Were you able to arrest Tope?"

Coleman shook his head. "I wish. When I went back to ask additional questions, he wasn't there. The maid said that Tope had gone down to the stables, but she was terrified. I think he threatened her. I just can't prove it. And he wasn't at the stables when I went to look. I couldn't find him."

"I'm almost positive he threw Vivian over the balcony

railing. When I talked to her, she didn't seem depressed." I thought back to that brief conversation. "She was planting flowers. A suicidal person wouldn't do that, I don't think."

"A terrified woman might jump," Coleman said.

"But wouldn't that be murder just the same?"

"Yes. In my book it is. Tope and his family are slick with the law. They've been involved in real estate deals in the past that were criminal in my book, but nothing ever stuck. Teflon Tope."

Warming in front of the fire and leaning against Coleman while we sipped wine was the perfect end to the day. My life was full, sweet, and happy. Why couldn't everyone find the people and things that fulfilled them and made them content? Why were some people only happy when they were making others miserable?

I told him about the photo we'd received and showed it to him, but Budgie had beat me to the punch. "Budgie said it looked legitimate," Coleman said. "He's checking into it. He's very clever with that kind of thing."

"I know, and thank you for letting him check for me."

"It's part of my case, too. If Lydia is alive, maybe she'll testify against Tope."

That was an excellent point.

"Did Doc say when he'd have the autopsy ready?" I asked.

"As soon as possible. I'll let you know what he finds. I sure hope he can give me the evidence I need to put Tope behind bars."

"Me, too, but I'm not counting on it."

The timer on the oven went off and all of us trooped into the kitchen for supper. Even Sweetie Pie and Pluto were ready for something warm in their bellies.

* * *

Coleman was gone by the time I woke up, and I stretched under the covers in perfect contentment. When my phone rang, I knew it was Tinkie. She was up early every morning to feed Maylin. That baby was growing by leaps and bounds, and Tinkie had to constantly eat to keep up with the dietary needs of her daughter. If anyone had told me ten years ago that Tinkie would be the ideal mother, I would have scoffed. But seeing was believing. Maylin was her first and last thought every day.

Coleman and I hadn't really talked about children. We both loved them, but I wasn't certain either of us was willing to bear that responsibility and the awful power of potential hurt and pain that would come if something untoward happened to a child. In other words, we were cowards. Or at least I was. Coleman would back my decision, because he loved me. Knowing that, I had to be certain what he wanted, and how badly, before we made any decision. My fear shouldn't dictate his future.

I found my phone and called Tinkie back. She was firing on all eight cylinders.

"Have you heard from Budgie about that photo Elisa received? Is Tope in jail? Will the district attorney prosecute? Have you had breakfast? I have coffee made."

"No, no, I don't know, and no. Don't ask any more questions or I'm going to have to duct tape your mouth."

"Well, that's rude." Tinkie laughed at me and at herself. "I've been up for a while."

"And had what, five cups of coffee?"

"Something like that. Maylin wakes up and she's ready for action. I have to be alert to keep up with her. Gone are the days of lounging in bed to drink coffee and read a newspaper."

"And you love every minute of your current life."

"I do, but I'm still allowed to complain. To my business partner. And Oscar would take her to work if I'd stop by every few hours to feed her." She paused. "I could do that!"

"Hold on, Mama Tinkie. You've got a great arrangement with Pauline caring for Maylin and you in and out. That way Oscar gets to do his job and you do yours and Maylin has the full attention of someone twenty-four/seven." As much as I loved being with Maylin, I had to admit she was a huge distraction. When she was near, I only wanted to hold her and be with her. It had to be even harder for Tinkie and Oscar.

Another call buzzed on my phone. Budgie was on the horn. I let Tinkie go as I talked to the deputy while I poured a cup of black coffee.

"That photo of Lydia was taken in the Memphis airport," he said. "The airport helped reconstruct the flights and arrivals and departures on the board behind her and the photo is recent. Ten days ago."

"Is this enough evidence to prove Lydia is alive?" Someone had seen her at a produce stand a week ago and now here was a photo of her less than two weeks old. Things were looking up.

"Unfortunately, no. This is a photograph of a photograph. The original could have been manipulated. But it is enough for Mrs. Redd to file a motion to stop the court from declaring Lydia dead. It will have to be battled out in court, but it will stop Tope for the immediate future."

"I owe you big-time, Budgie. Thank you."

"Maybe one day when it's nice and warm you could give me some riding lessons. I've always wanted to learn."

I was touched. "It would be my pleasure. In fact, if we teach you to be horse savvy, Coleman can have his own mounted patrol since DeWayne rides."

"I'd like that," Budgie said. "But when it's warmer. I know how frisky horses can be on a cold day."

He was right about that. And I regretted only that I didn't have time to give Reveler a chance to ride out his kinks this morning. Duty came first. I made a piece of toast and ate it walking upstairs to take a shower. Fifteen minutes later I was in the car with Sweetie Pie and Pluto. I explained the case to them as we drove to Hilltop. Some people would say I was nuts, but time and time again, the dogs and cat had come to my rescue. Tinkie's little dust mop, Chablis, was fiercely loyal, too. Even with an underbite, she could still take a chunk out of crime when necessary.

Tinkie, with Maylin in her arms, met me at the front door. Chablis greeted Sweetie Pie and Pluto and they all raced upstairs, I presumed to find Gumbo, Tinkie's sassy little calico. If they tore up a bedroom or ate shoes, Tinkie would never scold them. Her policy was that everyone in her house should have fun. I couldn't afford to let the critters eat my furniture or shoes, and somehow they understood the difference between the two households.

By the time I had grits, eggs, and bacon in front of me, I'd filled Tinkie in about the photo and she called Elisa while I ate. We were all on the same page. I wished I could be in the courthouse when Elisa filed to stop Tope's attempt to declare Lydia dead. The news would fly faster than a bat out of hell. Tope would be seething, a look I never tired of.

"We should call Cece and Madame to tell them." Tinkie dialed up Cece and I called Tammy, who sounded terribly flustered. "Are you okay?" I asked.

"Yes. I'm okay. Just another dream. The heart again. That beating sound. The vibration of it through the floorboards and into my heart. And I saw an old tree and a grave with a tilted headstone. Blood on the ground. Just . . . dark details that give me a feeling of disaster coming our way."

"I think the dream centers around Lydia Redd Maxwell's disappearance several years ago. But we think Lydia is alive. We may have evidence."

"That would be fabulous," Tammy said, and I could hear the relief in her voice. "Better than fabulous. I can't control my dreams but before I go to bed I'll focus on finding an answer to where Lydia and her friend Bethany are. Lucid dreaming."

"That would be spectacular." Tammy, much like Jitty, seldom came up with evidence or proof of anything, but her sixth sense sometimes presented itself in dreams that foretold the future. If she could dream those women alive, maybe there would be a clue.

"Especially in light of what happened to Tope's fiancée yesterday. I hate to blacken his name without proof, but I think he threw her out the window."

Tammy sighed. "Once you find Lydia and Bethany, you can turn your full force on putting Tope in prison where he belongs."

"That would be my pleasure. Now you try to take a nap. Maybe some shut-eye will revitalize you. If we can all get together later, I'll call you."

Tinkie was hanging up just as I did. She heaved a sigh of relief. "Cece has to go to Memphis on newspaper business and she said she'd stop at the airport there and see what she could find in the way of records or anyone who might have seen Lydia."

"That's a huge favor!"

"Yes, it is. We're lucky to have the friends we do."

I told her Tammy had had another nightmare about the beating heart.

"It's this case. I know it is. It's Poe. A body hidden under the floorboards. And that creepy vulture eye. It's all about Tope killing the women he claims to love." She brushed an angry tear from her cheek. "This makes me think they're dead."

"Let's follow the evidence. Lydia looks very much alive in that photo." I put my plate in the sink to soak and prepared to sit down at a computer to work while Tinkie applied her magic on Tope's financials. My phone rang and it was Elisa. I put the call on speaker.

Elisa was almost breathless. "We have another tip on the reward line. It's the same person who sent the airport photo. Or at least it came from the same number. Someone in Greenwood saw the flyers you put up. They want to claim the reward. They said they'd tell me where Lydia is once they have the money. It's all set up. I'm going to leave the ten grand at the drop they designated tonight."

Tinkie and I both tried to talk her out of leaving the money before she got the information, but she was determined. I had one more play to try. "Elisa, they won't hurt me, but they might try to abduct you. To extract more money, and that would be bad for Lydia. Let me make the drop."

Elisa was silent for a long moment. "Come by and pick up the money. I have the cash. I've had it for a while, hoping someone would call. The drop isn't until tonight, but that way you'll be able to pivot to another location if you need to."

"We're on the way," I said. Sweetie Pie and Pluto could spend the day with Pauline, Maylin, and the Richmond critters. They would be in hog heaven.

11

Elisa tried to serve us another breakfast, but I declined. My hobbit habit of two breakfasts was showing up on the scales. "Some coffee would be nice," I suggested. In the South, accepting hospitality is as important as offering it. Elisa had grown up during the time when people, especially women, used social networking to help their families. Parties, dinners, church, participation in charity drives or clubs that helped the community improve. These were a woman's arena of influence.

To my surprise, Elisa went to make the coffee herself. I knew she had a staff, but this was a personal touch that showed how much she appreciated our efforts.

"I sure hope Cece turns up something," Tinkie whispered.

We hadn't told Elisa that our friend was checking into the airport photo. "What are our plans for today?"

I wanted to see if Budgie could trace the call to Elisa's phone, but she wouldn't hear of it. "Let's see if Ole Miss will give us Lydia's file. And we have to follow up on the truck license plate that Gavin told us about. This evening I'll make the drop. I have a plan."

Elisa returned with an expensive satchel crammed with money and a short stack of emails she handed to Tinkie. "Tope's attempt to declare Lydia dead has stirred up the missing persons case again. It's all over social media. I suppose someone in the clerk's office spilled the beans. The tip line is getting more action than it has in years, but you can read these and see folks are grasping at straws." Her voice thickened with emotion. "Not everyone has good news or kindness in their tips. I swear the world has gotten meaner in the last six years. But I have to take everyone seriously."

As we sipped our coffee, Tinkie and I read through the tips and threats that had come in. Elisa was right. Some people got their kicks from making others feel terrible. Hiding behind the anonymity of an email address, they allowed their meanness free rein. Most were clearly false leads that someone had made up in an attempt to get the ten grand. One was threatening, one cruel, and several sorrowful, but only one troubled me.

I read the note aloud. "The bones of both women are buried in the Mount Zion Cemetery near an old sycamore tree known as the Hangman's Friend. Look for the grave marked *Salter*." Mt. Zion was a long-abandoned church off a narrow county road south of Zinnia. The church was white clapboard with a single bell tower. The cemetery sprawled behind the church. My mother had taken me there once, when I was a child, to look for the grave of a family member of someone she was helping. Even back then the cemetery had been overgrown with thickets of honeysuckle, wild huckleberries, and kudzu. My mother had never mentioned a hanging tree, but she wouldn't have.

"Do you know this tree?" I asked Elisa, thinking of Tammy's dream once again.

"I know the tree, the cemetery, and the legend. It's an old, old burial site on the edge of the Marsh plantation," Elisa said. "Slaves and local people are buried there, and there's a special elite section for the wealthy planters of the 1700s and 1800s. We were always told by our elders to stay out of the cemetery because that tree had been the official gallows for a lot of rural Sunflower County. We were told unhappy ghosts roamed, looking for the people who had unjustly executed them."

"Damn," Tinkie said, shivering a little. "That doesn't sound like justice to me."

"It wasn't. When a man was accused of a crime—most often Black men or slaves who attempted to run away—they were taken to that tree for a public execution. Folks would bring picnic lunches to watch the hanging."

"The tree was truly a community gallows?" I asked, chilled by the images her words conjured.

"Yes. That's the legend, and I believe it to be true. If you know the true history of this region, you know poor men of all colors had only the rights the elite gave them. Before the war, wealth ruled. After the war, the night riders or Ku Klux Klan meted out vigilante justice. Most often it was Black men lynched in that manner, but others, too. Mobs were easily stirred," Elisa continued. "There isn't a lot of written documentation about the dispensation of justice from those days. Mostly what we have is legend, but the Mount Zion hanging tree is well known. In the state archives there are oral histories of people who witnessed hangings there."

"How awful to make a family outing of an execution." Tinkie was outraged.

"How do you know all this?" I asked.

"Bethany was deeply involved with victims' justice organizations. She asked me to do some research on these rural public executions. She said she was interested in maybe writing a book."

"You liked Bethany." Tinkie made a statement.

"I did. And I came to believe she was Lydia's only hope of surviving Tope." Elisa looked down. "I wish she'd killed that bastard. And I would have helped her bring justice to other victims, too. Her heart was right. So many horrible things have been hidden from history books. When injustice is the basis for a society, it is doomed."

I understood her emotions. It was a history none of us could change, though the recent efforts to at least address the wrongs of the past were a step forward. Inspiration struck me. This would be a great story for Cece and Millie to cover. Not a pretty story, but a necessary one. The Sunflower County hanging tree.

"Why that particular tree?" I asked Elisa.

"It's a magnificent tree," Elisa said. "As I mentioned, that cemetery is located on the edge of the Marsh plantation. The Marsh family had a lot of power and influence. Davis Marsh often served as judge and jury over the proceedings. He'd 'hold court' on his front porch and then the mob would take the condemned man behind the plantation to the cemetery and hang him. Unmarked graves. No telling how many people are buried in the ground reserved for felons and nobodies."

My breathe caught as I recalled Tammy's most recent dream about a tree and a tombstone knocked askew. It was time for me and Tinkie to get busy. "We have several things to check out. The cemetery first. After that, if Budgie can get a lead on that Adams County truck, Tinkie and I will pay a visit to the owner. We have feelers out in Memphis for anyone who saw Lydia at the airport there. We're covering all the bases," I told her. "If you hear anything from anyone, call us."

"Be careful tonight and let me know immediately what happens, please." She gripped Tinkie's hand. "Let this be the lead you need to bring my daughter and her friend home." She offered the satchel stuffed with cash to me. "Just be careful."

"Of course," Tinkie assured her. "You've made the right decision letting Sarah Booth make the drop."

We left the Redd mansion and drove to the sheriff's office. Budgie actually had the telephone in his hand when we walked in.

He hung up and waved us behind the counter to his desk. "That license plate is registered to an Ernest Salter."

"That's great, Budgie, thank you so much." This was going much faster than my last case.

"It's not going to be that easy," Budgie said. "That plate is several years old. When I called Adams County to get an address, they informed me that relatives reported that Ernest Salter is dead. Has been for a while. He bought a place in Adams County, but it sold years back."

That took the starch out of my spine. "Damn. Did he die there?"

"No official record of his death is recorded in Mississippi. He probably moved out of state."

"How did he die?" Tinkie asked.

"Here's where it gets interesting. Rumor is that his body was found hanging from a sycamore tree in a local Sunflower County cemetery, burned beyond recognition. Or that's what I dug up when I searched for him. This was before Coleman's time in office, and there aren't any official records of his death in this county, but he and his wife did live here for a time. Adams County had no death certificate or cause of death. I got the address Salter listed when he paid for the tag in Adams County, but like I said, that was years ago."

"Any relatives?"

Budgie shook his head. "His wife, Florence, preceded him in death and she's buried in that same cemetery. Best I can piece the rumors together, Florence died and he moved to Natchez. The rumor is that both of them were suspected in the disappearance of several young women. The story goes that when Ernest came to visit his wife's grave, some locals caught him and hanged him."

"I think I know where this cemetery is," I said. "Elisa got a tip that Lydia and Bethany are buried in that cemetery near that old tree. I don't believe it, but Tinkie and I will check it out. We'll look for the graves of the Salters while we're there. Would they bury him without notifying the county?"

"In rural areas, a lot of things are done like that. Even more so before Coleman went into office. He's tried to make the paperwork less cumbersome for people, which has helped."

"But wouldn't someone complain? About folks just digging a hole and dropping a body in?" Tinkie asked.

"The cemetery is abandoned, and the Salters never had children. From what I could find out, Florence was said to be a conjure woman who mixed up herbs to help women abort unwanted pregnancies. She was either the biggest saint or sinner ever born. Folks said she'd help anyone who sought her out. There were other rumors, though. Suspicions that if things went wrong, she disposed of the girls. Her husband was suspected of worse."

"Worse?" Tinkie asked.

"Some folks thought he seduced those missing young girls and Florence helped him get rid of them."

"Damn," I said.

"Others say that Florence was no less than angelic with healing powers. She gave care to a lot of people who couldn't afford a doctor. Several attempts were made by the former sheriff to catch her in the act of doing something illegal, but no charges were ever filed. Then they were just gone. She died and he left."

"What about her husband? Did he work?"

"For a year or two it seems Ernest Salter stayed at the old farmhouse where they lived and farmed. He supplied two fruit stands with fresh fruit and vegetables and local legend said he had a green thumb and could grow anything, especially the herbs Florence needed."

"I heard he was hung and burned," DeWayne threw in. The handsome deputy had arrived on the feet of a thief— silently. I hadn't even heard him come in the door. "Before the cemetery became so overgrown it was a big deal for teenagers to go there on a full moon and spend the night. Ernest Salter was supposed to show up late at night looking for the graves of the women he murdered."

Oh, great. Exactly what I needed. Another ghost to haunt me and my case.

"In the days when Mississippi was rural and so many places were isolated, a lot of unfortunate things went on. Vigilante justice." Budgie was analytical. The hint of scandal—or ghosts—didn't attract him at all. "But let me add that there was no evidence anyone in recent years was hanged or burned in that cemetery. That's all just a ghost story. The former sheriff claimed there was no murder. Of anyone," Budgie said.

"If he was hung and burned, I would think that would be evidence that a crime was committed." Tinkie was perplexed.

"No doubt, but the sheriff at the time couldn't prove there had even *been* a crime. The society toffs were happy to let it go because the Salters were also gone. From what I remember, their homestead had been abandoned and there was no sign of them anywhere."

"Was Florence a conjure woman?" I asked Budgie.

He shrugged. "I remember the stories but I don't know anyone who ever used Florence to solve a problem."

"Have you heard any of this?" I asked DeWayne.

"There was talk in certain areas of the county. The Salters lived in an extremely rural area. A lot of the children born in that region never attended public schools. It was almost a different country unto itself."

"And no one did anything to get those children in school?" Tinkie asked.

"Those kids didn't even have birth certificates. A lot of them were delivered at home and not all granny midwifes were as conscientious as Ms. Bessie." DeWayne took a seat on the corner of Budgie's desk. "Your mama helped Bessie register every live birth she assisted in to be sure those little babies were citizens. Not everyone knew how to do that or that it was even important."

"Do you believe Ernest Salter was murdered?" I asked both deputies.

Budgie shrugged and shook his head. "No. That's just a tale."

DeWayne had stronger views. "I do. Possibly Florence, too. She was controversial in town. Folks in Zinnia only heard rumors about her, how she mixed potions and cast spells. Town folks, who were horrified and dismayed, enjoyed the high drama of titillating gossip, but there are people who are terrified of dark spirits. You know that. They're irrational about it."

I had to ask the hard question. "If there was a crime, do you know who did it?"

"I have my suspicions, but Coleman has taught me the importance of never accusing someone until you have proof. And there's no stomach to reopen the disappearance of Ernest."

"What happened to Florence? How did she die?"

"No one knows," DeWayne said. "I heard folks went out there one day and her grave was just there with a new headstone. It had some unusual inscription."

DeWayne's suspicions, though, might give me a new direction to look for Lydia. "Thanks, Budgie and DeWayne. I may press you on this later."

Budgie smiled wide. "Still going to give me riding lessons?"

"Any time. You don't have to do a thing for that to happen."

"You're going to make a cowboy deputy out of Budgie?" DeWayne asked. "Can I watch?"

"No!" All of us spoke together and then we burst into laughter.

DeWayne excused himself and picked up a ringing telephone. Budgie gave me a little salute and turned back to his computer. He had work to do, and I needed to quit pestering him. "Budgie, I'm sorry to interrupt you again. Where is that cemetery?"

He gave us directions that took us deeper into the heart of the Delta.

"Let's pick up the dogs," Tinkie suggested. "Going to a cemetery to look for graves of dead girls, conjure women, and men thought to be serial killers calls for canine assistance."

"Great idea." We each had a gun, but Sweetie Pie was a tremendous asset when it came to defense. Chablis, too. Even Pluto had been known to jump on a dangerous felon. We swung by Hilltop. Tinkie took a moment to kiss and snuggle Maylin, who rewarded her with a smile that made the sun outside seem dim. Then we were off, the critters in the backseat.

12

I drove right past the cemetery gate and had to reverse. The place was covered in weeds and brambles. If anyone living had been there in the last three or four years, I'd be surprised. But on the tip line, someone had mentioned this place specifically as the location of the bones of two dead women. I got the gun and a shovel out of my truck, and we walked up to the locked gate. The chain was thin and rusted. I wacked it hard three times with the shovel and it broke.

"Not exactly done with finesse, but it worked," Tinkie said.

The dogs and cat heard a rustling in the weeds and took off. Sweetie Pie struck the trail of something, and she bayed and hollered as she gave chase. I wasn't worried. Sweetie loved the game, but she'd never killed anything, to my knowledge. The only thing she'd ever hurt was someone trying to harm me or Tinkie.

My partner had slipped into a pair of knee-high boots, while I still had my walking shoes on. Looking at the tall grass, I regretted not having boots. I wasn't worried about snakes—the winter had been cold, and they would still be hibernating. Ticks were another matter. How I hated them! I'd have to be sure Sweetie Pie, Chablis, and Pluto were tick-free when we got home. Tinkie had been wise to leave Gumbo with the baby and Pauline. Gumbo was a house cat that disdained working in the wild. She might evolve into it, but only time would tell.

"Why would someone lock a cemetery?" I asked Tinkie. "Especially one in such a state of disrepair." I wasn't exaggerating. Weeds had taken over many of the graves. Tree limbs had fallen and knocked gravestones over.

Tinkie's blue eyes glinted with mischief. "They locked it either to keep us out or keep something in."

"I don't think that dinky chain would keep a ghost or ghoul inside." From experience I knew physical barriers were worthless in containing ghosts.

"Oscar sent me a text while you were driving. Seems this cemetery was abandoned because people thought it was haunted. Oscar said the rumors about Ernest Salter being killed here were the last straw. First the Marsh plantation burned to the ground while no one was living there. Then the youngest Marsh boy was shot to death in the woods around here. After that, the church and burial ground were abandoned."

Oh, if she thought she was going to scare me with a tale of ghosts, she was going to be shocked. I had Jitty, and no cemetery ghost could be worse than she was. Just to be on the safe side, I looked all around. It would be like Jitty to pop up behind a tombstone and scare me. Then I'd have a lot of explaining to do. Tinkie wouldn't be able to see her. The more I thought about it, the more it sounded like a plan Jitty would adore.

"Are you afraid of ghosts?" I asked Tinkie.

"I'll tell you if we see one." She grinned. "Just don't get in front of me. I'll mow you down."

The gate creaked open with a high-pitched moan as if it were a stage prop for a horror flick. We waded through the bushes and weeds, stepping over broken headstones and the forlorn neglect of a place where dead people rested, forgotten.

"This is sad," Tinkie said, kneeling at the tomb of Rufus Theodore Ward, born September 10, 1830, and died August 12, 1861. "He was thirty. He could have been in the Civil War."

"Maybe." I brushed mold away from the inscription: LOYAL IN LIFE AND DEATH. I read it aloud. "Look, he's buried beside his father, who died in 1862."

"Hard times." Tinkie had no fondness for the myths of the glorious lost cause, but she was tender about parent-child bonds and the loss of a loved one.

The burial plots were in sad shape, and I began to despair that we would find Florence Salter's grave. Or any indication of two dead women surreptitiously buried in a forgotten cemetery. Many of the headstones were toppled over or broken. As Tinkie had pointed out, this was not the grave site of the affluent planter class where shaded pathways and marble angels marked eternal resting places.

As we rounded a clump of dense cedar trees I saw the white skin of a sycamore reaching for the sky. The bare limbs were incredibly beautiful, so stark against the blue sky and also somehow melancholy. It reminded me of bones bleached by the sun. "I wonder why they used a sycamore tree for a gallows," I said. "Mostly oaks are used. Sometimes big cedars."

"The way the bark is white and sheds in peeling sheets, it's a beautiful and odd tree. The London plane tree, which is a relative, is smaller, but was very popular in the formal gardens of the royals."

"You know some strange things, Tinkie Richmond."

She laughed. "I was going to line my driveway with sycamores like your ancestors did at Dahlia House, but I didn't."

"Why not?"

She shook her head. "The impulse to do it passed. Your driveway is so beautiful, but it wasn't what was needed at Hilltop. We left the driveway open except for the flowering shrubs."

I glanced at her but she was transfixed by the tree. It was stout and strong and several lower limbs would have served to throw a rope over. In a momentary flash I saw a terrible scene from another century—a body dangling from a noose while a mob cheered.

"Let's find that grave," Tinkie said, rubbing her arms as if she were suddenly cold.

I felt the chill, too. We went in separate directions, radiating out from the tree, checking more tombstones. Some were merely wooden crosses that had almost deteriorated. Others were stone that time had weathered. Many engravings had been worn away. I found one stone that had been knocked askew and knelt to trace the information with my fingers.

FLORENCE SALTER, THE MOTHER. There were no dates of birth or death, just the simple inscription.

"Tinkie, come look at this. This might be where Lydia and Bethany are buried."

She navigated among the headstones to kneel beside me. The grave, like all the others, was untended, but a single artificial red rose had been laid on top of the marker. Someone still cared for Florence—or whoever occupied the grave. Though the artificial flower was weathered, it still indicated the grave site had been visited in the last few months. The colors were still bright.

Tinkie touched the flower. "'The Mother.' I wonder what that means?"

"I wish I knew. That could be a way to find Lydia."

Tinkie stood up and poked around in the weeds near the grave. "I don't see a grave for her husband, Ernest. We've lived around here all our lives and I've never heard of Florence or Ernest Salter. Have you?"

My mother had known almost every resident of Sunflower County by name, but the Salters were a mystery to me. "I haven't. But if he was hanged and burned here, they should have buried him here."

"And they could have, without benefit of a grave marking," Tinkie pointed out. "If no one really monitors this cemetery, anyone could be buried here." Even two missing young women. She didn't have to say that aloud because I knew we were both thinking it.

"I'll start digging. There are some water bottles in an ice chest in the backseat of the car. Would you mind getting a couple? This is going to be some hard work."

"We're really going to dig up a grave?" Tinkie asked, even though she was holding the shovel.

I gave her a look. "I didn't come out here to see if the chiggers were biting." The thought of a chigger made my ankles itch. The sensation of needing to scratch moved all over my body. Chiggers were worse than ticks or snakes. I wished I hadn't thought about them.

"At least it's daylight," Tinkie said. "I'll be back."

I watched her disappear as I stepped on the spade and hoisted the dirt. I bent to the task but stopped when I heard someone humming a sad tune. I eased behind a thicket of weeds and bushes to see who else was in the cemetery. Had someone come to visit a dead loved one?

Movement about twenty yards away drew my attention and I inhaled sharply. The humming woman, dressed in a torso-fitting, black, long-sleeved dress with a belled skirt, strolled through the cemetery, pausing to read the names of the dead. She carried a basket of artificial red roses and stopped periodically to place one on a grave.

She turned to face me, alerted by my gasp. Her face was young and lovely, pale, her brown hair parted in the center and pulled into a chignon at the back of her neck. She came toward me.

"I know a bit about grave robbing," she said, taking in the shovel in my hand and the piles of dirt. "It's always been a profession of scoundrels, thieves, and those desperate for anatomical studies. Which are you?" Her accent was British. She sounded educated but friendly.

"None of those." I answered before I caught myself.

"Grave robbing played a crucial role in my novel." She was in no hurry to leave.

This was surely Jitty in the guise of Mary Shelley, a woman whose literary creation was a monster made of stolen body parts. Now wasn't the time for Jitty's foolishness. I bent back to my task, hoping Tinkie would soon appear. That would send Jitty packing. I was a tad offended by her suggestion that I was a grave robber.

Jitty perched on a nearby headstone, prepared to "sit a spell" and watch me work. "Tinkie will be back any second," I warned her. "If I come across any stray body parts, I'll save them for your monster."

"I don't think I'll need them. And just so you know, it was the doctor who was the monster, not the creature. Tinkie won't be back for a while. She took off after Chablis and Sweetie Pie. Someone has to watch those critters while you're busy robbing graves." She had slowly transitioned back to herself. And she was wearing my jodhpurs and riding boots. She was safe from chiggers and ticks!

"Why are you here?" I was two feet down into the grave and had a long way to go. It was a crisp day, perfection, but sweat had begun to trickle from my forehead. I shoveled the dirt up to the pile.

"Do you think Lydia Redd Maxwell is buried in this grave?" Jitty asked.

"I don't know. But I'm going to find out."

"I could save you some effort, but you know it's against the rules. I can't be tellin' you anything."

"Jitty!" I leaned on the shovel. "It's good you're dead, because if you weren't I'd be tempted to kill you."

"Don't you ever get tired of threatening me?"

The truth was, I would much prefer to have her tell me something useful, but since she wouldn't, threats seemed like a good alternative. "Why are you here pretending to be Mary Shelley?"

"She was a genius, don't you think?"

I remembered reading *Frankenstein* in high school. As

the villagers chased the monster, who'd never asked to be born and only wanted to be loved, I'd broken down in tears. My classmates had teased me for weeks. "I think Mary Shelley had a firm understanding of what it meant to be an outsider."

"Indeed. Her life wasn't easy."

"Do you think artists always have to suffer?" Jitty was a fabulous conversationalist when she chose to be.

"Everyone suffers, Sarah Booth. Creatives and everyone else. I've watched the Delaney family for generations now. No one gets a free pass."

That wasn't exactly the heartwarming theory I wanted to hear, but I couldn't deny it. "So why Mary Shelley and Poe? I get the heartbeat thing from Tammy's dream, but *Frankenstein*?"

Her smile was slow in forming. "You'll figure it out. You always do."

I was three feet into the grave and done with being badgered by a ghost. "Spill the beans or move along."

"Watch out for lightning," she said before she disappeared in a flash so bright I was almost blinded for a moment. Her departure was followed by a crash of thunder. I counted eight seconds to realize the storm, which I hadn't noticed before, was closing in on us. I dug with renewed fury.

"Sarah Booth!" Tinkie arrived breathless. "Those dogs. They took off and it took me forever to find them." Sweetie and Chablis settled down in the pile of fresh dirt I'd thrown out. "Let me dig for a while. Looks like we may get some rain."

"Just dig. We need to find those bones and get out of here."

We were only a tad over three feet in when the shovel hit something solid. Tinkie jumped in the grave and helped remove the dirt with a vase she'd found in the grass. Another ten minutes of work and the wooden coffin was revealed.

Tinkie hopped out of the grave and wiped her forehead on her sleeve. "You're really going to open that casket?"

I inserted the tip of the shovel under the lid that had been hammered down with light nails. With a creaking sound, the lid came up three inches. I moved down the side of the coffin and applied the same technique. In a short time, the lid was free. All I had to do was lift it off. I joined Tinkie on the side of the grave, got on my belly, and reached down to grasp the lid. Tinkie helped me.

"Oh, no," Tinkie whispered.

I hadn't looked because I was apprehensive of what we'd find. Both Lydia and Bethany buried together, the bones of an old conjure woman—I had a lot of gruesome visions. "What is it?" I asked.

"It's empty." Tinkie's voice was a whisper. "It's empty."

I looked down at the bare interior of the plain wooden coffin. "Damn. Now we just have another mystery to solve."

I checked my watch. The day was sliding away from me, and I had that money drop later in the night. "Let's report back to Coleman and see if Budgie or DeWayne found anything we can use."

"I just want to know that Tope is behind bars. Do you think Coleman will charge him with Vivian's murder?"

"If he has the evidence, he will. Coleman isn't impressed by Tope's law degree or his powerful family."

"That's one of the things about Coleman I love," Tinkie said. "And wipe that grin off your face. Get your mind out of the grave and back to where decent women reside."

"My, my, my, do you need your smelling salts, Mrs. Richmond? You're behaving a little peevish and privileged."

We both laughed and I sat down in the dirt for a minute. "Should we fill this back in?"

Tinkie frowned. "Call the deputies and ask. No point filling it in if they're only going to have to dig it up again."

She was right about that, but admitting to grave robbing might carry some penalties, though technically, we hadn't stolen anything. Not for lack of trying. "Can they charge us with abusing a corpse?" I asked, knowing that would get her cranked up.

"They wouldn't dare!" Tinkie went from passive to indignant in a flash. "Besides, there is no body to abuse."

She had a point and I placed the call. Budgie answered and wasn't thrilled, but he told me to leave the grave open. He'd be down with someone from the forensics unit to take evidence.

"Don't touch anything else, Sarah Booth." He was a little testy.

"Got it. We're leaving now."

"I didn't think you'd really dig up a grave," Budgie added.

"I just saved you a lot of work, and you're welcome." I punched the phone off, stood, and offered Tink a hand up. "Let's ditch this dead zone."

13

As we bounced down the rutted dirt road, Tinkie was pensive. "So where is Ernest Salter buried if he was hanged and burned?"

"I'm doubting the veracity of those rumors."

"Me, too."

"What do you think happened? And who were Ernest and Florence Salter? I mean, what were they up to?" Tinkie was gnawing on the big questions.

"I'm not really sure what to make of Florence Salter and the empty grave. 'The Mother.' You have to admit that's a peculiar epitaph."

"Peculiar but kind of lovely," Tinkie said. "No one would ever say that about my mother. Her tombstone would read 'mother to none.'" Before I could offer any comfort, she nudged my shoulder. "I know, I know. I expect from her what she isn't capable of giving."

"That doesn't mean your need is wrong or inappropriate. It only means your mother isn't capable. But you're going to correct the balance by loving Maylin in the way you truly need to be loved. And that is the beauty of having a child. Or, I should say, the beauty of someone who truly knows the power of parenthood. You're stepping onto that path and living it as hard as you can."

She squeezed my shoulder. "Continue with your analysis of what we've discovered. I need to jump off the pity train."

I gave her a wry grin. Tinkie might feel sorrow for herself, but it never lasted longer than a minute. "Ernest Salter was a real, live person. Or at least he had a truck at some point. We can check into that, but I'm not certain how or if he's going to play into our quest for Lydia. This feels like a rabbit trail." What possible connection could there be between a society debutante and a backwoods conjure woman?

"While we're out in these parts, maybe we could stop at a few houses and ask about the Salters. See what people say about them, how they react."

"If some of the local men hanged Ernest, they may react by shooting us." When I was a child, it was generally safe for me to stop at any home in Sunflower County. Times were different now and some places were heavily armed. Plenty of people seemed to have a love of victim mentality and an itchy trigger finger.

"Let's pretend we work with the census bureau." Tinkie was pumped with her own idea. "They won't suspect a thing."

I didn't love the plan, but it wouldn't hurt to give it a try. Within reason. "We can only get shot once. Let's do it."

We got on the paved road, a farm-to-market route created to connect rural areas with bigger towns to ease the transport of goods the farmers produced. The storm had, thankfully, moved around us, but, as we traveled, the road was wet where it had passed. We were in a part of the county with barren, hardscrabble fields and the smaller houses of those who worked the land, not owned it. Creeks and drainage ditches crisscrossed the fields and large sections had been left wooded and undisturbed. The ground was too boggy to farm with industrial equipment. The land was populated with small, individual farms that grew produce, not cotton. Truck farmers.

We came to a crossroads where the intersection boasted two churches, a gas station, and a produce stand. It was the most civilization we'd seen in a while. We parked at the produce stand, realizing too late that it wasn't open. The season for fresh vegetables and fruits was still several months away. Our luck was with us when I realized someone was inside the building sweeping. Tinkie knocked and stepped inside.

"Can I help you?" an older gentleman in a flannel shirt and puffer vest asked. His white hair was carefully brushed.

"We're looking for Ernest or Florence Salter," I said, holding back any details.

"Good luck." He kept sweeping.

"Do they live around here?" Tinkie asked. "We're with the census bureau."

"You won't be able to count either Ernest or Florence as citizens," the man said. "Far as I know they're both dead or moved away."

"That's too bad." Tinkie pretended to write something on the notepad she carried. "Did they have any children?"

"None I knew of." He found a dustpan and swept his

trash into it. When he looked up at us, I knew he was no-body's fool. He didn't believe for a second that we were census takers. Or any government officials. "What do you really want?" he asked.

"We're private investigators." I made the introductions because I felt we'd get further with the truth than lies. His name was Alfred Nyman. "We're looking for two women who went missing a few years back. It's possible they might have had a link to the Salter family."

He thought for a minute then motioned us out to the porch where several rocking chairs had been recently cleaned. "Take a seat," he offered. "Before I give out any information, I want to know who I'm talking to and why you're askin'."

We told him about Delaney Detective Agency and how we'd been hired to find Lydia Redd Maxwell.

"Her husband, Tope Maxwell, was abusive." Tinkie just put it out there, the devil be damned. "We think she ran away from him and started a new life, but it's possible he killed her. There was talk that Ernest Salter was involved with several missing young women and that he was hanged in the old cemetery down the county road."

"You found the legends. Now you're lookin' for facts." He patted his shirt pocket, and I knew he'd once been a smoker. The gesture of reaching for a pack never left many of us who'd quit.

"We want to find Lydia. Maybe Ernest Salter was mixed up in helping her disappear. Maybe Tope paid him to kill her," Tinkie said. "We have no evidence. We're just looking for facts. We're not making any accusations, either. I'm just repeating what we've heard. You asked for honesty, and here it is."

He assessed us for a minute. "I wouldn't go asking these questions around here."

I knew why, but I asked anyway.

"I don't know if the local men killed Ernest or not. But if they did, they won't appreciate anyone sniffing around about it."

"But someone was hanged and burned?"

"I never met a soul who would admit that they personally saw that." His blue eyes were much paler than Tinkie's but they held the light of intelligence. "Did you find Ernest's grave?"

"No, sir," Tinkie admitted. "Not in Mount Zion Cemetery. A truck with an Adams County license plate in his name was seen recently. The plates were registered to Ernest, but the registration is from a few years back. There's no official death certificate in Sunflower or Adams County, where we believe he moved to."

"I'd sure like to see his death certificate." Nyman gave me a look.

"Because you don't believe he's dead." It was the only conclusion to draw.

"I don't know one way or another. But I knew Ernest and Florence. Salt of the earth. Kept to themselves, farmed their plot of land, took in injured wild animals and healed them. Florence sold potions and cures, but she made no guarantees."

"Ernest wasn't a child molester?" Tinkie asked.

"To my knowledge, he wasn't. Like I said, he and his wife stayed to themselves. They were visited by young women from the schools around these parts. Mostly college girls, from what I remember. I suspected Florence was helping them solve a problem, but I never asked, and I never heard anyone say she'd done that." He shrugged. "The things that trouble young women in college who're hoping to build a life."

It could have been grades or boyfriend problems, love or learning. But I suspected it was unwanted pregnancies. It had become next to impossible in the South to find legal abortion clinics. Now women who didn't have the money to fly to a safe clinic had to rely on whoever was willing to help. It put another question into my mind. Had Lydia been pregnant when she disappeared? Had she known that having a child would tie her forever to Tope? Had she been so desperate that she'd put her life at risk?

Judging from Tinkie's expression, the same thoughts were going through her head. "If women around here don't have a lot of money . . . they will die. They can't get the health care they need."

"If I knew a way to change that, I would." Mr. Nyman rocked for a minute. "Whatever Florence and Ernest were up to, they were kind, good people. The sick and the old never went hungry if Florence had something to cook and a way to get it to them."

"Do you remember the last time you saw either of them?" I asked.

He shook his head. "It's been a long time but, honestly, I couldn't pinpoint it. There's a grave in the old Mount Zion Cemetery for Florence, though. No dates."

Tinkie and I exchanged a look. We both agreed to keep the empty grave to ourselves. "We saw it. Someone had left a red rose there."

"Florence loved her roses. She often made bouquets for the local ladies when her flowers were in bloom."

"If you had to take a guess, would you say Ernest Salter is dead?" Tinkie asked him.

"No. I wouldn't."

"How old were the Salters?" I asked.

"They were barely middle-aged. I think they staged their deaths and up and left this area. I don't know why, but that's what I believe."

"Thanks, Mr. Nyman." It was time to be busy.

"Should we try any other places?" Tinkie asked when we were in the car.

"I think that's a waste of time. Maybe Cece unearthed something in Memphis."

I felt we were spinning our wheels. How did one go about tracking a young woman who disappeared six years before? "We aren't the first private investigators that Elisa has hired."

Tinkie nodded. "You're right. There must have been reports or something we could look at."

"You would think." I dialed the sheriff's office and got Budgie on the horn. "Did you get an address attached to that old tag?"

"I did, but you shouldn't go without Coleman."

"Why not?"

"Whoever is running that tag is breaking the law. Now, my theory is that if they're breaking one law, they're likely breaking others. You need backup."

"Okay, but I need that address. It's a long drive and we need to hit it."

"That's not smart, Sarah Booth."

"Budgie, time is of the essence here. We have two missing women and an abuser."

"Two women who have been missing for a long time," he pointed out. "Just wait for Coleman."

"Give me the address. I can't trouble Coleman every time I want to follow a lead."

"Okay." He gave me the address, which was on the north side of Natchez.

"We're driving there now. I'm happy to work with a deputy if one shows up."

"You make Coleman's life difficult, Sarah Booth."

"And he loves me anyway." I was laughing when I hung up.

"I'm calling Cece," Tinkie said. "Maybe she found out something."

14

Tinkie put the phone on speaker when Cece answered, and I could tell by her voice she had good news.

"I found a pilot who met Lydia in the Memphis airport just after Christmas. They had a drink together at one of the terminal bars. He said she was very much alive and healthy."

"What name did she use?"

Cece laughed. "He didn't remember a name, but he remembered her vital statistics. He said she was a good-looking honey blonde with a Mississippi drawl. Excellent manners, likely came from money. When I showed him the photo of her, he said it was her, then added how much he'd like to date her."

"Men." It was all that needed to be said. They remembered

the most bizarre facts about a woman. On the other hand, Tinkie would have name, phone number, and a Dun & Bradstreet report on any guy who interested her. I would have the name and arrest record. We all had our priorities. "I can't believe he didn't get a name."

"He was having a drink, not auditioning her to be the mother of his child." Cece was laughing. "You expect too much of the weaker sex, Sarah Booth."

Tinkie's laughter was light and easy. I had to chuckle along with them. "Aunt Loulane used to tell me that if I expected more than a person was capable of giving, the trouble was on me, not them."

"A very wise woman," Tinkie said.

"But the pilot made a positive ID on Lydia?" I pressed Cece to be sure I understood what she'd found.

"He did."

"Did he know where she was going?"

"He said he thought she was heading to Atlanta to hop an international flight to Afghanistan. She told him she had a life there."

"She really went to Afghanistan?" Tinkie asked. "How will we ever find her?"

"Coleman is going to have to step in here. The airport authorities won't give me squat."

Tinkie signaled that I should turn left instead of staying on the road to Natchez. I didn't ask any questions, I just obeyed.

"I'm almost back to Sunflower County," Cece said. "Want to meet for a drink at the Peppercorn?"

It was a hot new bar in an old, renovated hotel. "Yep." Grave digging had given me a big thirst. The storm that had passed us was building on the southern horizon. Natchez was a long drive and could wait until another day, especially since I had a money drop to make.

"We'll be there in about twenty minutes," Tinkie said. "We can share information."

I checked my watch. We'd missed lunch, which wasn't normal for me or Tinkie. "Want me to drop you at Hilltop so you can feed Maylin and I can leave the critters?" Sweetie Pie and the crew had been unusually quiet in the backseat. They were well behaved, but I didn't want to leave them in the car while we drank and ate. Pauline had a soft touch for all of them and I knew she'd find them something wonderful to eat.

"Good plan," Tinkie said. "You'll need your car for the money drop tonight."

"Call Millie and see if she can meet us at the Peppercorn."

"Okay." Tinkie obliged and in a moment had an agreement. "She'll be there at five," she said. "Before the dinner crowd hits her café. That'll give you a chance to eat and go home for a brief rest before the drop tonight at nine."

"Call Budgie, please, and tell him Natchez is off for tonight. We'll go tomorrow or the next day."

I'd come up with a big plan for the money drop. Elisa might want me to just leave the money and walk away, but if someone was holding Lydia hostage, I wasn't about to give them the money before I knew where she was. To enact my plan, I'd need Millie's help.

I waited until the late afternoon lull at Millie's Café and went to find Millie in the office going over her accounts.

"I need your help tonight," I told her.

"Me?" She looked around like I was talking to the invisible man.

"Yes, you. I want you to hide on the floorboard of the Roadster when I go to make the drop. Elisa insists on paying the ten grand and getting the information on where Lydia can be found later."

"Are you insane?" Millie asked. "You're going to drop money by yourself in the dark to pay for a woman you don't even know is alive? I know Elisa hornswoggled you into agreeing to this, but I don't think I want to participate."

"I need you." It was that simple. At least to me.

"Sarah Booth, I don't like this plan."

"Me, either. But it's what we have to work with. I trust you to do this and do it correctly. Tinkie needs to be home with Maylin, and I don't think Coleman can fit on the floorboard successfully."

Millie sighed. She checked her watch and looked out into the nearly empty café. "What time is the drop?"

"Nine o'clock."

"How are you going to ditch Coleman?"

I had actually thought of that. "Coleman and DeWayne are backup. They going to be waiting for my phone call so they can pick up the tail from you. We can't all be in the woods, and I figured they're better at tailing than you or I are. See, I got it covered."

"Then I'll do it. Reluctantly. If you get hurt or killed, I'm not responsible. I want that in writing. If you lose Mrs. Redd's money, I'm not responsible for that, either."

"I'll sign it in blood if that will make you feel any better."

"No. It won't." She gave me a sour glare. "You put our hearts on the line, Sarah Booth."

"I'm as careful as I know how to be." That was the truth. "What I need for you to do is follow the tipster when he or she leaves the wooded area. You'll have my car. Someone will come and pick me up when I call. I won't be stranded and I'm not going to try to apprehend anyone. I just want someone to follow them. Maybe the tipster will lead us back to Lydia or Bethany."

"That's a solid plan, I guess." She was less grumpy.

"It's a shot in the dark. I don't know if this person who called in to get the ransom has any useful information or not. I personally think it's a scam, but Elisa would rather lose the money than miss a chance at getting her daughter back."

Millie nodded. "Pick me up at eight o'clock, okay? That way if the plan changes, I'll be with you and ready."

"Thanks." I kissed her cheek. She was a mother hen to all of us, and I loved that. I hated worrying her or anyone else, but it came with the territory.

"Where's the drop?" she asked.

"They'll call in with a location, then I'll call Coleman and DeWayne. I have the money already. We just have to wait for them to contact Elisa."

"I'm going to set up for the supper crowd. I'll be ready when you come by here. Just blow the horn in the back. And you should take that hound dog with you, too. On a leash. Just to be on the safe side."

"You have a good head on your shoulders, Millie." It was a terrific suggestion.

I was eager to learn the details of the money drop, but I couldn't do a thing until the tipster called. It was slow waiting, so I went to the barn and groomed the three horses. Sweetie Pie lounged in the warm sunshine and rolled in the grass, scratching her back. Pluto was too dignified to perform such antics, but he was parked on the front porch, also basking in the sun.

Once the horses were sleek and shiny, their manes and tails free of tangles, I gave them the carrots they loved. When they realized the treat train was empty, they bucked, farted, and ran to the pasture to chase each other. I loved the way they moved in unison, like a flock of birds. The woman who taught me to ride had told me once that horses were the most psychic creatures she'd ever known. They could move together in perfect symmetry. Some riders developed that same bond and they became one with the horse. I was lucky with all three of my steeds. We had that close connection.

I went inside to shower and get dressed for the night. Dark clothes with plenty of layers. The days were perfect, weather-wise, but at night the temperatures dropped.

To keep Jitty off my back, I whipped up some baked chicken enchiladas and put the dish in the oven for Coleman's dinner. I had everything ready. My gun was in a shoulder holster under my arm, and I had two high-powered flashlights. It was after eight o'clock when Elisa called.

"I'm sorry, Sarah Booth. This location is kind of out in the boonies."

"Not your fault, Elisa. Just give me the location."

"The old Cunningham farm off Pesco Road. A mile or two beyond the Pesco Methodist Church."

That was, indeed, way out in the boonies. It made me wonder about who this tipster was that they'd know this long-abandoned farm. My mother had taken me there once as a child, for the burial of one of our family friends. There was a family plot in one of the fields. Even back then the narrow, rutted road with a thick canopy of trees had been intimidating. After all these years, there was no telling what condition the dirt road was in. The little community that had once surrounded the Pesco Methodist Church had dried up and blown away. The land had been acquired by the large agricultural conglomerates who were buying up the rich Delta soil.

"The drop is at nine, sharp."

"I have the money and I'll be there."

"Sarah Booth, the caller threatened me. He said if anyone but you showed up, he would never give me the information on Lydia."

"You did a good job convincing him I would make the drop. It was a man?"

"This time, yes."

"Did you recognize the voice?"

"No."

"Elisa, call Coleman and tell him all of this. Tell him to stay away from the drop, that I will call when I need him, but let him know what's happening. We have to take all precautions to make sure Lydia and Bethany have the best chance possible. If something goes south, we'll need Coleman and the deputies ready to help."

"Sarah Booth, do you think Tope is behind this?"

"Why do you ask?"

"One of my friends at the Club said Tope was in financial trouble. Big trouble. Something about an illicit development deal. Now he may be charged with murder. My friend said Tope is desperate."

That was an interesting tidbit. The Maxwell family, a law firm filled with family members, was very wealthy.

Tope seemed desperate for funds, though. It was possible he'd been cut off. Interesting, indeed.

"Would you relay that to Tinkie, please? She can start digging into that aspect of his financials. If he's desperate for money, that could work in our favor."

"Will do. Be safe, Sarah Booth. I couldn't stand it if I put you in harm's way."

"I'll be fine."

At least that was my intention.

15

Millie was hiding on the floor of the Roadster as I bumped over rutted roads to find the drop location. She'd insisted on ducking low in case the tipster was watching our car. For that same reason, I'd left Sweetie Pie behind at Dahlia House. If she sensed I was in danger, she'd jump the villain—which might result in never getting the information where Lydia was allegedly located.

"I'm sorry," I said as I hit a bad bump. "This road hasn't seen a grader in fifteen years, at least."

"But the tree canopy is beautiful," she said gamely.

"Silver Lining Millie." I couldn't help the sarcasm.

"Grumbling doesn't make it better."

She was right about that. "Another quarter mile."

The little TomTom GPS I'd borrowed from Budgie announced, "Stop. You have reached your destination."

"Great." There was nothing but woods on both sides of the road. Millie started to pop up to look but I cautioned her to stay down. I couldn't tell if we were being watched or not. Millie's job was to watch the tipster's car and discreetly follow it if they fled before I came out of the woods.

"Drive a little farther," Millie suggested. She was peeking out the passenger window. "There should be a pig trail into the property. If I remember accurately, the actual homestead is a little distance into the woods."

I drove slowly, taking in as much of the surroundings as my high beams afforded. Up ahead I saw the reflection of taillights and I stopped. I slowly backed up. I didn't want to box the other car in. I checked my watch. I was right on time.

"Stay down, Millie. I'm going to ease up to the car and make sure no one is in it right now."

"Got it." She held up the mirror I'd given her so she could watch without being a silhouette in the car. "Be careful."

"I will. You, too." I got out and slammed the door. They could be watching me, and I didn't want to act furtive. Once I was out of the car, a high-powered flashlight helped me find an overgrown trail, just as Millie had posited. I was about to check the other car, but I heard something in the underbrush. I stepped into the woods to the creepy sound of a hoot owl. I loved the night predators, but they were not comforting when I was going to an abandoned house on a dark winter night.

The satchel of money wasn't heavy, but it was awkward. Limber branches tugged at me. The trail was almost invisible. When I paused, I heard someone else stop walking, too. I'd have to add that to my list of most-hated noises: the sound of the AC dying, brakes squealing, an animal in distress, a gun cocking, or a stranger's footsteps following behind me.

I kept walking, glad it was winter and not summer, when the biting insects would have drained me of blood.

When I saw the wrought iron gate that marked access to the old homestead, I stopped. It was open, but I didn't want to go in. My directions had said "at the Cunningham farm," not inside. The gate was ornate and had once marked a working family farm. Now the fence was partially down and the old camellias were covered in buck vines and kudzu, a deadly combination to anyone who didn't see the thorns.

I put the satchel down right in front of the gate. I was to leave, and the tipster was to pick up the money, check it, then call Elisa with the information. It was a terrible plan. Everyone knew this, but it was what Elisa wanted. I was her agent, not her boss. As such, I had to comply or quit.

I waited a few minutes and realized no one would show themselves until I left. I went back to the trail, disappointed and wary. But here's where my own ingenious plan would kick in. I hid in the thick undergrowth to watch. Millie was to wait fifteen minutes for me to emerge. If the tipster made it back to leave, she was to follow them and call Coleman. If there was no sign of the tipster, then she should leave, which would hopefully signal to the tipster that it was safe to return to his car. Coleman was at one end of Pesco Road and DeWayne the other. We would catch the tipster red-handed.

I hunkered down behind a cluster of huckleberry shrubs and ferns, a safe and secure hiding place, where I could still see the drop. My legs were cramping but still no one appeared to take the loot. I checked my watch. It was time for Millie to depart. I'd be left in the woods until I called for a ride home.

I never saw the person who struck me from behind. I went down in the soft leaves and underbrush. The smell of the fecund earth was musty, and I had a strange vision of cornfields and cotton stretching to the horizon.

I felt a hand pull roughly at my shoulder and someone turning my face out of the dirt and leaves.

"Leave this alone. You're going to get someone killed if you don't."

The voice was female and Southern. I tried to turn over to look, but my body was too heavy. For a time, I blacked out. When I came to my senses, I checked my watch. It had only been ten minutes. Plenty of time for the attacker to make a clean getaway. I got to my feet and stabilized my balance, then went back to the farm gate. The satchel was gone. No surprise. They'd knocked me out and taken the money. They'd been hiding and watching me.

I started the hike back to the road, calling Millie as I went.

"I'm on the tail," she answered. "I'm doing just like you said. No headlights and staying way back. They're driving like fools, though. Are you okay?"

"Yes." I could fill her in on the details later. "Be careful."

"This tailing a person isn't easy. TV makes it seem so simple. I hope I don't lose them."

"Don't confront them." Nothing was worth Millie getting injured. "I'm going to call Elisa and see if they came across with the info to find Lydia. You don't do anything foolish."

I placed the call and Elisa answered before the first ring

was complete. I had my answer then. She was almost hatching the phone she was so close on top of it.

"They never called," she said, sounding forlorn.

"They knocked me out and took the money. I'm sorry. I thought I could trick them."

"You warned me, Sarah Booth, but I had to try. It's not your fault. Everyone tried to tell me they were likely scam artists just playing me for the cash. I'm just so desperate to find Lydia."

"You did what you had to. I'll check in tomorrow." I hung up. I didn't want to get her hopes up that I had Millie on the tail of the tipster. Besides, I had a long way to walk and I needed to watch my step in the dark.

The truth was, I didn't blame Elisa for her actions. She had plenty of money and only one daughter. I would have made the same bargain. Understanding didn't give us any better options. All my hopes were pinned on Millie and Coleman, but there was something else, too. I'd been warned to stop looking for Lydia. The person who'd hit me also knew who I was. And they knew I was searching for the missing women. So the tipster was either someone who knew what happened to Lydia and wanted to keep that information secret because they were culpable in the disappearance, or it was someone trying to keep Lydia from being found for other reasons.

I dialed my lover. "Coleman, they're headed south on Pesco Road. Millie is tailing the blackmailer. No one has called Elisa. The money is gone, and a woman warned me to stop looking for Lydia or someone would die."

"DeWayne is near the intersection of Pesco and Ladner Roads. He's in his truck so he can pick up the car. Tell Millie to drop back."

"Will do. She can retrieve me then." Good that I didn't have to call Tinkie out.

"Are you okay? You sound odd."

"Just aggravated with myself. What are you going to do?" I didn't want him fretting about my head.

"You said a woman warned you. Did you see her?"

"No, she hit me from behind." He needed the details, even if they worried him. I gave him the CliffsNotes version. "I'm okay. She leaned down and whispered in my ear to stop the search."

"Did you see the car she was driving?"

"I didn't. I parked far back from the parked car because of Millie." Damn, I should have gone to check it and gotten the tag number, at least. There had been a lot of missteps.

"That's okay. DeWayne will get the make, model, and tag. Just get home and make sure you aren't hurt."

"Where will you be?"

"Paying Tope an unexpected visit."

"Be careful." Coleman knew his business, but Tope Maxwell was most likely a murderer, possibly a double or triple offender. He was no one to mess with.

"Let me know you're home safe."

"Will do. You keep your eyes open." He gave me the freedom to do my work, and I owed him the same.

I started walking back to the county road. It would take Millie a good twenty minutes to circle back for me once DeWayne picked up the tail. Along the way, I called Tinkie to update her.

"Well, double damn," she said. "They got the money, and you got a lump on the head."

"We knew going in that Elisa risked losing the money and getting nothing, except maybe we did get some useful info." I told her my hypothesis about the woman wanting us to stop the search for the women. It had occurred to me that maybe, just maybe, that could have been Lydia or Bethany.

"Lydia may really be alive." Tinkie processed the clues at record speed.

"It could have been Lydia who picked up the money. Or Bethany. Or their agent."

"Why wouldn't she just ask her mother for cash? Elisa would give her the moon."

"That could put Elisa in danger. If Lydia is alive and in hiding, she may be desperate for money and in a really bad situation. That may be why she's stayed away. Out of fear Tope would take his vengeance out on Elisa."

"What could she be into that would be so dangerous?" Tinkie asked.

"I wish I knew. Hey, I'm on the county road and I think I see Millie coming. We'll talk tomorrow."

16

Coleman was late getting home, but I was waiting for him with hot food and a drink. He looked done in, but when he saw me, he perked up.

"It's been a day," I said, handing him a Jack on the rocks. I had one myself. I'd lit a fire and the crackling flames were too inviting to ignore.

"Sit down and I'll bring some food for you." The chicken enchiladas were still warm. The perfect winter meal. Coleman was suitably impressed.

While he ate, I snuggled near him on the sofa and filled him in on the details of my failed plot to snare the tipster. DeWayne was still tailing the person who'd picked up the loot, and he was keeping Coleman abreast of each development in real time. Coleman had decided that rather than stop and arrest the tipster, DeWayne should follow the car. He felt more information would be gleaned that way, and DeWayne would call when the "fly lit."

For the moment, it was good to have Coleman home, to see him eating as the firelight flickered on his features—to know that we were working together to bring justice to the people around us. I was a lucky woman.

When he was done, I took the dishes to the kitchen and brought the Jack to top off our drinks. He put a hand over his glass. "I could be called out any minute. Better not."

He was right. I put the Jack away and snuggled beside him. "Now tell me everything that happened with Tope."

"You are learning patience, aren't you?" he teased.

"Maybe a little. By the time you're old and fat, I'll be *really* patient. Now spill, or I'll have to hurt you."

He laughed and drew me against him. "Tope was extremely put out."

"A major understatement, I'm sure."

Before he could get into it deeper, his phone rang.

"It's DeWayne." He answered and listened intently for a few minutes. "Okay, thanks, DeWayne. Good work." He shifted so he faced me. "DeWayne followed a gray sedan, which turned out to be a 2010 Altima. The license plate is covered with red mud, so we can't run it."

"What?" I couldn't believe it. Another dead end. "Where is the car going?"

"South, toward Natchez. He's going to follow but once they leave Sunflower County he won't have arrest powers. It's either pull them over now or wait to see where they lead us. I suggest we wait. DeWayne says they aren't aware he's bird-dogging them."

I nodded agreement. As Aunt Loulane would say, we

were trading a bird in hand for two in the bush. But finding a location that we could search might be more beneficial than arresting someone who'd lied to Elisa Redd on a tip line. A fraud charge might hold up, but we'd be no closer to finding Lydia. Coleman was still talking to DeWayne, and I leaned in to catch the last of the conversation.

"Stay on his tail," Coleman told DeWayne before he hung up. "If he crosses the river into Louisiana, don't follow." He turned to me. "Whoever this person is, we can claim they've broken a number of laws. Deadly assault and fraud, to name two. Once DeWayne runs them to ground, we can get the local deputies to arrest them. We might not make the charges stick but we can bring them in for questioning."

"Well, damn." Tinkie and I had gone to a lot of work to lose ten grand and not even have a suspect we had a guarantee of arresting. I'd hoped to have someone to question tonight. And someone to hold accountable for knocking me out. I hoped we'd found the trail of Lydia Redd Maxwell.

"Coleman, do you know anything about Ernest and Florence Salter?" I asked. Coleman had cleaned up the sheriff's department since he took office. Before him, the law officers weren't on the up-and-up. But would they really have allowed a man to be hanged and burned without investigating a murder?

"I heard rumors, but never anything solid. Tomorrow Budgie will follow up with this Ernest Salter situation. If anyone was hanged, we'll know."

"And the girls who allegedly went missing?"

"It'll take some research, but we can look into it."

"And Florence? Her grave is empty. Maybe the hanging and the grave are just a convenient way for the Salters to leave and start over somewhere else."

"I'll check the state statistics to see if there's a death certificate for either of them," Coleman offered. "You might want to find someone who knew them. Ask Cece to check the newspaper for any local stories. The *Dispatch* keeps a pretty good file of old stories."

"In the morning." It was too late to call anyone in a nonemergency situation. "What about Tope?" Coleman wasn't going to plead exhaustion and evade my questions.

"He's a real piece of work."

"That goes without saying. Did he kill Vivian?"

"I'm one-hundred-percent positive. I just can't prove it. The house staff is terrified to even speak with me. Vivian's parents believe he's a man in mourning, a good man. They believe their daughter fell by accident. According to them, he's such a kind man he's paying for all the funeral expenses even though they were just engaged and not married. According to them, Tope is a king."

"Did you tell them about the black eye and the bruises?"

"They didn't want to hear it. Tope really has them snowed, which may explain why Vivian stayed with him even after the abuse began."

"Vivian never told them about the abuse?" It astounded me. Had anyone ever physically abused me, my father would have taken the legal actions to put them behind bars. My mother would have cut out their gizzard with a dull knife. "I wish we could have done something to save Vivian. She should have confided in her parents."

"If she did, they're denying it."

"That's incomprehensible." How did a child grow up and thrive without that kind of protective love from a parent? For all of Tinkie's mother's benign neglect, Mrs. Bellcase would have scalped anyone who deliberately hurt Tinkie.

Why have a child if a person couldn't love it with a whole heart? Or wouldn't put everything on the line to protect that child?

Tope had to pay for what he'd done. "You know why women don't talk. Chances are Vivian was too proud to tell her parents or anyone else. There's a stigma about being abused. There shouldn't be, but there is. The patriarchy has put the burden of physical consequences on the woman for eons—she isn't enough, not worthy of decent treatment, too needy, too bossy, too bold, too shy. Somehow it's always the woman's fault. Abusers even say it. 'Why do you make me hit you?' How many times have you heard that?"

"Too many," Coleman said, his hands soothing my back. "As a society, we need to truly examine the messages we give our sons and daughters. The Maxwell family has always been eaten up with entitlement. Tope is the monster they created. They've long believed they could do whatever they wanted without legal repercussions."

"And until you became sheriff, they got away with that attitude." I kissed his cheek. Coleman saw the worst of human nature—and sometimes the best—each and every day. Somehow he kept his balance in a world full of cruel extremes. "Where do you think Lydia is?"

"I don't think she's dead. Budgie can check international law enforcement sources to see if there's anything on her. If she went to Afghanistan at all, she'll be on someone's radar. He was going to do that today but ended up working a burglary at a furniture store."

"Thanks, Coleman." I wanted to kiss him, but his phone rang again.

"Okay," he said. "It's okay, DeWayne. As long as you

aren't hurt. Okay, okay, don't worry. They won't get away with this."

I knew it was not good news, but I didn't interrupt. When he put the phone down with a frown, I asked. "What?"

"The tipster who picked up the money ditched DeWayne."

"How?" DeWayne was an excellent tracker and driver.

"They scattered roofing tacks on the road. He got two flats and had to pull over."

"Someone watched a lot of Wile E. Coyote." It wasn't funny at all, but roofing tacks? Who would have thought of that? "Is DeWayne okay?"

"Yeah, he's calling a wrecker. He's mad as a hornet."

That I could understand. "Please thank him. I know he's aggravated."

"That he is."

"And thank you, Coleman. You didn't have to send De-Wayne to help me."

"I'm happy to help you, but remember, Lydia is a missing persons case in this county so it's my job, too. And Vivian's death won't be forgotten. There's something rotten going on with Tope Maxwell. I want to contain it before it spreads. Now let's go to bed. Tomorrow will be a hard day and I have to be up at the crack of dawn."

Coleman had the wonderful ability to find sleep almost instantly. As Aunt Loulane would say, he found the rest of the innocent, those with a clear conscious. The flip side of that was me—the perpetual insomniac. I was wide awake, going over every single thing I'd done and worrying over the decisions I could have made better. When my tossing and turning threatened to wake Coleman, I got out of bed and went downstairs.

I stoked up the fire, poured another Jack, and dove under a warm blanket to sip my drink and hope the fire could mesmerize me into sleep. Sweetie Pie jumped up beside me and Pluto came to sit on my chest and make biscuits. I had all the elements for a restful sleep. At last my brain calmed and I drifted.

I woke up to the sound of a typewriter. An older model, where the keys struck the paper on the platen with a loud clack. When I looked over the back of the sofa, I saw the silhouette of a woman at my mother's desk, pounding away. She pulled the page from the typewriter, cleared her throat, and read, "'Last night I dreamt I went to Manderley again.'"

That simple sentence, a marvel of hardworking storytelling, sent my mind spiraling back to the hard days when authors and books helped me through some impossible years. I remembered reading *Rebecca* down in the grove of old oaks where I'd played with the elves and fairies before my parents died. After the wreck that took my parents, I went there often to read. Daphne du Maurier had given me the fantastic and scary world of Manderley, a fictional British estate where an evil housekeeper sought to keep a ghost alive. For the amount of time I was immersed in the book I lived that life, not the one where I was an orphan.

"Ms. Du Maurier?" I asked. It wasn't possible, but I wanted to believe. "*Rebecca* saved my life." It wasn't exactly an exaggeration. Reading had given me a thousand other lives to live when mine became too painful.

The slender woman stood up from the desk. "Did you know my book hasn't been out of print a single time since 1938 when it was first published?" She came closer, but her features were still in shadow. She wore a shirtwaist dress, little heels, and her hair framed her face in soft chestnut curls. A style of the 1940s.

"I love your book. Well, all of them. But *Rebecca,* in particular."

"Thank you. That's gratifying to hear. There's a special contract between the reader and the writer. You give me your time and willingness to visualize my world, and I tell you a story."

"You honored that agreement."

She came closer and the firelight illuminated her clean jaw-line and regular features. She was slender and attractive. A string of pearls was the only jewelry she wore. "You read my books after your parents were killed. I kept you company."

I was surprised she said this, but not shocked. "You helped me through those impossible times." I'd almost forgotten that period where Daphne du Maurier was a beloved companion. Manderley was as real to me as Dahlia House. The wicked Mrs. Danvers was worse than a ghost. "Thank you."

"The character Rebecca was . . . always a shadow. There, but not there. Looming larger than life. When I first conceived her, I had to write her. I thought about using her point of view, but I found a better way."

"Yes, you did! The young narrator, so eager to fit in, to be worthy of love. Every word is perfect."

"Thank you."

I knew the phantom typist was Jitty in the guise of du Maurier, but I felt as if I were really talking with the writer. "Do you have a message for me?"

"In fact, I do. You have everything you need to figure out your case."

"Everything except a location for Lydia."

She smiled, genteel and kind. "It's there. It's only a matter of interpretation. Of point of view. You're smart and tenacious. You have good help. And thank heavens there isn't a Mrs. Danvers in Dahlia House to gum up the works."

17

Coleman woke me at first light when he scooped me up to take me upstairs to bed. I'd fallen asleep on the sofa under blankets, but the fire had gone out and my nose was a block of ice.

"Stay with me." I reached up to hold him to me when he shifted me into the bed.

"I have to work."

That brought me wide awake, and I kissed him before I let him go. "I'm getting up, too. I have a busy day."

"It's not even six," he said.

"I know." I reached up to him and pulled him down beside me for a long, delicious kiss. We both had to get moving, but a few minutes wouldn't kill either of us. And Coleman was certainly willing enough.

Before it got too heated, he sat up on his elbow, his finger tracing my profile. "I think you may be on Tope's payroll. Tempting me away from my work."

I laughed. "You think?"

"Not really. I know my girl. Money could never influence your affections."

Even though he said it in a mocking way, it made me happy. I pushed him almost out of the bed, then I escaped his grasping hands. Screaming, I made it to the bathroom and shut and locked the door. We were both laughing so hard we couldn't talk.

"Bring me a cup of coffee, please." I knew he'd made it. I had smelled it when I was downstairs. "By the time you bring it up here, I'll be ready to give you the shower." I turned on the hot water to let it run warm, and in two shakes I was lathering up and shampooing my hair. By the time he brought the coffee, I was drying off and he jumped under the stinging hot spray.

Standing in the bathroom doorway, I took a moment to appreciate the many blessings of my life. Then I was snatching up jeans and a sweatshirt to dress in the kitchen as I put bacon on to fry and four slices of wheat bread in the toaster. I wasn't a big breakfast eater, though I loved it. But on the cold mornings, a little food was necessary.

Coleman took his toast and bacon to go, leaving me with a kiss and a whispered promise. I put the dishes in the sink before I called Tinkie. "How do you feel about a ride to Adams County today?"

The day was incredible—the most perfect weather of the Mississippi Delta. Pale yellow sunlight warming the fallow fields, banks of white cumulus clouds in a robin's-egg sky. It was warm enough to put the top down on the Roadster since

I was wearing a coat, scarf, and gloves. Sweetie Pie and Pluto were snuggled in the front seat and Sweetie Pie's ears flapped in the wind when she stuck her nose out to test the air.

At Hilltop I tooted the horn. If I went inside I'd be caught up in baby adoration for at least half an hour, and we had ground to cover. Tinkie swept out of her front door with Chablis tucked in her arms. They wore matching houndstooth coats, and Tinkie had added black leggings and red boots. Each wore a red beret. They could have been ready to walk on a Parisian street.

"Looking very chic," I said as Tinkie shooed my critters into the backseat so she could take her place. Chablis jumped out of her arms and into the back.

"Chablis and I decided we would style together. Even though she is glitzed, trimmed, and totally fabulous, she's ready to work. Just like me."

At one time I'd considered Tinkie not very bright, thinking her shallow because of her emphasis on style, appearances, and money. I'd been so very wrong and was glad to admit how judgmental I'd been about her intelligence and value system.

"What are we doing?" she asked.

"Tracking down the vehicle belonging to Ernest Salter. And also seeing if we can pick up the trail of the deceitful tipster. DeWayne lost them last night because they threw roofing nails down on the road. DeWayne had to call a tow truck to get him because he had two flats and only one spare." I'd given her the basics, but now she had the details.

"Why Adams County?" Tinkie asked.

"Remember the truck that was registered to Ernest Salter? We can get the address and see what's there. I don't have a lot of other leads to follow. It's a drive, but we're getting an early start."

"Yes, a physical address. We'll get that and go look for ourselves." Tinkie was ready for action.

We took the famous blues road, Highway 61. While our mission was serious, we couldn't help but enjoy the day. Just as we were hitting the outskirts of Natchez, Budgie called us with an address.

"This is old," Budgie said. "It may no longer be valid, but I can't find any listing for Ernest or Florence Salter except this one."

"Mr. Salter was supposedly hanged in one of the rural cemeteries in Mount Zion. Tinkie and I searched the cemetery but couldn't find a grave for him, or for Lydia or Bethany, as someone had said on the tip line. They could be buried anywhere, though. The cemetery is pretty much abandoned. Florence has a grave and headstone there."

"An empty grave." Budgie let me know he was paying attention. "And there's no evidence to show that Ernest Salter was hanged or died in Sunflower County. In fact, the old Salter farm is still standing but abandoned, from what I could find out."

"Do you know anything else about the Salters?" I asked.

"I always thought the talk was without basis, just meanness aimed at two people who were reclusive. Florence tried to help people, from what I heard. But you know how cruel people can be. I never knew a single girl who went to Florence for an abortion. No one who could verify it was true." Budgie hesitated for a moment. "I've come to believe that the Salters were likely moonshining. They created those rumors themselves to keep people away from their property."

That theory also made good sense. Distilling corn liquor

was a tradition in a lot of rural families. The old joke was that a bootlegger never bought all of his sugar from the same place because it was a dead giveaway. "Was there any proof of that?" I asked.

I slowed and pulled off the road at a scenic overlook with a view of the Mississippi River. The bluffs in Natchez were famous for many things, including spectacular views.

Budgie continued, "I never bought any liquor from Ernest, but my friends swore they did."

"What about the girls who went missing?" Tinkie asked. "What happened to them?"

"That's a good question. I've been digging around in some of the old records, and I've found three reports of young women who went missing. They were there one day, then gone the next. No explanation. It's very strange." Budgie had an ace up his sleeve but he was holding it back.

"Isn't that a bit unusual?" Tinkie asked.

"A lot unusual for people in your social strata, Tinkie. But for the poor, sometimes a fresh start is the only answer. I'm thinking some of these girls got in trouble and then just left the area, either to have the baby or to have an abortion. They'd have to go north to find an out-of-state clinic in Memphis or Cincinnati to find a doctor who might help them."

"Unless Florence Salter would," I said. "So what happened to the Salters?"

"That's what you're going to find out," he said. "If they're in Natchez, you can get a lot of answers from them."

18

Natchez had a colorful history, and at one point in time, before the Civil War, more than half the millionaires in America owned homes there. For the wealthy and privileged, it was a land of beauty and graciousness. Most of the plantation owners in Mississippi owned a home in Natchez or Vicksburg or Greenville—those river towns where the transport of cotton from inland to the river, then down to New Orleans and, eventually, the textile mills of England brought them boundless profit. There was also a great cost, but those who upheld slavery seldom wanted to count that expense. They preferred to pretend it didn't exist.

I loved the river town, which had such fabulous stories of river pirates, witches, and ghosts, not to mention estates that had survived the rigors of war and the climate. There was beauty there.

We decided to stop off at Natchez Under the Hill for some coffee and to explore a local map. We had the Salters' address, but I wanted to study the topography and community a little. The day was very warm, and without the rushing wind of the convertible, we began peeling off the layers of clothes. Sweetie Pie and Chablis found a shady spot under our table on an outside patio. Pluto was being a diva and refused to sit anywhere other than on a chair. He made it clear he had menu selections he wanted us to order. Why not? Tinkie and I only wanted coffee, but we got eggs, cheese, and bacon for the critters, served in take-out cartons.

We took our time, enjoying the view of the river, where the *Delta Queen,* en route from New Orleans to Memphis, had docked. Tourists swarmed off the boat to visit Natchez Under the Hill, which at one time had been notorious. Pirates and thieves frequented the bars and saloons that had been replaced by high-end restaurants. The boats traversing the river were often set upon and robbed. Natchez was a wild and wooly place.

The Mississippi was a broad, brown ribbon; deceptively docile looking. Those of us who knew the history of the river were well aware of the currents and eddies that could trap a swimmer and pull them down to the watery embrace of death. Natchez was built on bluffs, and across the river, the sea-level terrain of Louisiana spread out.

I remembered the old legends, which used to spook us as school kids, about inmates from Louisiana's notorious Angola state penitentiary escaping, swimming across the river, and traveling up to the Delta to find and kill us. It never happened, as far as I knew, but at the age of ten, I believed it. One thing about the South was that gossip and stories often had a Gothic tinge to them. Escaped murderers on the rampage, hanging trees, women disappearing, ghosts popping up—a fact I could attest to. We loved our haunted houses, decrepit cemeteries, and legends.

As we drank our coffee and watched the traffic on the river, I thought about the section of Adams County we would soon visit. The ruins of a very large plantation were near the address listed as belonging to Ernest Salter. It was said Mark Twain had often visited the old plantation, which was not far from the river, drawing inspiration for his stories. I studied the map a little more, making sure I knew where I was going.

"Do you think we'll find the Salter residence?" Tinkie asked. She bent to pick up the dishes from our animals.

"I don't know. In truth, I don't know whether to hope we find Ernest or not."

"What I'd really like is to find Lydia or Bethany," Tinkie said.

"From your lips . . ." I didn't finish the old saying. I was turning into Aunt Loulane and that was scary. Tinkie would have to drive a stake through my heart if I continually spouted adages and sage wisdom.

"Let's hit it." Tinkie whistled up the dogs and Pluto followed them to the car. In no time we were on the road, taking in the smell of the river.

Tinkie gave directions as I drove, and half an hour later we turned down a long gravel driveway beneath the arch of McTavish Plantation. The plantation house was long gone. But tucked in the overgrowth of vines, brambles, and bushes were heritage camellias and other plants that told of a once-incredible landscape. It was impossible to tell how long the area had been neglected. In the South, with the subtropical weather, the undergrowth could take over in a matter of months.

"I'll bet this was once a showplace," Tinkie said, pointing at the Corinthian columns and marble steps that were all that remained of the big house.

"I've seen photos in history books. It was a beautiful place."

"What happened?" Tinkie asked.

"A fire." I didn't remember the details, only that the house went up fast. No one died, but every stick of furniture was lost. "I think it was lightning, but I don't recall the exact story. I was a kid when it burned. I remember my parents talking about it. There aren't a lot of the big houses left in the rural areas. Most are in town and now tourist attractions."

"Such a shame." Tinkie had a soft spot for the old mansions that were part of a gracious past. "The truth is that the maintenance today would break the average homeowner."

"Or even someone wealthy," I pointed out.

We left the ruins behind us and continued along the well-maintained gravel road. The map was unclear if we were still on the plantation grounds or if we'd left them behind. When we came across wooden shotgun houses and cottages, I knew we were getting close to the object of our quest. A few of the mailboxes were even numbered, and I saw the address we were seeking. I stopped the car and looked at the house.

It was a plain white cottage, well maintained. Adirondack chairs and a swing decorated the front porch, and a man was seated on the swing. He moved back and forth, watching the road and us.

"Do you think that's Ernest?" Tinkie asked.

"I don't know. But we're going to find out." I turned in to the driveway and pulled up near the house. Five dogs came out from under the porch to bay at us. They wagged their tails so furiously it made them wiggle. Hounds were just like that. Sweetie Pie and Chablis barked a greeting, and we were forgotten by the pups. Tinkie and I got out of the car and approached the gentleman I could now see was elderly. Too old to be Ernest Salter.

"Can I help you?" he asked.

This was the graciousness of the South I admired. If he was suspicious of us, he didn't show it. "We're trying to find Ernest and Florence Salter. Do you know them?"

He shook his head. "What you need them for?"

"I need their help," I said.

He gave me a long look. "You look too old to be in trouble."

That stopped me. My brain whirled, connecting the dots. Ernest or Florence or both *had* been involved with young girls in "trouble." "Not that kind of trouble. I need their help finding a missing woman they may know. From Sunflower County."

The man stood up with a limberness I didn't expect. "Don't know anything about missing people." He stepped backward and opened his screened door. "I've got work to do. Have a nice day."

"Mister!" Tinkie was up the steps in a flash. "We need some help. We're not trying to start anything. We just need to know if you've seen these women." She pulled out her phone and showed him pictures of Lydia and Bethany. "There's a ten-thousand-dollar reward for information leading to them. No strings attached."

He glanced at the photos but shook his head. "Never

seen them. Now I need to work, like I said. Pleasure meeting you." He stepped into the house, but Tinkie grasped his arm.

"Please," she said. "This woman's mother is heartsick with worry and grief. Sarah Booth"—she pointed at me—"and I are private investigators. We heard that the Salters may have helped Lydia and Bethany. Lydia was in a terrible marriage. Her husband abused her."

The gentleman stepped back outside. "How long those women been missing?"

"More than six years." Tinkie sighed and shook her head. "The ex-husband, Tope Maxwell, is trying to have Lydia declared dead. Maybe he killed her. But he sure wants her money. There's nothing we can do to stop him if we don't find her. We're hoping she's with Bethany."

"And why did you come here?" he asked.

"Truck tag traced back to this address. Do you have a truck?"

"Yeah." He looked to the left of the porch. I figured the truck was parked behind the house.

"Look, Mr. . . ."

"Riley. Frank Riley."

"Mr. Riley, we are trying to help this family. Now, what we know is that the women were seen driving a pickup truck at a produce stand. The truck tag was spotted and when I had it checked, it was an old tag issued to Ernest Salter. I'm assuming you know him."

"I bought the truck from him. I just never bought a new tag. It's a farm truck. I seldom drive it to town."

"But you loaned it to two women?"

He nodded. "I did."

"And where are these women?" I asked, hope surging

through me. Could we possibly be that close to finding them?

"I don't know," he said. "I loaned them the truck. They brought it back this morning. They left."

"To go where?" Tinkie asked.

"They didn't tell me."

"Are you sure it wasn't the women I showed you?" Tinkie asked.

"No. They needed the truck for something, and I let them have it. I didn't memorize their looks or pry into their business."

"Did they say why they needed a truck?" Getting information from Mr. Riley was a chore. I had to drag it out of him.

He thought a minute. "Yeah, they did tell me."

"Well, why?" I asked.

"They said they had to move a dead body."

19

Tinkie and I stood speechless for a long moment. We looked at each other, and finally Tinkie spoke. "A dead body?"

"That's what they said." Frank Riley looked up and down the quiet street.

"Do you think they actually had a body?" Tinkie pressed.

Frank shrugged. "They *said* they did. Why would those women lie to me?"

"Did they say it was a human body?" I asked. "Maybe it was a dog or cat or some pet."

"Folks wouldn't borrow a truck to bury a pet. They'd just dig a hole in the yard and have the funeral. This is the country, not some asphalt city."

Frank was a little testy with me, but he had a point. In

the country, each family generally had a pet cemetery near the house. Family cemeteries on the grounds were also popular. In the South, keeping the dead close at hand was something of a tradition.

"Wish I could be more help. Now, if you'll excuse me, I have chores to do."

"Mr. Riley, please." Tinkie put on her saddest face. "We're only trying to help the missing women and Lydia's mother."

"I can't tell you what I don't know. I left the keys in the truck while I had some farm work to do. They left me fifty dollars. They took the truck and then they brought it back, and with a full tank of gas. I never saw them."

Tinkie's face told me she didn't believe this for a minute. "You'd just let two people you never even met use your vehicle?"

"I told them not to go on the main roads, because of the tag. I guess they didn't follow directions very well."

"You don't mind that your truck was used to haul a dead body?" Tinkie pressed.

"Doesn't mean they murdered someone. Maybe they were doing that natural-burial thing. I've found that the best way to get along in this world is to mind my own business. They didn't ask for my help or advice, so I didn't give any."

"When did they borrow the truck?"

He shrugged. "Couple of weeks ago, it seems. Said they had a lot of work to do. At my age, time slides by fast, and I wasn't paying that much attention."

He loaned his truck to two women—whom he'd never met—who said they wanted to move a body, and he just sort of ignored it? Wow. Frank Riley was either incredibly callous or not mentally right. This just didn't add up. Tinkie nudged me with her elbow and whispered in my ear, "Do you believe he doesn't remember?"

I didn't respond. I was trying to figure out the best way to play this. In a two-week period, someone resembling Lydia and Bethany had been spotted, together, in Natchez *and* Greenwood. If the ladies were in the area, why in the heck wouldn't Lydia get in touch with her mama? It was either very cruel, careless, or dangerous, and I couldn't help but wonder if Lydia or Bethany was trying to protect Elisa or someone else by staying away. Tope was capable of anything, and threatening Lydia's mother was not out of the question.

"Would you mind if we took a look at the truck?" I asked.

"Suit yourself. It's in the back. I'm going inside to sit by the fire. My old bones don't like this cold."

"Before you go, do you own another vehicle? A gray Altima?"

"Only the truck," he said. "I don't have a lot of driving needs. Now I'm cold."

"Thank you," Tinkie called to his back as he closed the door. "Let's check out that truck." Tinkie skipped down the steps ahead of me and cut around the corner of the house.

The truck was parked near an old shed beneath a leafless sycamore tree, and I thought of the Hangman's Tree in the old cemetery. Sycamores were such beautiful trees, but they appeared so naked and vulnerable, too. In the fall, their big leaves turned a rich shade of yellow, and in a good wind they'd flutter to the ground like falling stardust.

The old F-150 had seen better days. It looked to be a

1998 model with a V-8 for hauling things. Truly a farm-work truck. The bed was cluttered with old potting containers and organic soil bags. I climbed in and moved the debris around until I could see the metal of the truck. If a body had been there, it might have left some trace evidence. I examined the bed inch by inch but found nothing other than dirt, leaves, and a few twigs.

"The body could have been wrapped up good," Tinkie pointed out.

"True."

"It could have been frozen."

"True." I couldn't help myself. "Like those Popsicles we used to buy at Nixon's Grocery. Remember?"

"That is gross!" Tinkie made a face. "You have a sick sense of humor."

"So I'm told." I jumped out of the truck bed and went to the driver's door. Maybe the women had left something in the cab.

"Sarah Booth, are we tampering with evidence?"

Tinkie's question held no hint of hesitation. It was purely informational. "We don't have enough evidence for any legit law officer to investigate so, no, we aren't interfering." That was my story, and I was sticking to it.

Tinkie opened the passenger door, and we began our interior search. I imagined Lydia behind the wheel and Bethany in the passenger seat, then changed it around. Bethany would likely be driving, knowing the dynamics of the women as I did. Bethany was take charge, and Lydia more retiring. Or at least that was the way I visualized them.

We found gum wrappers, dirt, some loose change, and, at last, some success. Tinkie found a hair tie with several blond hairs in it. "These could be Lydia's," she said.

"Yes." I felt a thrill of success. Bethany was a brunette and, from all the photos I'd seen, had shorter hair, but over the years it could have grown out. The elastic hair tie could well be the proof we needed, assuming there was a DNA sample to test against.

Tinkie heaved a sigh. "Not a lot to go on, but better than nothing."

"Yes. Do you think this is his only vehicle?" I asked.

"Why would he lie? He doesn't know DeWayne was bird-dogging an Altima."

She was right, but still. If the truck was a farm truck—with an invalid tag—what did Frank drive when he had to go to town? "I'm going to take a look in that old barn." I pointed to a wooden structure half hidden in Chinese tallow trees.

"It might fall on your head," Tinkie said.

"Maybe. Maybe not." I glanced at the house and found Frank Riley looking out a window, watching us.

"Why don't you go to the front door and distract him for a minute?"

Tinkie grinned. "Sure. Just be quick. He pretends to be an old man, but he's a crackerjack. He doesn't trust us as far as he can throw us."

"No kidding." I started walking back toward the house with her. Frank disappeared from the window. The minute he was gone, I darted behind some trees and headed back to the barn. Tinkie trotted toward the front of the house. She had a way with men, young or old, and she'd divert his attention for a few minutes. Just long enough for me to examine what might be in the barn.

The door squealed on rusty hinges, and I stepped inside, the winter sunlight filtering through cracks between the boards. The car was right there, under a cover. I lifted the corner and identified the type and the license plate covered in red mud. Now I had a real dilemma. Was it possible Frank Riley was with the woman who'd struck me in the head? Should I press charges? My gut told me to back off. I checked the front seat of the car as thoroughly as I could in the dim light. It was clean, almost as if it had been vacuumed. I took a photo of the license plate, put the cover back, and slipped out of the barn, circling around until I was at the car waiting for Tinkie. I tooted the horn to let her know I was safely out of the barn.

Through the branches of a bottlebrush tree, I watched her say her goodbyes and walk to the car with all the confidence of a queen. This was the advantage of being trained as a Daddy's Girl. Composure sat on her right shoulder and decorum on her left. Tinkie was the person you wanted in a pinch.

"Did you find anything?" she asked as she slammed the car door.

"I found the car. I didn't have time to really search it."

"Coleman can get the sheriff here to impound it and search it for clues."

He could, but would he? I doubted he'd be willing to. Not because he didn't want to help, but our evidence was pretty flimsy. The Adams County sheriff likely wouldn't comply, and Coleman wouldn't want to put him in a situation where he refused a fellow law officer.

"The car was clean. There weren't any roofing tacks or anything in it that could be used as a reason for a warrant. I think we should let that part go for now, but we have gained vital information. The people who took the ransom were here, at Frank Riley's farm, to at least borrow the car. That's a fact we know. I don't believe for a second Frank doesn't know them. He's protecting them for some reason."

"All very true," Tinkie agreed.

"We also know one of the ransom thieves was a woman—because she spoke to me before I blacked out. I believe that woman was either Lydia or Bethany. If it wasn't one of them, then it was someone who knows where to look for our missing heiress."

"And the dead body?" Tinkie asked. "I don't know why they needed a truck, but I think it was Lydia or Bethany who borrowed his truck. We must find them, and Frank Riley is not going to help us," Tinkie said.

"Not intentionally. And I think that whole dead-body remark was his way of trying to scare us off."

She gave me a quizzical look as I pulled onto the road and headed toward downtown Natchez. "So he's working with Lydia and Bethany?"

"Frank is important to the women who went to the produce stand. If one of them was Lydia, then she'll show up at his place again. We'll be prepared when she does." That seemed to be our best lead, as unsubstantial as it was.

"We're going to stake out Frank Riley's place?" Tinkie balked at the thought. "That's going to take more manpower than we have."

Tinkie's total devotion was to her baby. I understood that. "Not we, just me. I can take you home and drop back by here. I'll get a thermos of coffee and I'll be just fine. It isn't even very cold. Honestly, I don't think the women will be back here today. But they'll be here before long."

"Not while the sun is shining." Tinkie rolled her eyes. "You can't do this alone."

"Tinkie, you have a responsibility. If one of the horses was sick, or the critters, then I would have to say no to the stakeout. But I'm free and willing."

"You might have to be here for days," Tinkie wailed. "That's just not fair. I'm a partner."

"A good partner. Do your computer thing. I honestly think this will turn out to be a waste of time, but what else are we supposed to do?"

The perky jingle of my ringtone perfectly ended a conversation that only made both of us anxious. "Hello, Budgie," I said.

I didn't get a chance to say anything else. Budgie talked a mile a minute, and what he had to say was very interesting. When we got into downtown Natchez, he was still talking, and I took the road to Natchez Under the Hill. Terrific restaurants had replaced the cutthroat bars of the river-pirate days.

He was still talking after I'd parked the car and we'd walked to the front door of the restaurant. Tinkie went in to get a table while I stood in the sun watching the boats on the river.

"Thank you, Budgie." His information was disturbing, but I was glad he'd called.

"I'm sorry, Sarah Booth. I know this isn't what you wanted to hear."

"No, it isn't. But we deal with the facts, not the fantasies."

"What are you going to do?"

I honestly didn't know. "I'll give Elisa a call. I know she's very upset. I'll do whatever she wants us to do."

"Call Coleman when you start home. He specifically asked me to tell you that."

"Will do." I punched off the phone and entered the restaurant. Tinkie sat at a table in the bar nursing a glass of iced tea. When she saw my face, she knew the news was bad.

"What?"

"Someone called the tip line and told Elisa to pull us off the case. They said that Lydia and Bethany were working as CIA operatives in Afghanistan and that our questions were causing serious trouble for both of them. If their covers are blown, they could be killed."

Tinkie burst into laughter. Suddenly, I was laughing, too. First Lydia and Bethany were hauling dead bodies around in a borrowed pickup and now they were CIA operatives in Afghanistan. "That is insane," Tinkie said. "And, trust me, the CIA wouldn't call a tip line to leave that information. You and I would just disappear," she said.

She was right about that. And it felt so good to laugh. For a moment I'd been swept up in despair. Tinkie instantly recognized the absurdity of the moment.

"Call Elisa and tell her that whole scenario is bogus," Tinkie said. "She'll be worried sick."

"You get her on the horn," I said. "I need to talk to Coleman."

"Perfect. As soon as we order. I'm suddenly starved to death."

20

Tinkie calmed Elisa down, and I riled Coleman up by telling him about the car and truck at Frank Riley's address. He was still mad about the person driving the Altima throwing roofing tacks in the road. It could have seriously injured De-Wayne, or anyone else who happened to hit them. Coleman was right about that. A blown tire could be dangerous. To avoid that, DeWayne had swept the road with some brush he'd cut from the verge while waiting for a wrecker. He was that kind of guy.

We finished our brunch and decided to go back to Zin-nia. Tinkie could take care of Maylin for a few hours, and I could decide whether or not to take Sweetie Pie and Pluto on a stakeout with me. I didn't relish the long drive or the hours of sitting in a cold car waiting for something to happen, but it was part of the PI gig. Sometimes the longest odds were the ones that paid out.

I dropped Tinkie and Chablis at Hilltop, and I stopped by the sheriff's office with Sweetie Pie and Pluto. The critters regularly visited the office and they were behaved, so no one ever objected. Coleman hadn't returned, but Budgie was there. I pressed him about the caller who said Lydia was a CIA operative.

Budgie failed to see the humor. Instead, he was unnervingly solemn. "I finally got some response to the feelers I put out, Sarah Booth."

His face told me it wasn't good. "What?"

"Those women may actually be working undercover."

"For the CIA?" I found that hard to believe. Bethany seemed tough enough to be a secret agent, but what I'd learned about Lydia didn't lead me to that conclusion.

Budgie shook his head. "I don't know what agency. But there's some indication those women were in Afghanistan. My source couldn't get a clear answer." Budgie sighed. "If they are working undercover, it could explain a lot."

He was right. But I didn't like any of the explanations that came to mind.

"Is there any real evidence they were even in Afghanistan?"

Budgie looked down at his feet. "Maybe."

"Maybe? What does that mean?"

"There's an old report that my friend found. Keep in mind that he risked a lot looking for this."

I didn't like the direction this had taken at all. "And? What did he find?"

"The bodies of two females buried on the Pakistan–Afghanistan border. The bodies were never identified or claimed. But they were listed as teachers, as activist troublemakers who'd gone into the region to stir the women up to rebel against the Taliban. They were executed. Beheaded."

"You're thinking it could be Lydia and Bethany?"

Budgie held his answer for a moment. "It could be them. That was all the information my friend could get."

"What's the likelihood it's them?" I asked.

"That I couldn't tell you. This was a tip he followed up on for me. He couldn't give any more details. He didn't know who took the bodies or if they were autopsied or not. That's what made him suspicious they were undercover. It was all brushed under the rug. His thinking is that the two dead women were working undercover, were discovered, and then killed. I'm sorry."

Was it possible that two American bodies were found in Afghanistan and they were never reported to the American authorities? I knew the answer to that. The U.S. government could do only so much to protect its citizens around the world. When a person went off the grid and into dangerous places, often they were on their own. And if Lydia and Bethany were working undercover in the guise of teachers . . . Would our government ever admit to that? I didn't know.

"The location of the bodies was near a small settlement with a school for girls," Budgie said. "A school that became illegal in the last few years."

"This sounds worse and worse." It was exactly the kind of place Lydia or Bethany would go.

"Yes, it sounds bad."

"Where are the bodies?" I asked.

"Gone."

"When were the bodies discovered?"

"The report didn't have a date, but it was within the last four years. That was when the file was established. I can't ask my friend to risk more by poking at this further."

"I fully understand. Thank you and him." I'd never really considered that Lydia or Bethany had traipsed off to Afghanistan, because I wouldn't have done such a thing. Now I had to give it some thought. It was possible, though I didn't want to believe it. I had no option but to do my best to check out the report of two bodies found overseas. For that, though, I would need Coleman's help. We had pressed Budgie's unnamed friend as far as I was willing to.

"I wish I could tell you my source, but I promised."

"It's okay. I'm going to keep checking through other channels. If you hear anything more, please let me know. And thank your friend. He's at least given me something to check. Any additional details would be great, but he can't risk his safety."

"You bet."

"The only good news in this whole conversation is that if the women are dead, nothing I do here can impact them negatively."

"If it's true," Budgie reminded me. "The truth eludes us too often."

Our conversation was interrupted when DeWayne walked in the door. Pluto literally hurled himself off the counter and into DeWayne's arms. "You're wooing my cat's affections away from me," I told him. "And I heard a little birdy talking about your friendship with Marletta Bounds." Ever since I'd returned to Zinnia from Bay St. Louis, I'd heard swirling rumors of a budding new romance. "Pluto harbors jealous tendencies."

DeWayne flushed until the tops of his ears were a bright red. "Marletta is a great gal."

"Yes, she is. Is this serious? You know I ask because if you continue to house-sit the pets and Marletta is part of the package . . . I need to know." Not exactly the truth, but it sounded like a plausible excuse for my nosiness.

Budgie was laughing so hard he had to leave the room. DeWayne shifted back and forth. For a man who was such an excellent deputy, he was hamstrung by romance. "Marletta is . . . Now, that's really none of your business, Sarah Booth."

I couldn't help but laugh. DeWayne had been pushed as far as he could be, and I'd had my fun. When I caught my breath, I asked where Coleman was.

"Out at Tope Maxwell's house."

"For what?" I was instantly back to business.

"Elisa Redd paid her son-in-law a visit. She and Tope got into it. He slugged her in the face. Coleman took her to the hospital and then went back to arrest Tope, but, the last I heard, Tope was nowhere to be found. Coleman's questioning the staff there."

"Is Elisa okay?"

"Doc Sawyer is still checking her out. Coleman said Doc was mad as a hornet that a man would strike Elisa. Tope better not show up in the emergency room any time soon."

Doc would never hold back on treatment for an injured person, but he might prescribe some unpleasant tests for Tope. Just to be on the safe side, of course.

"Thanks, DeWayne." I decided to go to the hospital to check on Elisa myself. I needed to tell her what Budgie had discovered and about our trip to Natchez. It depressed me that I didn't have better news for Elisa, but my job as a private investigator was to find the truth, even if it was hard or unpleasant.

Sweetie Pie slept under DeWayne's desk and Pluto circled and curled up in a box beneath the counter. Both deputies agreed I could leave the critters while I ducked over to Sunflower County Hospital, which was only minutes away. I left the courthouse, stepping out into the warm sunshine of another spectacular January day. The bitter cold rain, hail, and ice—winter companions for most of the Delta—would come, but not today. While the trees were bare of leaves around the courthouse square, the sky was lit with a brilliant blue. Across the street, Mrs. Doty's camellias were a luscious red against dark green leaves. Each season brought a bounty of beauty.

I hopped in the car and drove the four blocks to the hospital. The emergency entrance looked deserted, but I hustled inside. With the help of a nice young nurse, I found Elisa sitting on the end of an exam table, waiting for Doc to return with test results.

"Are you okay?" I asked. She had a huge red mark on her cheek, which was beginning to swell. Tope had hit her hard.

"My neck is sore, but since my vision cleared up, I'm okay. I was seeing stars for a little bit. Did Coleman catch Tope?"

"Not yet, but he's hot on the trail."

"The coward slugged me and then took off running."

"He won't get far and his family wealth or name won't keep him out of jail, as long as you're willing to press assault charges."

"What?" She looked up, startled.

It had never occurred to me she wouldn't press charges.

This was her opportunity to give it back to Tope at ten to one. "He slugged you. You *are* going to press charges, aren't you?"

Elisa looked out the hospital window, where I could see the high school marching band practicing on the field. She didn't answer.

"Elisa, you must press charges. Coleman needs that leverage to squeeze Tope into talking."

"That bastard told me he knew where Lydia was buried. He won't tell if I put him in jail." She started sobbing softly.

"He said she was dead, and he knew where the body was buried?" This on top of bodies in Afghanistan and sightings of live Lydias in Greenwood and Natchez.

"That's what he said."

"Did he own up to killing her?"

She shook her head.

"What about Bethany? Does he know where she's buried, too?"

"He didn't say." She pulled a tissue from a box and dried her tears. "I can't continue not knowing where Lydia is. Dead or alive. I need closure."

"I wouldn't trust anything Tope Maxwell said." I understood why she wanted to believe him, but the man was a brute and a liar. "Why did he hit you?"

"I told him he was going to jail for killing Vivian. I know he murdered that poor girl. Coleman will prove it. Tope probably killed Lydia, too." She lifted her chin, her tear-streaked face defiant. "I confronted him, and he came out slugging. He will tell me where her body is. One way or the other."

"I think you're accepting manipulation and, ultimately, defeat." I said it flatly. "You're letting Tope dictate the terms of your search for your daughter. If he knew where she was buried, he would have dug her up years ago and gotten his hands on her money. Put your thinking cap on, Elisa."

The harshness of my tone snapped her out of her funk. She sat up straighter on the end of the exam table. I could vaguely hear the drum section of the band beating a rhythmic tattoo as they left the practice field in formation and marched toward the band hall. Practice was over. And so was my patience. Elisa had decided to aid and abet the man who may have killed her daughter. I was about to quit the case when she spoke again.

"I'll press charges, if that's what Coleman recommends. Tope won't tell me the truth anyway. I just let desperation get its claws in me."

I sighed, compassion replacing anger. "It's okay. If Tope knows something about Lydia, it's in his best interest to tell it. Coleman will get it out of him. Once Tope is in jail." But I had another big question for Elisa. "Do you have any reason to believe Lydia was working undercover for a federal agency?" I didn't want to say CIA. No point in scaring Elisa. Not yet, at least.

"Lydia? Absolutely not."

"Why are you so sure?"

"In one of the last conversations I had with her, when she mentioned Bethany and the program Bethany wanted to start in Afghanistan, Lydia said that Bethany had been approached to be a spook for the CIA. They were both ethically opposed to that."

The information shocked me. "Are you sure this happened?"

Elisa bit her bottom lip. "No. I mean I never questioned

it. Until now." She searched my face. "Lydia believed it, and I believed her. Why?"

I shook my head. "Just something a friend of mine heard."

"That Lydia was working undercover for the CIA or some federal agency?" Shock colored Elisa's face, which was now swollen from Tope's fist. "She would never. I can say that without any qualms. Neither would Bethany."

I had no intention of telling her what Budgie's friend had said. It would only worry her more, and I lacked evidence. I would continue checking, but Elisa didn't have to know every single step I took.

Elisa stood up. She swayed slightly, but caught her balance and stiffened her back. "Can you take me home?"

"Has Doc released you?"

She shrugged. "I'm fine. I just want to go home and lie down on the sofa in front of the fireplace."

She sounded totally defeated and I regretted the role I had played in that. But allowing Tope to brutalize her wouldn't help us in any way. I was glad she finally accepted that. "I'll take you home, but first let me talk to Doc."

"Sure." She slumped, defeated by the load she carried.

I hurried down to the nurse's desk and was directed to the X-ray department to find Doc. He was just coming out the door when I got there.

"Sarah Booth, you must be here to take Elisa home."

"Yes. Is she ready to go?"

"She's been ready, but I had to be sure she wasn't injured. The X-ray showed no damage to the bones of her face. I was afraid he'd cracked her cheekbone."

"She's really low, Doc."

"Yes. She's trying hard to hold up, but the idea that

Lydia is really dead hit her hard. It's consumed her. Now she wants her daughter's body. That bastard Tope is just playing with her emotions."

"Why would he do that?"

"Why do some children pull the wings off flies? Tope is and has always been that kid. His money and privilege have made him feel protected from any consequences. He's only going to get worse the older he gets. I can't give a clinical diagnosis of his mental illness, but, trust me, he has some serious and dangerous psychosis."

Doc didn't bandy mental issues about carelessly. I could see he was angry, but he was also worried. Tope was a loose cannon. He'd tried bribing Elisa with information about her daughter's grave—how macabre and cruel was that? And when it failed to keep her in line, he struck her hard enough to send her to the ER. "I'm sure Coleman will put him in jail when he finds him."

"If he finds him," Doc said darkly. "Tope has unlimited funds."

"Maybe not. I've heard he's run through his Maxwell inheritance."

"Perhaps he has, but his family will bail him out. They may kill him in private, but they won't allow him to be publicly held accountable for his crimes. They're too egocentric to have that stain on the Maxwell name."

"Then you would say he's been a stain on the family name?"

An idea was forming at the back of my little brain. How much did the Maxwell family want Tope to disappear into the ether? It was a question that Tinkie Bellcase Richmond had all the social moves to pursue.

21

I left Elisa at her beautiful home with some misgivings. She had staff, who seemed to care about her, but she needed a close friend or family member to lean on. I mentioned that and she promised to make some calls. The critters loved the sheriff's office, but they loved a car ride more, and they left the courthouse happily: Sweetie Pie howling and baying the melody of hound-dog joy, Pluto exited as if he heard the wedding march in his head.

The case was so fragmented and all over the place that it had killed my appetite. When I called my partner to report in, she suggested meeting at Millie's. I told her to go ahead. She could feed herself and Maylin and put the baby down for a nap before she joined me. I gathered up my critters, hoping for a moment with Coleman, but he wasn't in the office. I headed to Dahlia House, where I continued pacing in the PI office. I didn't know what else to do. That I was driving Sweetie Pie and Pluto to distraction with my nervous energy, I didn't doubt. I needed a horseback ride but there wasn't time.

I heard Coleman's truck pull up to the front of the house and rushed outside. His face told the story—Tope was still on the loose. I made him a sandwich while we caught up, and though he didn't say it, I knew he was hopping mad. Coleman was most deadly when he was quiet and calm. Tope Maxwell would have to run far and hard to avoid the long arm of the law.

"Any leads on where Tope might have gone?" I asked him as he kissed my cheek at the front door, leaving once again. Work awaited him.

"Memphis, I'd say."

"Hiding out with his family?"

"More likely. But I'm not going to try to have him arrested and brought back here."

"You aren't?" This wasn't what I expected. Coleman was the lawman who never gave up until he had the criminal in cuffs.

"I've given it some thought. If Elisa agrees to press charges—"

"She will. I talked to her."

"Good." A grim satisfaction touched Coleman's face. "Then we're going to wait him out. I don't want a court fight about arresting him. I'm not going to make a single call about him. When he thinks he's in the clear, he'll come home. He has to. Court appointments and all of that if he wants to pursue declaring Lydia dead."

Coleman was lethal when he was calm. And he was

smart. Tope would begin to believe that his entitlement gave him complete cover. Then, surprise! The jail door would clang behind him.

There was little I could do to check the espionage angle. If Budgie came back with more details, I'd ask Coleman to intercede. I did have an angle to pursue, and it would require Tinkie's special skill set. Change of plans. As soon as Coleman drove away, I called her and arranged to pick her up. We were going to pay a visit to the Maxwell family in Memphis. Not a social call, but a very rich woman seeking legal advice for her will. Tinkie wouldn't even have to pretend.

The Maxwell law offices were plush and designed to give the impression of affluence, good taste, heritage, and all the things wealthy people valued. Interior design rigorously applied to create image. The overstuffed leather chairs, the expensive carpeting, the decanters of Irish crystal that sparkled in the sunlight slipping through designer sheers. It was all done with taste and care.

Oswald Maxwell had time to see Tinkie about setting up an estate plan for little Maylin. To sell the image we'd brought the baby with us. She wore a designer leopard-print onesie that matched Tinkie's blouse and turban. Tinkie completed the look with black matador pants and tall boots. As the chauffeur, I didn't have to dress up, thank heavens.

Tinkie didn't need me, so I stayed in the lobby reading magazines on history and the natural world. Tinkie's main objective was to find out where Tope had gone, if she could. Mine was to watch the people coming in and out of the offices in case our errant abuser showed up.

A lot of my friends had spent time in Memphis, the closest big city to the Delta. The Maxwell law offices were in one of the older, elegant downtown buildings, and I had a primo view of the city and the river. I called Cece to check on any developments with the airline photo, and to fill her in on Tope assaulting Elisa. Once we'd learned the truth about what happened to Lydia, she and Millie could spin the facts into a clever story for "The Truth Is Out There." Maybe they'd be able to work in the ghost of Elvis.

"I can't believe he hit his mother-in-law." Cece was outraged.

"He killed his fiancée, and maybe his wife. A slug to the face is rather ! . . . minimal."

"Elisa is his mother-in-law. An older woman."

She had a point. If anyone had ever punched my mom, I would have made them pay no matter how long it took me. "Sorry, that was insensitive."

Cece laughed. "How rare to hear you admit that."

I had to laugh, too. She was right. "Look, thanks for the help. Did you ever hear from that pilot fellow?"

"He's been out of the country, but he's expected back tonight. He said he would call me if he had any new information."

"Where's he been?" Maybe one day I'd get a chance to travel. When I'd lived in NYC, the international airport just a few miles away, my theater friends and I had planned European travel trips. We were very poor, and every time we ate Italian, we'd plan our trip to Italy, Spain, and Portugal. Maybe one day I'd actually make it happen.

"Afghanistan. He had a hop to NYC, then to Amsterdam, and then Kabul."

"Afghanistan." I repeated it as if it were magic.

"I know," Cece said. "The destination of Lydia and Bethany, according to some."

I really wanted to tell her about Budgie's tip that the women were CIA operatives, but I didn't. Once this was all done and we'd found Lydia, I'd tell Cece and she could do with it what she would as a journalist.

"That's only a rumor," I reminded her. "There's no evidence they ever got on a plane."

"I understand your reluctance to think about it," she said with a hint of melancholy. "If they went over there to do good, that's not a magic cloak able to keep them from harm."

"I know."

"As far as I can find out, Lydia was only in the airport. No one ever saw her get on a plane and there is no record of her buying a ticket. To Afghanistan or anywhere else."

The inner office door of the law firm opened, and Tinkie came out with a tall, slender, handsome man at her side. "I have to go," I told Cece as I put my phone away.

Tinkie and the man shook hands, and he went back inside the office. Grinning like a possum, Tinkie came toward me.

"Mr. Maxwell will visit Oscar and me in Zinnia next week to talk about the estate. He's bitterly disappointed in Tope."

"Yeah?"

"I explained that I had tried to get in touch with Tope to set this up for me, but Tope didn't respond. His uncle says he's 'on the Continent' traveling after the horror of Vivian's suicide."

"Suicide?"

"Exactly. I told you they'd close ranks to protect him."

She'd been right. "Did you get a reading of how they view Tope's potential involvement in Vivian's death?"

"Publicly denying it, but, privately, they are very angry that Tope has brought this on their family. They'll defend him, don't get me wrong. They won't abandon him, unless it begins to affect their bottom line. If that happens, they'll erase him from the family like he was only a bad dream."

That was sad, even if Tope deserved it. Family was all about the hard times. If I'd ever committed a serious crime, my family would have stood by me. They wouldn't have tried to block consequences, but they would never have made me feel I was dead to them. "Tope is smart enough to know he's in serious trouble with Coleman and the law. I guess he took a runner to Europe before Coleman could pull his passport. Did they say when Tope would be back?"

Tinkie's grin widened. "He never left. He's in Mississippi."

"How do you know that?" I asked.

She nodded toward the exit. "Let's get out of here first."

22

Tinkie didn't have to ask twice. It was a bit of a drive back to Zinnia, and I was eager to get home. My body was sore and achy, and I felt like I'd been on the road for half a year. Hanging over my head was the possible trip back to Natchez to stake out Riley's house. I'd driven all over Mississippi today and it was a large state.

When I'd picked up the critters from the sheriff's office, I'd left the hair strands Tinkie had found in the pickup truck. Coleman—because he, too, was looking for Lydia officially—had agreed to cover the cost of running them against Lydia's DNA, which Elisa gladly provided. Everything seemed to be caught in a waiting game.

Tinkie drove so I could call Coleman and tell him that

Tope was in Mississippi. He enjoyed the news and asked how Tinkie had found out.

"No man is immune to her feminine wiles once she puts her mind to it," I told him. "Oswald was selling the family line that Tope had taken off for Europe, but he got a phone call and she overheard him talking with a delivery service about booze and food for a residence on the river. We're pretty sure Tope is there. You know people often don't take Tinkie seriously because she's so sweet and pliant."

"Yeah, she has that lip-popping thing, too, which is mesmerizing," Coleman said, much to my amusement. I hadn't realized he'd noticed.

"I just said what he wanted to hear about Tope, with the proper concern for Tope's well-being, of course," Tinkie explained. "When he got the call I pretended to be putting on lipstick and digging around in my purse. He was only too eager to express his disappointment in his nephew. And he also said that Tope was a financial incompetent. His exact words were that Tope had been handed a golden ticket and he'd used it for strip clubs and casinos."

"He *has* hit financial hard times." This was the best news so far. A desperate man would attempt desperate things. We might be able to force Tope into a mistake. If Coleman could ever get his hands on him, a few nights in county hoosegow, for a man like Tope, might give him a preview of life to come in Parchman penitentiary. The state prison was a far cry from our little county jail. Tope's privileged and entitled life had not prepared him for a system where no one cared about his money, only what he could do for them in the moment. And those services were often brutal.

"Do you know where he is in Memphis?" Coleman asked.

"I do." Tinkie was almost preening. In a half hour she'd

infiltrated Oswald Maxwell's brain and sucked out all the information she wanted. Damn, she was good! He'd revealed a lot more than he knew.

"Where?" Coleman's voice had that steely edge to it that spelled trouble for Tope.

"His family has a houseboat on the river just below Memphis. It's in Mississippi. I got directions when he gave them to the delivery guy."

Even though she was driving I lightly punched her arm in congratulations. "You are the bomb!"

"Don't go there." Coleman was firm, because he was worried about us.

"We won't," I promised. Tope Maxwell, I believed, was a killer. I wouldn't put Tinkie at risk like that, or myself. The law would get him. Coleman had friends in every county in the state. In the next thirty minutes, Tope would be under surveillance.

"He's a dangerous man. Don't ever doubt that. On another issue, Doc has the autopsy reports back on Vivian Dantzler."

I didn't really want to hear this, but I had to. "And?"

"Her fingers were broken and there were signs of petechia. She was strangled before she went over that balcony."

"He strangled her?" Tinkie asked, trying hard but failing to hide the horror in her voice.

"That's what Doc found. He's ruled her death a murder."

"Now maybe her parents will come clean with details," Tinkie said.

"I wonder what pushed him to kill her when she was still useful. I don't think he ever meant to marry her, but she was a grand reason to begin the process of having Lydia declared dead. A man in love, wanting to move on. Some people would have bought that. Vivian did, and she paid the price for it."

As a kid, I'd loved the fairy tales of Sleeping Beauty and Prince Charming, but I wondered now if the stories of honor, white-knight rescue, and soulmates set women up to be victims. I didn't want to believe that, but Vivian had embraced the fantasy Tope offered and he had killed her. I knew he had.

"Thank you for telling us, Coleman. We're coming home. I may drive back to Natchez to stake out the Riley farm. If Lydia and Bethany are using Riley's vehicles, that might be the best place to catch them."

"No need, Sarah Booth. DeWayne's cousin is an Adams County deputy. He's volunteered to stake out the place whenever he's off duty."

I was stunned. "That's incredible. Why would he do that?"

"I told DeWayne you'd teach him to jump horses. Once he heard Budgie was upping his horsemanship game, he decided he wanted some lessons, too. As soon as the weather is warmer. It would seem your horses have a reputation for winter friskiness."

"You made a good bargain, Coleman."

"I know. I was determined to get my fiancée home and in bed."

"Make a video," Tinkie said loudly. "You two could become a viral success. Coleman, I see you as an influencer. A man for all seasons."

"Oh, Tinkie, I'm not the shy lawman you bullied back when I first started dating Sarah Booth. Be careful. I can focus my investigative skills on your bedroom antics with Oscar."

"You wouldn't!" Tinkie was honestly taken aback.

"Oh, but he would. And I would help him." It gave me a certain evil pleasure to give Tinkie a little payback.

"Some partner you are." But she was grinning. "I am so glad to have a little bit of fun back in our conversations. Now, let's solve this. What's the next step?"

"Coleman, can you use your law enforcement contacts to have someone check out that houseboat? If Tope is there, we need to keep an eye on him. I'm pretty sure if things break badly for him, he'll attempt to flee the country. Maybe if he's there, Elisa will hire another PI to shadow him."

Most Mississippi sheriff offices were not staffed to allow for continual surveillance of suspects. But it would be money well spent to Elisa if she put up the fee.

"That's an idea, and sure, I'd be happy to ask. Tope is a suspect in a murder case. I'm sure they'll help all they can."

"Coleman, did you find any reports of young women missing in these parts? Back in the days of Ernest and Florence Salter?" Coleman had been checking around for me, hoping for a name that would give us a lead.

"Have I ever let you down?" Coleman asked.

Tinkie pretended to fan herself as she winked at me.

"No, you have not."

"Budgie found three young women who simply disappeared. One from Sunflower County. The other from two neighboring areas very close to where the Salters used to live."

"They were reported missing?" Tinkie asked.

Coleman hesitated. "That's unclear. There is no official paperwork in the sheriff's office on Tillie Randall."

"How do you know she went missing, then?" I asked.

"DeWayne remembered her," Coleman said. "He knew her from high school. Then she stopped coming home from college. He had a mad crush on her, so he stopped by her house and her parents said she'd moved to California, but they wouldn't give him an address. That was a few years ago. But he stopped by to see them this morning on his way to work to check on Tillie. They said she'd died out in California. You know DeWayne, he checked the California statistics. No death certificate filed. No obituaries. He said the Randalls were lying."

We were getting close to Zinnia, and I eased off the gas so we could finish the conversation. "What do you think happened to Tillie Randall?"

"Good question. If she was abducted, I don't think her parents would try to hide that. If she ran off with a no-good man and he hurt her, I really don't think they would hide that, either."

"And if she was pregnant?" Tinkie asked.

"That's the scenario that gives me the most trouble," Coleman said. "If she went to some back-alley abortionist and died? That's what keeps popping up in my brain."

"Her parents would hide that, wouldn't they?" Tinkie asked. "The shame of it all. If Tillie was dead, they wouldn't want to ruin her reputation."

"If my daughter was dead—" I stopped. Because I couldn't say what I might do. Would I fight to prosecute the people who harmed her, or would I retreat to protect her from public condemnation? More important, why did we live in a world where getting an abortion was a source of shame?

"It's not fair," Coleman said, as if he could read my mind over the phone. "It's wrong. But it does happen."

"I'll check with the Randalls and see what I can learn about Tillie," I told Coleman. "Maybe it will pan out into a lead."

My voice must have conveyed more emotion than I thought. Tinkie put a comforting hand on my lower arm. "We'll check it out," she said to Coleman. "Bye, now. We're rolling into Zinnia."

"Later, ladies," Coleman said. "Don't despair, Sarah Booth."

"Not when she has you to make it up to her later," Tinkie said archly. "And she's making a video of you two together to put up on TikTok."

Before she could say anything else, I disconnected. "I'll get you back," I warned her.

"I'm counting on it."

23

It didn't take long to find the Jason Randall farm. It was not a cotton plantation but a truck farm just below Clarksdale, where the soil was rich and well drained. A small tractor moved back and forth across a field, turning the earth so that the old stalks of corn would serve to help fertilize. Jason Randall was an organic, sustainable farmer. I was eager to talk to him about that, even as I dreaded bringing up his missing daughter.

Tinkie had refused to let me drop her off at her house. She'd held and nursed Maylin while she helped me do a computer search for Tillie Randall. She'd found Tillie's parents' address, and here we were.

The farmhouse was modest but gracious, with a front porch that offered shade and rocking chairs. Well-tended ferns swung gently in a breeze. The leaded-glass front door also included a screened door. This was a house built long before central air-conditioning. Screens were vital to survival back in those days. It was also a house that was well loved. The paint was fresh, no dust or cobwebs, a fact that made me cringe in comparison with Dahlia House. I loved my home, but it was a big, expensive place to keep up. So many things I couldn't do on my own. The Randall farm showed the hand of a hardworking, loving family.

A woman not much older than my mother would have been answered my knock.

"Can I help you?" She was wiping her hands on an apron just like someone in a movie set in 1960. She was still pretty, but when she was younger, she was probably a great beauty. "Faded" was the word that came to mind. Hard work and worry showed in her face.

I introduced us and explained we were looking for some information about Tillie Randall. She stepped back from the door and I realized a toddler clung to her leg. The apron had hidden the child. The little girl looked up at me and smiled.

"Is this your granddaughter?" I asked.

"No, she's my great-niece. My sister's daughter's girl. She lives with me and Jason now."

"She's a beauty and she sure favors you."

"Thank you." She hesitated. "I don't have any new information about Tillie. Jason and I don't talk about her anymore. It's just too painful."

"We're searching for two other women who disappeared nearly seven years ago. We're hoping you can help us," Tinkie said. "It would be a real act of kindness if you could just talk to us a few minutes. I know this is painful. We only have a few questions, and we won't stay long."

She picked up the child and came out onto the porch where she walked to the edge and watched her husband on the tractor. Back and forth. Back and forth. "I'll tell you what I can, but you need to be gone before Jason gets off that tractor."

"We can do that," I said, relieved that she'd even consider talking to us.

She pushed the screened door open, and we stepped into a front room with a beautiful antique sofa and matching wing chairs. "I'll put on a pot of coffee. Let me take Elvie to her playroom."

"Don't bother with coffee," I said.

"It's not a bother. I generally have a cup this time of day."

Tinkie and I looked at each other when she left the room. We were about to rip the scab off a very painful part of her past. Did we feel guilty? We did. But we had to do it.

When I heard her coming from the kitchen, I got up to lend a hand. "Let me help you with that, Mrs. Randall."

"Call me Jane." She allowed me to take the tray with coffee cups, saucers, milk, and sugar.

When we were seated and sipping the coffee, Tinkie broached the painful subject. "We understand that your daughter disappeared several years ago. Can you tell us about it?"

Jane Randall put her coffee down on the small table beside her chair. "The worst day of my life. Yes, I remember. Tillie was attending Ole Miss. She was supposed to come home one Friday in March. When she didn't come home, we searched for her. No one had seen her that whole week in school. No one called to tell us about it. The law searched for her. They didn't have anything to go on. She simply vanished. There was talk she'd gone to California but it was only rumor, as far as we could tell."

The story was similar to the disappearance of Lydia and Bethany. "Jane, have you ever heard of a woman named Florence Salter?"

She paled and nodded. "Yes, Florence was well known in the rural parts of the county. In fact, Jason often grew herbs especially for her. She used them in her medicines. She was quite the healer."

"She really healed people?" Tinkie asked.

"She did."

"Have you ever talked to someone she healed?" I asked.

Her smile said it all. "I talk to him every day. My husband Jason had an autoimmune disease. Florence concocted a remedy for him with her herbs and whatever else she used. Folks said she was a witch, an abortionist, a hoodoo woman, a ghost—there was all kinds of talk. The only thing I know is that after working with her for several months, Frank was back to his old self. This farm takes a lot of work, and he'd gotten down to the point he just couldn't go on. She healed him. That's the truth."

Whatever had happened to Jason Randall, his wife believed he'd been healed by a conjure woman. "Did Mrs. Salter ever come to your house?" I asked.

"Sure. She came to treat Jason and to pick up the things he'd grown for her. They were close friends."

"Have you heard any rumors about Florence and her husband, Ernest, being involved in the disappearance of several young women?" I thought for a minute Jane would slap me, but she merely sat back in her chair.

"That's the most ridiculous thing I've ever heard. A finer woman than Florence Salter has never walked this earth. She gave my family a miracle and I won't have anyone speaking negatively about her." She stood up. "Please leave."

"We didn't mean to offend." Tinkie popped to her feet and took Jane's hand. "We sincerely didn't mean to upset you or imply anything about Florence Salter. But we have to ask. That's our job."

She nodded slowly. "I do understand, but I can't have it."

"We're also looking for the Salters," I said. "Do you know where they are?"

"I do not. Two or three years ago, I went to their house and it was empty. They'd gone. Thank goodness Florence shared how to make her remedy with Jason, but I'd give a lot to see Ernest and Florence. They were good people. I don't know why you're hunting them, but you should leave them alone."

"What did Ernest Salter do? For work?" I asked.

"He helped."

"Helped how?"

Jane put her hands on her hips and her face might have been carved from stone. "The Salters are good people. Good people. They never refused to help a single person who asked. They went the extra mile. Didn't matter to them who you were, where you came from, what you believed or didn't believe, or how you worshipped. They wouldn't harm a living creature, much less a young woman."

It was a solid endorsement, but it wasn't evidence. Only opinion.

"It would help us if we could talk to them in person. Or maybe they're dead."

Jane reacted with shock. "What? Who said they were dead?"

"We found a grave for Florence Salter," Tinkie said. She didn't mention it was empty. "And we heard that Ernest had been hanged in the old Mount Zion Cemetery. Not so far from here."

"The Hanging Tree." Jane put a hand on the back of a chair to steady herself. "I know the stories, but I never heard them applied to Ernest or Florence. I can't believe they're both dead."

Her response was enough to convince me she was telling the truth about not having seen them lately. I was about to ask another question when a commotion in the back of the house stopped me short.

"Mimi! Kyle won't let me play ball!" A little girl about six whirled around the corner and took her place beside Jane, cowed into silence by the unexpected visitors.

"This is Cadence." Jane put a hand on her head. "Now go play with Elvie and tell Kyle to behave or he'll be in trouble." She turned to face us. "I'm too old for those young children, but I love them."

The little girl wheeled and ran back down the hall.

"She's beautiful," Tinkie said. Maylin had melted her heart toward all children.

"I have work to do." Jane was ready for us to depart.

"Just another moment. Can you tell us about your missing daughter?"

"No." She walked toward the front door. "You should go now. I really have work to do."

"I'm sorry, Jane." And I was. Deeply. "We want to find Lydia Redd Maxwell and her friend Bethany Carter. We might turn over some clues to find your daughter Tillie, too."

"No. My girl is gone. Tillie is never coming back. The Salters didn't harm her." She eased around us and opened the front door. "Thanks for stopping by."

"If we find anything, we'll be in touch," Tinkie said as we walked past her and out into the afternoon sunshine.

24

It had been a long, long day, and I dropped Tinkie at Hilltop and fetched Sweetie Pie and Pluto. I was too tired to ride, but I'd take them to the barn with me to feed. The winter days were shorter, and my energy seemed at a low ebb. A walk around the yard was the best I could offer.

I was brushing the horses when my phone rang. I didn't recognize the Mississippi number, but I answered.

"Drop this case," said the voice on the other line. "Please. Drop it. People are going to get hurt. Just stop." The woman sounded desperate, and scared.

"Who is this?" I asked, but the line went dead. I called back, but no one answered.

I immediately dialed Budgie, who was still at the sheriff's

office. I gave him the number that showed up on my phone and told him what had happened.

"Was the caller male or female?" he asked.

"Female. And she sounded super stressed. Desperate." I thought for a minute. "We stopped by the Randall farm coming home from Memphis. Jane Randall was upset by our questions." I didn't connect the dots to see what Budgie would say.

"You think that was Mrs. Randall calling you? That she knows something about Lydia and Bethany?"

"I don't know what I think, but her daughter Tillie is missing, too. I can't say that it sounded exactly like her, but it could have been her, talking deeper. But why would she want me to stop looking?"

"Maybe because she has something she's hiding. If it was her. We'll know as soon as I can trace that number. I'll call you back."

I relayed all the new info to Tinkie while I was waiting on Budgie to work his magic. After I finished with my partner, I called Millie's and ordered hamburger steaks smothered in onions and mashed potatoes for three—sans the onions for Sweetie Pie, who had worked up an appetite at Tinkie's. Coleman would be hungry, too. I also ordered some pan-fried trout for Pluto. He was looking a little rotund, but fish was good for him.

The phone rang as I was putting the critters in the car to pick up the food. Instead of Budgie, it was Coleman. "The phone belongs to Miranda James."

"Who is that?" I'd never heard of her.

"It's Jane Randall's niece. She and her children live with Jane and Jason. Miranda's husband was killed working offshore, and I think Jane missed Tillie so much, she and Jason took Miranda and the kids in."

"I think that's a good thing."

"Me, too."

"But why would Miranda be calling me about dropping the case?"

"Because you probably upset Jane, bringing up old memories and losses."

Well, that did make sense. I'd be protective of my loved ones, too. There was no doubt I'd poked around in an old, sore wound. It was possible she'd broken down after we left. I was sorry, if that was the case.

"Do you want me to talk to Jane and Miranda?" Coleman asked. "She shouldn't be threatening people, even with the best of intentions."

"It wasn't exactly a threat," I clarified. "More like a plea. Just let it go. I don't feel threatened in the least."

"Your wish is my command."

Coleman said that too often and one day I would make him pay the price. Just not today. "When will you be home?"

"Shortly."

That was exactly what I wanted to hear. "I ordered some food from Millie's. I'm starving and I'll meet you at Dahlia House." Coleman hadn't exactly moved in with me. He still rented a house south of Zinnia. He spent most of his time at Dahlia House, though.

"I'm hungry, too. I'll head home."

When I got home, I set the kitchen table because it was warm in that room with the oven on. While I was waiting for Coleman to arrive, I did an internet search on Tillie Randall.

The *Zinnia Dispatch* had covered the young woman's disappearance. Tillie had been attending Ole Miss, as Jane said. When she didn't arrive home one weekend, Jason had reported her missing. The university had been notified, her room searched—nothing. Her possessions were in her room. Only her purse was gone. She didn't have a car, so she couldn't have driven away.

Oxford, Mississippi, police and the Lafayette County and Sunflower County sheriffs' departments had put up roadblocks and conducted searches. Students and friends had been interviewed. Tillie's boyfriend, Alan Chisholm, had been brought in for questioning, but had an alibi—he'd been in the hospital having his appendix removed. Tillie's friends were upset and cooperative, but they thought she'd caught a ride home. The trouble was that no one knew who she might have ridden with.

According to her roommate at Ole Miss, who was the last person to admit to seeing Tillie, she'd been in her dorm room after her last Friday class saying she planned to go home for the weekend for a family dinner on Saturday. The roommate went out with friends, and when she came back, Tillie was gone.

Tillie had disappeared into thin air. I rubbed my eyes and searched more, but the basic facts of her disappearance remained the same. The account was briefer in the Memphis and Jackson papers, but the disappearance was covered. After two weeks, the coverage faded away. Tillie was gone, there were no new leads, folks got on with their lives. Except for Jane and Jason Randall. They would never get over the loss of their only child. Much like Elisa Redd would never give up looking for Lydia. And wherever Bethany Carter's parents were, I was positive they still longed to find her.

Speaking of which, Bethany's parents would be an excellent lead. And while I had time on the computer, I looked her up and found George and Alma Carter. They lived in a rural area of the county, and I thought about driving over. For now, though, a phone call would work.

Tinkie had installed software that allowed me to do a skip trace. I didn't suspect the Carters were bad debtors, but the same tactics could be used to garner general information about any person. I wanted an address and phone number. And I got both.

Coleman still hadn't arrived, so I called. A woman answered the phone, and I suddenly wished I was standing in front of her. The phone truly was inadequate, but it was a first step.

"Mrs. Carter, I'm Sarah Booth Delaney, and I've been hired by Elisa Redd to find her daughter Lydia. It's my understanding that your daughter disappeared at the same time Lydia did, and that she and Bethany were friends."

"Yes, that's true."

"Have you heard from Bethany?"

"Not in a long time. Almost seven years. Have you found her? Is she alive?"

I felt my heart cracking at the hope in her voice. "No, ma'am. But I'm hunting for both of them."

"Oh." Hope faded from her voice. "We hunted for Bethany and Lydia the first years. George and I followed up on every person who saw Bethany. We tracked down and talked to every single client from her self-defense classes. We never believed she was dead. Not for the first few years, at least. Bethany was such a force, so vital and alive and filled with energy."

I heard the past tense. Now she did believe Bethany was

dead. Was it easier hoping or not hoping? Had I done a terribly cruel thing by digging up a hard past for the Carters and the Randalls? "I just wanted to ask about where you thought Bethany might be. Did she ever travel to Afghanistan to help the women she'd talked about?"

"I don't know."

I wasn't certain how to proceed. She didn't know because . . . "Were you estranged from Bethany?"

"Yes. That is the biggest mistake of my life. George didn't approve of all her activism. I let him put up a barrier between us so that the last year, before she disappeared, I didn't talk to her. But I always thought she'd be right down the road where I could find her. Don't ever delude yourself about time. You don't have as much as you think you do."

I blinked back tears. Tinkie was the softie, not me, but Alma had gotten to me. Regret was a bitter banquet. And no, there was never enough time. The night my parents died in a car crash I'd gone to sleep planning a picnic for the next day down in the oak grove. I woke up to a completely different world. But drifting into the past wouldn't solve my case.

"Mrs. Carter, where was Bethany last seen?"

"As far as the law officers could find out, she was in Zinnia. She had that martial arts studio in Jackson for a while, but her friends said that she had planned to visit a friend in Zinnia. I'm presuming that would be Lydia. They weren't seen after that weekend."

"Were they traveling together?"

"Lydia was married. Tope kept her close, or that's what I was able to find out. Everyone seemed to believe that Bethany showed up in Zinnia to convince Lydia to flee her marriage. Tope caught them and got angry. That's what everyone thinks. I'm not certain anyone actually saw them together, though."

"Why would their friends think they left together?"

"Until Lydia married, they did everything as a team. They were two parts of a whole. Bethany was bold and stood up for herself. Lydia was passive and tender. Bethany would have given her life to protect Lydia, and Lydia loved her like a sister."

I believed that. "How did Bethany feel about Lydia's marriage?"

"Bethany hated Tope Maxwell. I was worried that my daughter would harm him, not that he would end up harming Lydia and Bethany."

"And that's what you think happened? That Tope killed them?"

"I don't want to believe it but, yes, that's what I think happened. And he's never going to pay." I couldn't see her face, but I knew it was drawn in angry lines. "The Tope Maxwells of the world never pay."

I wondered if she'd heard about Vivian Dantzler and her death at Tope's home. I wasn't going to tell her to add to the bitter brew. "I promise you if we can prove that Tope did anything to anyone, the sheriff here, Coleman Peters, will see that he pays. Mrs. Carter, would it be possible for my partner and I to visit with you? We have other questions, and it could really help us."

"George is at work on weekdays. Come when he isn't in the house. I don't want this all stirred up again. George blames himself, because he was at odds with Bethany when she disappeared. The guilt has eaten at him all this time. I don't want to make it worse."

"I understand. We'll call before we come to make sure

it's convenient. And thank you for talking with me. Just one more thing. Was there anyone else who might have wanted to harm Bethany?"

"She got under a lot of men's skin. She wasn't compliant and she didn't give a good damn what anyone thought of her. Some men are threatened by an independent woman. One who doesn't need a man and makes sure they know it."

"Any names?"

"Not off the top of my head."

"Are you familiar with or did you know Ernest and Florence Salter?"

"Why, sure. Florence was a blessing in my life. I didn't know Ernest very well, but Florence was an angel on earth. Always helping people and seeing that the old people living alone were fed. I miss her."

"What happened to her?"

"I don't know. One day they were just gone. There were all sorts of rumors, but having raised Bethany and heard some of the foolish cruelties people make up, I didn't believe any of it. Whenever I think about Florence, I see her with that big sunhat, coming to the front door with a basket of strawberries or sweet potatoes or okra. We'd have coffee and chat and she'd go on her way."

"Thank you for talking with me. I'll be in touch."

"Maybe I can help financially with your fee. I mean, Mrs. Redd shouldn't pay for the whole thing. It's my daughter who's missing, too. I don't have a lot, but we have some savings."

"I wouldn't worry about it, but I will tell Elisa that you offered."

25

I smelled the coffee when I woke the next morning. Winter temperatures had taken a dive overnight, and it was brisk in the bedroom. I put my bare feet on the hardwood floor and quickly drew them back into bed.

"I'm awake. Can I have some coffee? Please!" I called down to Coleman. I could hear him bustling in the kitchen. Dawn was just breaking so it had to be close to seven. I hoped Coleman had time for a ride. He wasn't afraid of frisky horses. As for me, I wallowed a little longer in the warm bed.

Coleman and I had caught up with each other the night before as we ate the terrific food from Millie's. When we and the critters were full, we'd lit the fire in the bedroom and compared notes as we snuggled under family heirloom quilts. There were definite advantages to being in love with a good man, especially a lawman.

I ran through the things I'd learned. Tinkie's lead about Tope had panned out. Coleman had discovered he *was* living on the river. Coleman had called the Mississippi Bureau of Investigation and they'd agreed to sit on him. Coleman didn't have the goods to charge him with Vivian's death, but Coleman was working on finding the evidence.

Since the autopsy had shown that Vivian was murdered, I'd asked Coleman to arrest Tope, but he was holding off in the hope that Tope might lead his tail to the place he'd buried Lydia. Since I hadn't made progress in finding her, it was at least one thing we could try. It was a long shot, but Tope might feel cornered and do something dumb.

Budgie's relative in Adams County had reported in on the Frank Riley house. No movement of any kind. No one coming or going. The deputy had casually talked to some neighbors down the road who said Frank Riley was a very private man. He wasn't social and he didn't leave his property often.

Our last best hope was the DNA profile of the hair found on the hair tie in Frank Riley's pickup. That report should be in later this morning.

I heard Coleman's footsteps on the stairs and I fluffed my pillows to sit up so I could drink my coffee. He came into the room and handed me a steaming cup.

"Have time for a ride?" I asked.

"Sure, if you pop out of bed ASAP."

I gulped some coffee and swung my feet out from under the covers. I gave a little scream as I ran to stand in front of the fire. Dahlia House had air and heat, but the old fireplaces brought so much comfort and good memories that

I preferred using them. Coleman, too. But today was truly cold. Maybe I'd turn on the heat when we left so we could both shower without turning into icicles.

It only took us a few minutes to call up the horses and tack them. Coleman chose Ms. Scrapiron and I rode Reveler. The horses danced in the driveway with eagerness to run. It was going to be a fast and frisky ride. Once we were across the road and in the open field, it was as if they'd been shot from a bow. Clods of dirt flew behind us as we gave them their heads and let them enjoy the wild pleasure of a run. When they slowed of their own accord, we headed home.

The cold wind had whipped tears in my eyes, but the day was clear and sunny. It was a day where the pale winter sunlight bridged the past and future. Memories were in every smell and scene. The bare limbs of the trees held stark beauty against the bluest sky. A cloud bank was building on the horizon, and I figured a storm would be upon us by nighttime.

The horses were content to walk home, their warm breath blowing from their nostrils in puffs. Coleman's hand sought mine as we rode side by side, glad of the warm gloves that kept our fingers from freezing. I had a headband for my ears, but my nose was cold enough to break off. Coleman's smile was worth freezing for, though. I'd found someone who loved the horses as much as I did, whether riding or caring for them. In so many ways, my life was very lucky.

"Plans for today?" he asked.

"When we get the lab report on those hairs, I'll know more."

"It was good of Elisa to provide us with something to test against."

I nodded. "What if they belong to Lydia?"

"Then we'll find her. Frank Riley knows more than he's letting on. I'd be willing to bet on that."

I had the same gut feeling, but proving it was a different kettle of fish. "What are you planning today?" I asked.

"I have some papers to serve around the county."

Normally DeWayne or Budgie did this work. "What's up?"

"One is to the Randall farm. I thought I'd take it myself. It's a summons for jury duty for Jason. He was supposed to show up yesterday and didn't. I'm hoping I can talk him into just appearing. He can ask the judge for compassion and dismissal of duties, but he can't ignore his duty to serve. I know his plate is full, running his farm. I have sympathy. I'm hoping to avert serious trouble for him."

"He works that farm alone," I said.

"He can make that case, Sarah Booth. Otherwise, he won't be working the farm if he's sitting in a jail cell. It's a civic duty. I don't have any leeway here."

"I don't think Jason Randall believes in the justice system."

"Sometimes I doubt it myself," Coleman said. "Poor people always pay. People like Tope too often buy their way out of punishment."

"I hear you."

We stopped in the driveway to admire the lane of sycamores and the flashing black horse that ran toward us, greeting his missing pasture-mates with a loud whinny. Reveler bunched beneath me, and I tightened my legs, ready if he decided to pull a stunt. He thought about it for a minute and then relaxed, stepping out in a full, swinging walk. Good for my boy. He'd rather eat his grain than buck me off. Life was good. It was time to take a shower and go to work.

Coleman had just left when my phone rang. Budgie was on the horn, and he had the goods I was waiting on.

"Do the hairs we found match Elisa Redd's DNA?"

There was a hesitation on the line. "I'm sorry, Sarah Booth. They don't."

I hadn't realized how much I'd counted on the match. My stomach lurched. "Are you sure?"

"They ran it twice. I'm sorry."

I was all out of questions or ideas of what to pursue next. My best hope for finding Lydia alive had just ended. And with it my hope that I would find her at all. "Thanks, Budgie. I appreciate all the work you did."

"I'm not done yet."

His voice stopped me. He sounded . . . gleeful. "What else did you find?"

"The person wasn't a natural blonde. It was from a brunette who bleached her hair."

I struggled to grasp his meaning. "But Lydia is blond."

"And Bethany was brunette. We need a sample from Bethany's mother or dad."

My hope rose again. "I'm on it today. Right away."

"The FedEx guy comes at ten. Have it here before then and the lab can get to it today."

He didn't have to tell me twice. I was grabbing my coat and keys and was halfway out the door when Sweetie Pie and Pluto rushed me to get outside. They weren't going to be left behind. I called Mrs. Carter as I was driving toward her home. I didn't want to just show up, possibly creating turmoil. Luckily, she answered and told me to stop by.

I called Tinkie and told her where I was going. I put a heavy foot on the accelerator as we rocketed down a long, straight stretch of roadway between fallow cotton fields. No matter what was on my mind, I could always find a moment to take pleasure in the rich soil of the Delta. It was a place of bounty and poverty, culture and racism, tradition and false allegiance. The extremes of the human soul seemed represented by the landscape of the Delta.

When I pulled into the Carter yard, I took in the neat clapboard house built in the style of country homes—tall ceilings, lots of windows. Air circulation had been of utmost concern. Before I could get out of the car, Mrs. Carter came toward me. She had a plastic baggy in her hand. "This is my hair and my husband's. I got his from his comb. But you need to go. He forgot something and he's coming back. I don't need a scene."

"Thank you." I took the bag and turned around. I was only a few hundred yards down the street when I passed a car driven by a man I presumed to be Bethany's dad. I'd barely missed him.

I made it to the courthouse with thirty minutes to spare before the FedEx driver showed up. Budgie had the paperwork ready, and we sealed the hair in an envelope. "Thank you, Budgie."

"Coleman wants to find those women, too."

"I know."

Sweetie Pie and Pluto had followed me into the courthouse, and they were hovering over a hot-air vent in the floor. Budgie had bought beds for them, and he moved the beds closer to the vent. "You spoil them," I teased him.

"They're well behaved. Coleman is all the time remarking about how obedient they are, compared to you."

"He'd better not—" I saw on his face that I'd risen to the bait. "He didn't say that."

"But you thought he did."

"Budgie, just remember that I can always put a burr under the saddle when I tack up the horse for you."

"Your point is taken." He did a courtly little bow. "By the way, I discovered two additional missing women from the area." He sat down at his desk and rifled through a stack of papers, pulling out two. "Right here. Andrea Mc-Caw and Bella Osborn. I got addresses and phone numbers for the families of both if you want to check it out."

"How long have they been missing?"

"It's odd because they went missing together, like Lydia and Bethany. That's what originally caught my interest. They've been gone about five years. It's possible they might have been found and no one bothered to let the authorities know."

"I can always hope." I didn't relish talking to more grieving parents. A happy outcome would be nice for a change. "I'll find Tinkie so we can get after this." I put a hand on Budgie's shoulder. "Thank you. You've gone above and beyond."

"Just doing my job," he said. "I may tease you about Coleman, but the man loves you to the ends of the earth."

"Always good to hear. Don't tell him but I love him back that much, too."

I whistled up Sweetie Pie, who'd warmed up and was ready for more car adventure. Pluto blinked his green eyes at me and curled back up. "Pluto!"

"Leave him," Budgie said. "He knows I have some creamed salmon in the refrigerator for him."

"Budgie! That's too much."

"I enjoy his company," Budgie said. "I'll bring him home at the end of the day if you don't stop back by for him."

"All I can say is thank you."

Sweetie and I sped out the door, down the steps, and into the car. I should have left the motor running because it was so cold. By the time we got to Tinkie's, the heater was going full blast and we were warm again. Tinkie met me with a cup of hot coffee and chicken-jerky dog treats for Sweetie.

While Tinkie looked over the paperwork Budgie had pulled on the two missing women, I checked emails and called Elisa to find out if she'd ever heard from the tipster who stole her ten grand. It was unlikely she ever would, but I had to ask.

"Can I call you later?" Elisa asked. Her voice was stressed.

"Sure. Are you okay?"

"Yes. Just in the middle of something. I must hang up."

"Is Tope there?"

She didn't answer. The line went dead. "Tinkie, we need to check on Elisa. Right now."

"Pauline!" Tinkie called the nanny and handed sleeping Maylin over to her. "We'll be back as soon as we can."

Sweetie Pie and Chablis were at the door, so it was quicker to take them than try to leave them behind. We jumped into the Roadster and took off. The Redd home was on the fringes of Zinnia. The family owned thousands of acres of farmland, not counting the big hunk of land Tope had stolen from them. But Elisa and her husband chose to live in town. They leased their fields to farming concerns. It didn't take us ten minutes to pull up in the driveway of her house.

The front door was open, and I felt a chill run down my spine. Sweetie Pie bounded past me and entered the house first. She went to the back of the house while I checked the rooms systematically. Tinkie had taken the upstairs and we met in the kitchen.

"There's no one here," Tinkie said.

"Maybe she wasn't here when we were talking," I said, hoping that was the truth.

"What about her car?"

We both rushed to the garage. Her SUV was parked there with her purse on the hood.

"This looks bad," Tinkie said.

"It does." I dialed the sheriff's office. "Budgie, you and Coleman need to get over here. Elisa Redd is missing. Her house is wide open, and her purse is on the hood of her car. There's not a sign of her."

26

Tinkie and I stood in the yard while the crime-scene spe-cialists worked over the house. Coleman was with them for a while, but he came outside and put his arms around us. "Now, tell me again," he said.

I went over the phone call to Elisa, how odd she'd acted, how she hadn't responded to my questions about Tope. And now she was gone.

"Okay, I'm waiting to hear from the law officer who had Tope staked out." Coleman frowned. "He should have called by now."

Sweetie Pie and Chablis appeared at the edge of the yard. I'd been looking for both of them. "Sweetie, Chablis, come here." I called to them, but they hung back at the edge of the lawn. Sweetie Pie howled and Chablis gave her ferocious bark. They had no intention of coming to me.

I didn't have any leashes on hand, but I walked over to them intending to get them to follow me back to the car. Coleman knew they were good at a crime scene, but there were other agencies involved in this. The other law officers were giving my pets the hairy eyeball. I didn't want to make Coleman look bad in front of fellow lawmen, so it was just easier to round up Sweetie Pie and Chablis and put them in the car until I was ready to go—which would be very soon.

When I was within reach of Sweetie Pie, she bolted into the azaleas and bottlebrush trees that landscaped the yard. "Hey!" I spoke in a strained whisper. I didn't want to call attention to the ill-behaved critters. "Come on, you two. We'll go to Millie's and get a hamburger steak." When all else failed the animals responded to bribery very well.

Not this time, though. They backed even deeper into the shrubbery. I felt Coleman's gaze drilling into my back, so I went in the bushes after them. "You guys, come on. Coleman is giving us the death stare. We need to clear the crime scene and start looking for Elisa."

Logic held no sway with Sweetie Pie or Chablis.

I managed to wiggle my fingers in Sweetie's collar, but she backed up and it came off over her head. She snuffled at the ground and flipped a bunch of molding old leaves into my face. Chablis gave her ferocious little bark.

I was about to scold them when I stopped. What were they up to? Sweetie Pie was an easygoing hound, and when food was involved, she was always docile and agreeable. Unless she was trying to show me something.

"Sarah Booth."

Coleman's voice made me jump and a branch from the

shrubs stabbed me right between the eyes. Blood trickled out.

"If you think you're hiding, you're wrong. Your butt is sticking out into the yard and everyone is watching you," Coleman said. There was a hint of merriness in his voice. When I came out of the shrubbery with blood flowing, his attitude changed to one of real concern. "You're hurt!"

"No kidding. You startled me and I jumped into a sharp limb." I wiped the blood dripping off my nose.

Coleman handed me a handkerchief. "Let me take a look."

I let him turn me into the light and examine the wound.

"It's minor. The stick just hit a bleeder." He pressed the handkerchief into the wound to stanch the flow. "Why are Sweetie Pie and Chablis hiding in the azaleas?"

"I think they found something. A clue."

"Here, hold this." He put my hand on the cloth on my forehead. Squatting, he crawled into the bushes. "Can you get me a flashlight?" he asked.

I didn't point out that I had been wounded in the line of duty. I sucked it up and went to the patrol car and got his high-beam light. He took it and scuttled deeper into the leaves. I could hear Sweetie Pie whining. "Find anything?" I asked.

"Not yet."

Coleman was moving through the bushes, following Sweetie Pie and Chablis as they shifted to the side of Elisa's house.

"Here it is," Coleman said.

"What? What did you find?"

"Footprints. Get DeWayne to bring me the materials to make a cast." Coleman stood up and he was in the middle of a giant azalea that came up to his chin. "Look." He nodded toward Elisa's house. "From this vantage point, I can see directly into her study. Someone stood here watching her."

"Before they took her," I said.

I hustled over to DeWayne to tell him about the plaster. Coleman's cell phone rang just as DeWayne arrived with the plaster. He came out of the bushes and DeWayne got busy making the cast.

"Are you certain?" Coleman said, an edge to his voice. "How long ago?" He listened and hung up. "Bad news. Tope knocked out the deputy watching him, tied him up, and then disappeared. Tope has been gone since very early this morning."

"He had time to come here and take Elisa," I said, keeping emotion out of my voice.

"Yes, he did. I should have worked with the city to have someone watching this house," Coleman said. "I just didn't think Tope would be so . . . reckless. I really thought MBI would be on top of him."

"You're not any guiltier than I am," I said. "I should have been watching her. She could have stayed with me or at Hilltop with Tinkie. I hate that she was alone."

"We'll find her." Coleman's jaw was set with determination. "We need to find out if those are Tope's prints, and we need to find some clues as to where Tope has taken Elisa."

"It may not have been Tope." I put it out there. I believed Tope was guilty of numerous crimes, and kidnapping Elisa could be one of them. But the worst thing a detective could do was start with an assumption and build a case around it. Coleman and I both had reason to hate Tope, but that wouldn't help us find Elisa or the missing women. We had to find the facts, interpret them, and work the case.

Coleman put his arm around me. "You're right. Thank you. Just so you know, nothing appeared to be disturbed in the house. I didn't really get a chance to check thoroughly, but it seems Elisa answered the door and exited of her own accord."

"Could she have left on her own?" Tinkie had been talking with the city officers and came to join us.

"Her car is in the garage," I pointed out. "She could have gone out with a friend, but why leave the front door open? And leave her purse?"

"No calls were made asking for help. The house has a very high-tech alarm system, and it wasn't triggered. The neighbors didn't see or hear anything." She sounded discouraged.

Coleman put a hand on her shoulder as he still held me to his side. "I'm going to let the city officers worry about this, but I have to find Tope. He's in big trouble now, assaulting an officer. I have enough to arrest him and hope the judge denies bail."

"You go on," I said. "We'll call if we learn anything. And DeWayne will know more than we will. How is the officer Tope attacked?"

Coleman nodded. "He's in the Memphis hospital. He was conscious and talking, but I don't have an update. You two be careful. Don't put yourselves at risk. Tope has always had a big problem following the rules, but this seems unhinged. If he's harmed Elisa, not even all of his family money can buy him out of that."

"I hope you're right," I said. "Tinkie and I will track down the other two missing women's families."

He kissed the top of my head. "Just be careful. Both of you."

It wasn't a long drive to Hilltop. Tinkie bustled to the kitchen and put on some coffee.

I settled into our quiet office. Maylin was off with Pauline, taking a bath. A good thing since she was an irresistible temptation. I had work to do. When Tinkie arrived with two steaming cups, we split the telephone chores. I took the McCaw family and Tinkie called Bella Osborn's parents. Sweetie Pie and Pluto were toasting in front of the fire in the office while we worked. They looked so innocent.

Mrs. McCaw answered the phone, and I felt relief shower down on me when she told me that Andrea had been gone about three weeks before she returned home. "She'd gone out to California to be an actress," Mrs. McCaw said. "You know young girls and their dreams. We wanted Andrea to dream big, but we never thought about Hollywood. She didn't tell us because she knew we'd disapprove, but that's what happened. Once she got there, it wasn't what she thought it would be. I think she believed some movie mogul would find her sitting on a stool at the lunch counter at Kress's. She couldn't even get a job waiting tables, and she didn't know a soul there. Bitter disillusionment, so she came back home. In the end, I think it was a good thing. Now my girl is married with two children. She's an accountant and her husband is, too. They work together and they're happy. They're in Aspen right now skiing."

"This is a great comfort," I told her. "I'm so happy for you and her."

"Yes, I try not to think about those days when she was missing. It felt like my skin was on fire with worry. No one knew where to look. It almost broke me . . . but that's far in the past. I am sorry for Elisa Redd. We weren't friends, but I saw them in town and Elisa doted on her girl. I wouldn't wish that kind of hurt and loss on my worst enemy."

I thanked her and hung up.

Tinkie had also finished her call, and she plopped down in an office chair with a sigh. "Bella disappeared from Ole Miss, dropped out of her classes. She was gone about three weeks and then suddenly reappeared. She said she'd gone to New Orleans to see about work, but it hadn't panned out. Her parents moved heaven and earth to get her reinstated in school, but she lost a semester."

"Did Mrs. Osborne say why Bella had gone to New Orleans?"

"I don't think she knew for certain. She said Bella went to find work but wasn't successful. She didn't sound like she believed that, but she doesn't care. Bella is safe. She got her nursing degree from Delta State, and she's happily married. No children."

Another instance where fate had dealt a kinder hand. "That is good news."

"Not for Elisa," Tinkie said, echoing my thoughts. "Why didn't Lydia and Bethany come home? It would seem those other girls left on their own and returned when they were ready."

"Yes, it seems that way." But another thought had occurred. Why would Bella leave a college degree program and lose an entire semester of work? And why had Andrea worried her parents sick? Why worry the people who loved you instead of just telling the truth? "I think both of those women had another reason for disappearing."

Tinkie caught my drift instantly. "You think they were pregnant. That they went somewhere to take care of the pregnancy."

Once she said it aloud, I nodded. "I do. And I think this also involved Ernest and Florence Salter."

"A conjure woman who knew herbs." Tinkie put it

together fast. "There are plenty of natural ingredients that can help a young girl. In the hands of someone educated in the craft, it's safe."

My mother had connections with several midwives in the area. She supported them and their valuable work. I had no doubt she would land on the side of a woman's right to control her fate and future. My father would support that, too. Had they lived, though, I felt certain they would have adopted children. I was their special, golden child. Their gift. I had their undivided attention for those early years. But I had been heading into my teens and itching for independence and to kick off my acting career. Even as a sixth grader, I'd known what I wanted to do. After college, they would have helped me get to New York. To try. They would never have stood in the way of me testing my own wings. But I believed they would have found Dahlia House empty, and with so many children in need . . . it would have been inevitable.

"You okay?" Tinkie asked me.

"Absolutely. Just thinking about my folks and if my mama might have known Florence Salter."

"You can bet my mother didn't." Tinkie wasn't exaggerating. Mrs. Bellcase had a select group of friends. Wealthy, white, and privileged. It was how she'd been raised. Thank goodness Tinkie had refused to conform to that.

"We need to talk to Madame Tomeeka," I said. "She may have known Florence and Ernest better than she let on."

"It can't hurt, but how will this help us find Lydia or Mrs. Redd's stolen money?"

I had to laugh. Tinkie kept her eye on the ball. "It probably won't. but I don't have another lead, and I want to know. After all, it was Tammy who dragged us into this case to begin with."

27

Pauline was putting Maylin down for a nap, and Tinkie and I took off to Madame's house. Tinkie called while we were on the way. I didn't want to interrupt one of Tammy's consultations. She gave tarot readings, psychic messages, and dream analyses for anyone who asked.

The smell of apple pie drifted out the front door and made my mouth water. I wasn't hungry, but Tammy made an apple pie so delicious a person could die happy after eating a slice.

"Come on in," she called out when we knocked.

The day was still cold, so we hurried inside. The kitchen was warm and smelled like heaven. Cinnamon, sugar, baking apples, pie crust browning. I peeked in the oven before she popped my behind with a dish towel. "Stay out of that oven. It has fifteen more minutes."

"Where'd you get the apples?" Tinkie asked.

"Mr. Payton brought them to me from his trip to Upstate New York. Sweet and crispy. Perfect for pie."

"Tammy, tell me what you know about Florence Salter and her . . . healing work."

Tammy's face fell into worried lines. "Florence helped a lot of girls who were in big trouble."

"What kind of trouble?"

"Safe havens. Money to run and build a new life. Medicine, when they wanted it. You know how poor this area is. People didn't and still don't have reliable cars to go several states away. Getting to a medical clinic for lifesaving care was another issue altogether. Some of those women were married to brutal men who would have killed them. Until you don't have money or privilege or health care, you can't understand what it's like."

"I can," I said. "I'm not criticizing anyone. I'm just wondering if Lydia needed the special help Florence offered and that's what happened. Lydia could have died accidentally, and Bethany may have felt responsible, so she ran. Look, everyone is gone. Lydia, Bethany, Florence, Ernest. There's no sign of them."

"Ever since I've had that dream, and many others like it I'm sorry to say, I've wondered that exact thing. And I may be as responsible as anyone else."

"Why would you say that?" I asked. My friend worried me. Clearly, she hadn't slept in days. She'd lost weight, too. "Haggard" best described her.

"I have my reasons." Tammy was closing off to me. That was a terrible sign.

"Tell me about the dreams," I said, hoping to back into the conversation we needed to have.

"More of the same. Beating hearts, blood leaking up from the floorboards, a strange blue eye peeping through cracks in the wall. I'm in a shack of some kind. Never meant to be a house. Old, maybe a farm shed. I'm paralyzed and I can't even lift my hand. All I can do is blink my eyes. It's hideous. It's like being buried alive."

That was another favorite Poe theme, but I was wise enough to keep silent on that. Besides, Tammy probably knew Poe's work better than I did. "Where are you?"

"This cabin." Frustration made her tone sharp.

"Where? Just think. What do you hear or smell? Just think back and tell me everything you remember."

Clear directions did calm her. "I smell dust. Not house dust but field dust, like someone not too far away is tilling the land."

"Can you hear anything?"

She listened with her eyes closed, remembering. "The wind rustling tree leaves. Bird calls. A mockingbird. Yes, a mockingbird trilling. And a caw, like a crow. A big crow." She closed her eyes. "I remember now. It was a huge crow, I can see it at the window." Her face paled. "I remember! I remember!" She opened her eyes and looked directly into mine. "It wasn't a crow; it was a raven. It said, 'the door.'"

For a long moment, we said nothing. Tammy's distress silenced us. While at times it was wonderful to have visits from the Great Beyond and intuitive insights into events, it could also be terrifying. I only had Jitty to worry about, but Tammy interacted with a lot of dead people.

"You sure the raven didn't say 'nevermore'?" Tinkie asked. She wasn't making light of Tammy's revelations.

Looking at Tammy's face, no one would make light. She was afraid.

"No. It wasn't the Poe poem. This was so clear. I didn't remember it until just now. Something made me think about it."

A light pecking made us all turn to the kitchen window. A huge black raven sat on the outside sill. It pecked the glass again. When it had our attention, it spoke. "The door," it said as clearly as if it was giving us an elocution lesson.

"Holy shit," I said, equally eloquent.

"What the heck?" Tinkie added. "Is that your bird, Tammy?"

"I've never seen it before except in my dream."

"What does it mean?" Tinkie asked. "I know that some birds, like cardinals, are said to be messengers from the other side. They arrive to let us here on this plane know our deceased friends and relatives are watching over us."

I gave Tinkie a long look. "Since when did you go all woo-woo on me?"

Tammy shook her head at our bickering. "The raven is a magical bird that has the power to heal and to see into the darker corners of the spirit world. Some people say it is a forewarning of death." She looked at both of us, and she wasn't pulling our leg.

"Who is the message for?" Tinkie asked.

Tammy shook her head. "I don't know. But the raven is a messenger bird. It's here for a reason. And it gave us a message."

"What does it mean, 'the door'?" I asked.

"I don't know." Tammy walked to the window. The bird never fluttered a feather. It watched her, watched us all. It turned its little head to the side and again said, "The door."

"How did it learn to talk?" I asked.

Tammy rolled her eyes at me. "I don't know. I've never seen the bird before. Maybe it belongs to someone and got out of a cage. Ravens can talk, to an extent. That's my entire knowledge of ravens, so don't ask any more questions."

Still the bird lingered on the windowsill. It made no attempt to peck the glass again, but it didn't have to. It had our full attention.

"What should we do?" Tinkie asked.

I shrugged. "It's not hurting anything."

"The door," the bird said again. It pecked the glass for emphasis.

"It's trying to tell us something," Tammy said. "It's a message from the spirit world."

That made chill bumps dance across my skin. "How do you know?"

"From the Greeks to Native Americans, the raven has been considered a messenger from the underworld, the spirit world. When a raven comes to you, be prepared for contact with that world."

I wasn't afraid of the spirit world. After all, I had Jitty as a constant companion. But I preferred to talk to Jitty than take dictation from an oversize crow. "If the bird has something to say, he should speak up."

The raven pecked the window glass and said, "The door."

I didn't have an answer to that, but I got up and hurried to the front door of Tammy's house. As soon as I left the kitchen, the bird flew away. Tammy and Tinkie rushed to the back porch to see where the bird had flown.

I opened the front door. Right on the doormat was an envelope. Sealed but not addressed to anyone. I picked it up and examined it. It wasn't mine to open, but I stepped outside to see if anyone lurked in the yard. There was no sign of anyone, no footprints, no car tracks, nothing. I had the crazy idea the raven had delivered the mail.

I took the envelope into the house. "This was left for you." I handed it to Tammy.

She took it with reluctance but quickly opened it. There was a folded page inside and she pulled it out and spread it on the table. It was one of the flyers Tinkie and I had left in Greenwood. A note scrawled in red marker across it said, "Stop hunting now! Or bad things will happen."

This wasn't the first request for us to cease and desist that we'd received, but this one had more teeth. "Bad things will happen." That wasn't a warning, it was a threat.

Tinkie got a plastic bag out of a drawer and Tammy deposited the letter and envelope in it. Maybe Coleman could get some fingerprints. My problem was that we'd had anonymous tips and phone calls and now an unsigned letter warning us to stop. It was easy to be threatening when you didn't sign your name.

"Any idea why someone would leave this for Tammy?" I asked.

"Maybe it wasn't for Tammy," Tinkie said. "Your car is parked out front. Maybe it was for you and me."

She had a point.

"Do you think it was Tope?" Tinkie asked. "Surely he wouldn't show up in Sunflower County with everyone on the lookout for him. But it sounds like him, trying to intimidate us into backing off."

"But who is in danger?" Tammy asked. "Us, Lydia, Elisa? Who will bad things happen to?"

That was the most dangerous part of the threat. It could

be anyone. Tinkie and I could take our chances, but was it fair to put Tammy and others at risk?

"It's a coward's message," Tinkie said.

"But cowards can be dangerous," Tammy warned.

"You're right about that. Privileged people often think it's their right to do whatever they want. They think they'll get away with it. They never expect to pay any consequences, and when they're caught and held accountable, they cry like little babies." I was over Tope Maxwell. Whatever had happened to Lydia Redd Maxwell, Tope was at the bottom of it. He'd hurt her and forced her to do something desperate. She was at fault as well for not filing charges and giving law enforcement the tools to stop him, but I understood being afraid. I would not want to be alone in a house with Tope. He had the ability and willingness to do true bodily harm. If Vivian could talk, I had no doubt she'd tell us exactly that.

"Call Coleman." Tinkie didn't care about blame, she just wanted to be sure we were safe. "Tammy might need protection."

"I don't think this was intended for me," Tammy said. "I'm more worried about you two. And Elisa."

"I have to tell Coleman about this." When he answered, I told him about the note. "We'll drop it by so it can be fingerprinted," I said.

"I have some news for you from Adams County. Frank Riley was pulled over for an expired tag in his old truck. The deputies were watching for him, and they got him. Which allowed them to go over the truck with a fine-tooth comb. There was no indication of a body ever having been in the bed. No blood or tissue or anything like that. Mr. Riley was pulling your leg about the dead-body part."

I was somewhat relieved, but I had questions. "Why would he tell us that? And why would the women who borrowed the truck say that?"

"As to the latter, we don't know that it's true. They might not have said that. Maybe Frank was after getting a rise out of you and Tinkie."

"Thanks. It's possible," I said. "I'll see you as soon as I finish talking with Tammy."

"Be cautious. If Tope left that threat, then he's watching you. No matter who left it or who it is meant for, precaution is always for the best."

"We're on high alert." I hung up and shared the news about the truck.

"Can we question Frank Riley?" Tinkie was ready to roll all the way to Natchez.

"I don't think an expired tag is enough to hold him in jail. It's a fine." Like Tinkie, I wanted some leverage to make him talk. He knew more than he was letting on. We'd appealed to his better angels and gotten nowhere. We needed something to hold over his head.

"As much as I want to make him talk, I think we should focus on Tope. If he's on the loose . . ." Tinkie didn't have to finish. Tope was a danger to everyone.

"Tinkie, would you take the threatening note over to the sheriff's office?"

"What are you going to do?" She was instantly alert.

"And remember, you don't even have a ride. They won't let me in, but I want to look around the area where Vivian died."

"Why can't you wait for me?" Tinkie asked.

"I can." I knew not to push. I didn't want Tinkie to be in the line of fire if Tope happened to be hiding out at his mansion, but she wasn't about to let me go on my own.

That was my partner—and everyone said I was the head-strong PI.

"Let's go." She picked up the plastic baggie that held the note. "We're going together. Or no one is going anywhere."

It wasn't worth an argument. "If you have more dreams, Tammy, please let us know."

28

Coleman took the letter and quickly set up to dust it for fingerprints. He didn't have the high-tech equipment of a CSI television show, but he had a lot of experience. Too bad it didn't pay off.

"Nothing. I would say the person who did this wore gloves. Y'all didn't hear a vehicle or anything?" he asked.

"No. And I checked outside. No footprints or tire treads. There was a raven—"

"Don't try to fool Coleman." Tinkie grasped my arm and dug in with her fingers.

She didn't want me to talk about the raven. I didn't get it, but I closed my pie hole.

"We have to go," Tinkie said as she almost frog-marched

me out of the courthouse and to the car. "Drive," she said. "Hurry."

"Pushy, some?" I asked. "And why didn't you want me to talk about the raven?"

"Because linking a wild bird to a threat makes you sound demented. Now watch where you're going," Tinkie said as I pulled into the driveway of Tope's place and nearly ran down a man standing in the road, flagging me to stop. Tope had hired a private security firm to a protect his compound.

"Turn around and leave. You aren't authorized to enter," the guard said.

Not even Tinkie, with her magic manipulation, could talk our way in. I turned the car around and slowly drove away before the guard called Coleman to come collect us.

When we were back on the main road, I took a right and then stopped at a pig trail that led into a thick brake. The trees and vines were almost impenetrable.

"We can sneak in through the woods," I told Tinkie. "Bit of a walk, but doable."

"Is it worth that much effort?" she asked. Clearly, she had a better option. "Let's go talk to the Randalls again."

"I don't know. They've been hurt a lot with Tillie's disappearance. I think they were telling the truth." I was reluctant to stick the blade of remorse and regret into them again.

"I don't."

I was surprised. Tinkie held the tenderhearted award. I was normally the hard-ass. "What's going on?" I asked.

"It occurred to me that if Andrea McCaw and Bella Osborn returned home after missing for several weeks or so, maybe the same is true for Tillie Randall." She grasped my hand so that I looked directly into her eyes. "I think the young woman posing as Mrs. Randall's niece is Tillie. Those are Jane Randall's grandkids. I think Tillie came home under a new identity."

"What?"

"Think about it. I don't believe any of those girls were ever actually missing. There would have been a lot more uproar. Those girls likely got in trouble and went away to have a baby or took care of it with help from Florence or a doctor, if they could afford to get to medical care. For whatever reason, Tillie needed a new identity. I suspect she had the baby, and the father was someone she didn't want in their lives."

Truth is sometimes like a sledgehammer to the head. The blow stunned me for a second, but then I realized Tinkie might have resolved the big issue of missing girls. "But then where are Lydia and Bethany?"

"Hiding from Tope." Tinkie had worked it through to the end.

"Elisa has been grieving for all this time. Why would Lydia be so cruel to her mother?"

"I don't think it was cruelty," Tinkie said. "The opposite. She was protecting Elisa from a man that Lydia knew was capable of extreme brutality."

The very worst possibility reared its ugly head. "Do you think Tope believes Lydia is alive? And near?"

"That concept terrifies me. He will kill her. With an investigation into Vivian's death, Tope is already at risk. He might think it's worth it to get rid of Lydia, too."

"And maybe Elisa. The Redd fortune. If Elisa dies, could Tope get all of it?"

"I don't know if Elisa has a will or not. And if she croaks

before Lydia is found, I'll bet Lydia is her heir. That would all then go to Tope if both women died in that order."

Tinkie had been spending way too much time online with conspiracy theorists. She was beginning to sound like Millie and Cece. Soon we'd be talking about Princess Diana living in Tahiti and pregnant with Elvis's baby. "If you're right, finding Lydia will only endanger both women."

"Yes. That's what I think the note was about. 'Stop looking. Leave us alone. We're in danger.'"

"Should we tell Elisa?"

"I think Elisa should fire us in a very public place. And Cece should cover it for the newspaper."

"You are a genius!" Even if Tinkie was wrong in her calculations, this move wouldn't harm our investigation. We could take it underground and accomplish more. Coleman and Elisa and everyone that mattered would know the truth. The general public would see it as a failure for Delaney Detective Agency, which would make the resolution in the end all the sweeter. Once we found the missing women.

"All we have to do is find the evidence, which will be Tillie Randall." Tinkie was justifiably proud of herself.

"Buckle your seat belt!"

If we were opening old wounds, we had no option. If Tinkie was correct, our entire game plan would change to one of aggressive defense. Maybe it was crazy to hinge the belief that Lydia and Bethany were alive on the fact that another missing girl might be alive and living under an alias.

"If Lydia and Bethany are alive, where do you think they are?" I asked.

"Greenwood," Tinkie answered without hesitation. "I

think they may be living there, and that's what's fouled up their plan. They got too close to home and someone recognized them."

There had been the call to the tip line, and then the second call where Elisa had dropped ten large for information that never came. "Do you think the people who took the ten grand were Lydia and Bethany?"

"It's possible," Tinkie said. "In fact, it's probable. What I don't understand is why she didn't give her mother a shred of relief, though. Taking the money and never saying a word . . . I can't accept that. I know, she might be protecting Elisa, but still. Surely there was something she could say to offer a little comfort."

"I hear you, but let's find Lydia and then you can take a switch to her bottom." We pulled up at the Randall house and I cut the engine. "This could be awkward."

"Which is why you're going to the front door and I'm going to the back."

Tinkie had sunk her teeth into this case and far be it from me to balk. "Aye, aye, Captain," I said as I prepared to confront a woman who I now believed had lied to my face. Tinkie disappeared around a corner of the house. I gave her a minute before I knocked on the door.

Jane Randall answered the door, and I couldn't tell if she was annoyed or afraid. "Why are you here?" she asked.

"You weren't straight with me."

"I don't know what you mean."

"Yes, you do." I put a foot across the threshold in case she decided to slam the door. I was waiting on a signal from Tinkie. She'd bang very loudly on the back door while I had Jane busy at the front.

There was a scream from the back of the house, and I figured that was my cue. "Where's your daughter, Jane?"

"You are a cruel woman. Get out of my house." She backed up, though, and gave me space to enter.

"Where's Tillie? We know it isn't your niece living here. It's your daughter."

She burst into tears just as Tinkie barreled into the parlor with a young woman trying to drag her backward.

"Tillie!" The name cracked with such power that Tinkie and Tillie stopped in their tracks. I pointed at the young woman. "You're Tillie Randall and there's no point denying it."

Tinkie gave a nod of satisfaction. Tillie looked at her crying mother and at me.

"Who the hell are you people?" she asked.

"They're private investigators," Jane said, brushing the tears from her cheeks. "They're looking for Lydia and that friend of hers. They think all of the disappearances are linked."

"Somebody needs to explain some things," Tinkie said. Her face was thunderous. "We've been played by you both and there are lives at stake."

"Yeah, mine. And my children," Tillie said. "You bust in here and put my family in danger. Who do you think you are?"

"The person who is going to see that you're charged with identity theft, fraud, and a host of other crimes." That made her clamp her lips shut. I pointed to the sofa. "Sit and answer some questions."

Jane and Tillie took a seat. I saw a shadow in the hallway and felt a jolt of adrenaline, but it was only a young girl.

She was soon joined by a little boy. They ran into the room to their mother.

"These are my children," Tillie said.

"You are Tillie Randall, aren't you?" Tinkie asked.

"I was. No longer."

"Why did you pretend to be missing?"

Tillie glared at me. "I was protecting my daughter."

That wasn't exactly what I'd expected her to say. "How so?"

"You're going to blow up a lot of people's lives," she said. "Are you prepared for the fallout from that?"

"We're trying to find two missing women. I don't know how you're involved in the disappearance of Lydia Redd Maxwell and Bethany Carter, but it seems you are. Care to explain?" Tinkie said.

"Tope is my daughter's father," Tillie said with surprising savagery.

"You pretended to disappear to keep her away from him?" I asked.

"To keep her alive, you fools. If Tope knew Cadence was his, what do you think he'd do? He doesn't want an illegitimate heir. He told me he would kill me when I suggested I might be pregnant. That's when I decided to leave the county. I stayed gone as long as I could, but I came home a few years ago when Mama had some surgery. I don't want anything from Tope except to be left alone."

"You really think he would harm your daughter?" Tinkie asked.

"I do."

"You were dating Tope?" I asked.

Tillie put her face in her hands for a moment to compose

herself. "Mama, would you make us some coffee, please? I'm tired of hiding and lying."

"I hope you know what you're doing," Jane said. "Putting yourself at risk won't help find Lydia or that other woman."

"It's not about that," Tillie said. "I've lived the last few years like a felon, hiding out here at your house, trying not to draw attention to myself or us. I'm done with it. Cadence starts kindergarten soon. She deserves to have friends over, to bloom. I've turned her into a mouse."

Jane started crying silently. "I know. I know. But she's been safe."

"That isn't enough any longer." Tillie turned to me. "I didn't date Tope. I went over to his house, which was extremely poor judgment. He was pretending to have found a lead about Lydia. He seemed really upset about her disappearance and he said maybe I could help with a clue. I was curious, so I went. We had a few drinks, and I woke up naked. I found out six weeks later I was pregnant."

"Okay then," I said, unsettled by the horror of her story. "And Tope is the father?"

"That's my assumption. That's why I disappeared for a while. When I came back, I came as a niece. It was the only way I could be sure my baby would not be in jeopardy. Tope might kill the women in his life, but now his own child would have no escape from his cruelty."

Tillie knew as well as I did that her daughter stood to inherit plenty from the Maxwells. Money was no lure, though, when her daughter's health and happiness were on the line.

My cell phone rang, showing a number I didn't recognize.

"I'm going to step outside to take this." My primary motive was to give Tinkie time to connect with Tillie and Jane, to make them feel safe that we wouldn't blow her cover.

I stepped out on the porch, snugging my coat closer. I answered the phone, but the line was dead. Foreboding settled around my heart.

Gray clouds heavy with rain were building to the west. They'd move east, over us, and likely bring freezing rain. If enough rain came down and it got cold enough, sometimes the power lines froze and snapped. The wide-open spaces of the Delta gave a chilling wind permission to create havoc. "Chilling wind" made me think of Tammy's dream and the raven that had settled on her sill. "'A wind blew out of a cloud, chilling my beautiful Annabel Lee.'" I spoke the line of poetry aloud.

The sense of foreboding that slipped over me was doubled when I heard a raspy voice. "Help me."

I walked to the edge of the porch before I saw the raven perched in a leafless tree. The bird was big. It stared directly into my eyes, unflinching. Unafraid.

"Shoo!" I tried to send it away, but my efforts had no effect. "You are getting under my skin," I told the bird. "Go away."

It fluttered to a higher limb.

The bird was framed against the steadily building storm clouds, and I had an urge to rush home and get the horses into the barn. It was dangerous to confine them, but it was risky to leave them out in the pasture. If the hail came and it was big, it could really harm them.

The bird flew to another branch, and I shifted on the porch so I could watch it. My new perspective gave me a glimpse of a secluded bench by a small fountain where a woman sat reading. She wore a dark skirt, white shirt, and sweater pulled over her shoulders. Whatever she was reading held her rapt attention.

Curious, I stepped off the porch. I assumed the raven would fly away when I walked toward him, but he didn't. He merely watched, and said, "Help me."

The woman either didn't hear him or ignored him. Maybe I was delusional and only I could hear the bird talk.

"Talk," the bird said, as if it had heard my thoughts. I hurried my footsteps across the lawn to the bench. The woman looked up. Her dark hair, curled, framed her face. Expressive eyes seemed to read my thoughts.

"Who are you?" I asked. Clearly, she was not of this time or place. I knew instantly that Jitty was at work, but this woman wasn't the normal flamboyant alter ego Jitty preferred.

"Anya Seton," she said, waving for me to take a seat on her bench. "Novelist."

"*Dragonwyck*!" I'd read her Gothic romance when I was in high school, and I'd been addicted to the movie starring Gene Tierney. Aunt Loulane had loved the movie, too. We'd watched it together numerous times. I was at that tender age when a dark romantic interest appealed to me greatly. The dangerous lover. The man with a shadowy past who captured my heart. But in my fantasies, the man was also good, just misunderstood. Righto. At that time in my life, naïveté ruled. Now Jitty was giving me a graduate course on Tope Maxwell and how dangerous he might be. "Why are you here, *Ms. Seton*?" I hit the name hard to let Jitty know I was onto her.

"I came to see you. You need to think things through, or you'll be hurt."

Definitely Jitty. "You're here, no doubt, to lecture me."

The writer laughed. She closed her book and put it between us on the bench. It was indeed *Dragonwyck*. I remembered the story line of a young, innocent woman falling for and marrying a nefarious man. The heroine, Miranda, dreams of an exciting life beyond her Connecticut farm and agrees to a job as companion to the daughter of Nicholas and Johanna Van Ryn. Infatuated with Nicholas, Miranda marries him shortly after Johanna dies suddenly.

As Miranda learns more and more unsavory facts about her husband, she meets a doctor who is opposed to the class structure of Upstate New York. In the end, Nicholas is brought to justice and Miranda realizes that the good doctor is a far better man to love. One of my favorite parts of the book was Dragonwyck Manor, a dark estate filled with old ghosts and hauntings.

"Aren't you glad you're not running around the Hudson Valley today?" I asked. "It would freeze your earlobes off."

"You're correct. The most beautiful place to be in the fall and spring, but not winter." She looked around. "No snow here. Perfection."

I pointed to the building clouds. "We could have freezing rain or hail."

"Nothing a nice fire can't hold at bay. The best days to sit at my desk and write. Or read." She pointed at the book. "You're not innocent enough to make the terrible mistakes of Miranda."

I didn't even want to argue that. She was right. I'd lay a cast-iron frying pan against the head of any man who tried to harm me or those I loved. "So the lesson is never to trust those who win your love?" I knew that would get Jitty up and going.

"I did not say that!" The calm countenance of Anya Seton began to morph to that of my fabulous haint, who was more than a little agitato. "You twist my words. I'm just saying women should stand up for themselves."

"I agree. But this whole love thing is too risky. I think I'll have to stay single. Wouldn't it be awful if I married and my husband killed me? What would happen to you and Dahlia House?"

"Stop it. Stop it right now." Jitty's furrowed brow told me I'd gotten her good.

Before I could gig her again, the raven circled out of the tree and landed on the bench beside Jitty. "Help me," the bird said.

"Is that your bird?" I asked her.

She shook her head. "It's yours."

"No, thanks. Birds should be free to fly."

Jitty had collected her emotions and she gave me a long, assessing stare. "We'll see about that."

"Tell me what you know about the missing women. What do you see in the Great Beyond?" I was desperate for a good lead.

She spun up into a little dust devil of fallen leaves and feathers. Before she could completely escape, I called after her. "'Nevermore!'"

29

Tinkie was ready to go when I returned to the Randall house. As soon as Jitty disappeared, the bird had flown away. And from the looks of Tillie and Jane, they were ready for us to be gone. We thanked them for helping and left.

"Tope could demand parental rights of Tillie's daughter," Tinkie said as we pulled down the drive. "No wonder she ran scared."

"Do you think Tope is involved with the McCaw or Osborn girls?" Tope was bursting with entitlement and privilege, and he had the kind of personality to take what he felt was his due, including young women.

"Like a serial rapist?" Tinkie frowned. "If that's the case, maybe we can just shoot him."

"Some men just need killin'," I agreed, knowing my

partner was all bluff and no action. She might want to plug him, but she'd never do it unless she was defending herself or someone else.

"Should we go back and interview those young women?"

I shook my head. "Not right now. I think we should leave that to Coleman. He'll get more out of them than we can."

She nodded agreement. "Then we should follow up on the DNA from that hair we think belongs to Bethany."

She was correct. "If it is Bethany's, that'll be a sure sign both women are alive."

"Sarah Booth, this is a hard question to ask: Do you think there is any possibility that Elisa Redd is working to keep Lydia dead?"

I didn't follow her thinking. "How so?"

"It doesn't make any sense. It's just that if Lydia is close, like Greenwood, why in the world wouldn't she give her mama a sign that she is okay?"

This was the question that threw a monkey wrench into my belief that Lydia was alive. Hair samples could be staged. But why? Tinkie and I were missing some aspect of this case that didn't make sense. Maybe the women had been CIA operatives. Maybe they had done things that would perpetually haunt them and anyone they cared about, so it was better to pretend to be dead. Safer.

"Let's check in with Budgie and DeWayne about the hair. Maybe they've heard from Elisa."

"The results should be in," Tinkie agreed. "Let's roll."

I hit the gas and we were sailing down the empty county road that would take us to town.

*　　*　　*

The FedEx driver delivered the results ten minutes after we arrived. I was still warming my backside by an electric heater. DeWayne, who was manning the desk, handed the packet to me to open. I didn't waste any time. I scanned the results and then gave it to DeWayne to confirm.

"It's a match," he said. "The hair you found in that band in the truck matches the Carters."

It was what we'd hoped for, but none of us reacted. Finally, Tinkie spoke. "We should tell her parents."

"Bad idea," DeWayne said. "This doesn't prove conclusively that she was in the truck. Those hairs could have been planted. Don't get her folks' hopes up until you have solid proof."

"I agree," I said softly. "Now we need to focus on finding those women alive. Any more info on their potential work overseas?"

DeWayne pulled up some websites on his computer screen. "Right here near the Pakistani border, there was a village that also contained a school for women and girls. No one has identified Lydia or Bethany as being the teachers there, but the school was run by two American women, a blonde and a brunette."

"What happened to the school? Is it still there?" Tinkie looked at me. "I know we can't go traipsing off to Afghanistan, but Elisa can hire some international PIs to look for them if that's what it takes."

"True. If we have enough evidence that they're alive there, we'll certainly recommend it. And whatever strings can be pulled with the State Department to get those women out."

"If they're viewed as spies, they'll never come home," DeWayne said.

"Are there any indications they were working for any government agency?" I pressed the point because it was crucial.

"None. And no real evidence they ever set foot on Afghan soil."

That was a relief. Finding those two missing women in America was tough enough. "Okay, since the hair we found matches the Carter family, we can at least assume she is alive. And she was with another woman. Possibly Lydia or maybe someone else."

DeWayne nodded.

"What's the next step?" Tinkie asked.

"Another trip to Greenwood and an unannounced visit with Nettie Adams." I couldn't help but wonder if our horticulturist debutante might have misled us deliberately.

"Be careful," DeWayne said. "I'll tell Coleman where you're headed so he won't worry."

Tinkie and I were out the door and in the car in record time. Greenwood was an easy drive, and, on the way, we set our plan. First, a revisit to Gavin Jerome. After that, we'd see what was happening at the Four Corners Farmers Market. In our jaunts around town, we'd leave a trail of bread crumbs for anyone helping the missing women to follow. At the end of the trail would be a tantalizing pile of money. Or at least the promise of such. If I was correct in assuming that Lydia and Bethany had stolen the ten grand in tip-line money, then they had a desperate need for cash. Dangle the right bait and even the wiliest fish would snap.

When cotton was king, Greenwood was a major transport city by river and rails. Like most settlements built around the cotton economy, though, hard times walked hand in hand with history along the city streets.

Tinkie loved the architecture, and we took our time exploring little boutiques and window-shopping. When we got to Turnrow Books, we stepped inside to warm up and talk to the local owners. I had a hunch if anyone had seen Lydia or Bethany, it might be the folks who ran the bookstore.

We browsed through local authors and Tinkie found a book she was dying to read. When we went to the cash register, she chatted with the owners.

"Would you mind taking a look at a picture?" Tinkie asked.

"Not at all." The woman took one of the flyers we had brought. "I saw this posted in some store windows. I've seen this woman, but not in the last week." She pointed at Bethany.

"Where did you see her?" I asked.

"Why do you want to know?" she asked. She was nobody's fool.

"We've been hired by their relatives to find these women." Tinkie gave the abbreviated answer.

"They look full-grown and able to find themselves." She handed the flyer back.

"We were afraid something had happened to them," I said. "Lydia's mother," I touched Lydia's face on the flyer, "is deeply worried and just wants her daughter home. Lydia stands to inherit a lot."

"Interesting." The bookstore owner was not impressed with bread-crumb mentions of money.

"She's an only child," Tinkie added. "Her husband is petitioning the court to have her declared legally dead. If it happens . . ." She shook her head. "It's going to be bad for the mother. And especially for Lydia if she is alive and unable to claim her inheritance."

The bookstore owner was stoically silent. If she knew secrets, she was going to keep them.

"Could you tell us where you saw Bethany?"

"Four Corners produce stand. The vegetables aren't coming in yet, but now's the time to buy and plant fruit trees and such. They do a good business with seasonal fare."

Tinkie pulled a card from her purse. "Thanks. Call me if you see her again. Or maybe just tell her that she needs to check in with her mama."

We continued down the street. "Do you think she really saw Bethany?"

"I don't know who or what to believe. Let's head over to Grand Boulevard and check in with Gavin Jerome."

Even though the clouds were building on the western horizon, they didn't appear to be moving our way. In the distance I could hear the rumble of thunder and see internal lightning illuminating the clouds, giving the afternoon a scary-movie feel. If the storm came, it would be a real blowout.

"We need to be home before that hits." Tinkie had been through too many Delta hailstorms. "I don't want to be trapped on the road."

"Let's talk to Gavin and see what's up. Then we'll head back."

"What about Nettie?"

"If the storm is moving this way, we'll talk to her another day."

"You're a poet, Sarah Booth."

I laughed out loud. Tinkie caught me by surprise. "Right. Actress, poet, Mata Hari. That's me."

We fell into silence as we walked along Grand Boulevard. The beauty calmed me a little. It was a grand and beautiful street. The three hundred oaks had been planted by Sally Gwin, a member of the Greenwood Garden Club.

The shade of the trees made the day colder, but we picked up our pace. When we arrived at the big house, we both stopped to take in the landscaping and simple beauty of the home with a wraparound porch and a balcony sunroom upstairs over a portico. Following the path back to the rental cottage, we kept an eye out for Gavin. I had a sneaking feeling he'd try to run if he saw us.

We were in luck. Gavin came out of the apartment just as we reached the bottom of the stairs. He had nowhere to go but back inside.

"Can we have a moment to chat?" I asked.

He sighed and gave a grudging, "About what?"

"Missing girls. Ten grand in reward money. And what you know about both subjects."

Just as I started up the stairs, my cell phone rang. "I'll talk to Gavin," Tinkie said. "Take it."

Since it was Coleman calling, I did.

"Where are you?" Coleman asked, and the tension in his voice told me he was worried.

"Greenwood."

"Good. Stay there."

"What?"

"Tope was in Zinnia earlier."

"What did he do?"

"Another state law officer picked up his trail. Tope made the officer and shot him in the abdomen. He's in serious condition in the Memphis hospital."

"I'm so sorry."

"Me, too. But he identified Tope."

"Did Tope drive back to Zinnia?" My gut clenched at the thought of what he might be doing to Elisa.

"He did. He was seen hanging out at the Redd house. And he's been out to his house to get clothes and things. The maid told me, though she was terrified to talk about him. She said he was brutal and unpredictable."

People might wonder why someone would work for a man they feared. I knew. He likely paid well. In a rural county, it was hard for a woman without skills to find a steady job. Housecleaning was an option that often paid better than anything else. And it was steady. In some of the homes of the wealthy, the "staff" got little to no time off because the homes wouldn't run without them. They were essential, but almost never acknowledged.

"And Elisa? Have you located her?"

"Still no sign of her."

"Coleman . . ." I knew he was doing everything he could. As were Tinkie and I. My guilt ate at me. I should never have left Elisa alone. She was a mother desperately searching for her child, grieving the possibility that her only baby had been hurt, or worse.

"This isn't your fault, Sarah Booth. But it tells me how dangerous Tope is. I don't want you tracking him."

"But if he has Elisa—"

"I don't care." Coleman's voice was iron. "Promise me you'll steer clear of him. Hunt for the daughter, but do not go after Tope. Swear it."

I didn't have to swear. I knew how destructive lying to a loved one, even for a good reason, could be. "I won't chase him."

"The MBI, highway patrol, and I think the FBI have

been called in. They're hunting for him. Stay out of their way and stay safe. Promise."

"I promise." The truth was, with that manpower, Tinkie and I truly weren't needed. If they didn't turn up Elisa soon, then I would renegotiate with Coleman and offer the use of Sweetie Pie to track Tope. Maybe if Coleman accompanied us, he would feel better about it. I was certain the state agencies had tracking dogs, but none were as good as Sweetie. That was a fact, not a brag.

"If you see him or any hint that he is near, you call me."

"Will do."

"What are your plans?"

"I don't think those missing women DeWayne turned up for me are actually missing. Tillie Randall is home with her parents and raising her children, one of whom belongs to Tope. He raped her, she told us. Now we're in Greenwood at Gavin Jerome's place. He called in a tip to Elisa but never followed through. I want to know why."

"Stay in Greenwood."

I laughed. "We aren't even married, and you don't want me to come home."

"Sarah Booth," he chuckled, "I never figured you for a drama queen."

"I can be, if you like it."

"No, thanks. Report in and I'll do the same."

"Find Tope and Elisa. I am worried."

"Me, too. Later."

I bounded up the stairs to the apartment where I could hear Gavin's voice raised. I stepped inside, wishing I had Tinkie's clever little cannister of Mace she kept on her key ring.

"Gavin, you are lying." Tinkie was in his face. "Why?

If you've seen the women and help us find them, you'll get ten grand."

"I can't tell you."

"Why not?"

He sighed. "I was trying to do those women a solid. That's all. They asked me to make that call, and I did. I don't know anything about them. They said they'd give me two grand if I helped them."

"Did you get the money?"

He shook his head. "No. I didn't follow through. I got cold feet. Something just seemed wrong."

"Where did you see them?"

"I told the truth about that. At the produce stand on the outskirts of town."

"Why would they drive all the way to Greenwood to buy produce they could get anywhere?"

"Probably to meet that woman they were talking to."

I was ready to choke the facts out of him. "You might have mentioned this woman earlier."

He shrugged. "Sue me."

I didn't want to sue him; I wanted to pop a knot on his head. Tinkie was gripping her heavy handbag like a potential assault weapon. "What did she look like? If you value your health, you'd better talk and tell the truth."

Tinkie hefted the handbag, which contained a gun and god knew what else. She brought it down on the table beside him with a smack that made us all jump. "The next one will go upside your head."

"Okay, okay. I kept hoping those women would get back in touch and give me another chance. I need the money. The job market in Greenwood isn't exactly on fire."

Tinkie lifted the purse. "Talk."

"It was someone they knew from school, from what I could tell. She was delivering some cold-hardy plants that folks were going wild for. There are always fools who want to get a head start on the garden, failing to remember that almost every year there's a freeze in February that kills all tender young plants."

"What did she look like?" Tinkie asked, at the very end of her patience.

"Tall, slender, pretty. She had these very cool muck boots with skeletons all over them. Pointed toes like cowboy boots."

Gavin wasn't the brightest bulb in the house, but he had, at last, given us a clue. I remembered those boots from a visit with our Daddy's Girl turned horticulturist, Nettie Adams. Tinkie gave me a look that told me she remembered, too.

"Gavin, if you hear from those women, call us. I'm not asking, I'm telling. Elisa Redd has gone missing and I'm afraid the man who brutalized Lydia has taken her. If Lydia's mother is hurt or killed, she will never forgive herself."

All of the buffoonery left his face. "I swear. If I see her, I will call you."

I had another thought. "What were you supposed to tell Elisa to get that money?"

He thought a minute. "I can't say."

"You damn well better say." Tinkie was ready to grab him by the throat.

"Okay, okay. I was to tell the woman to find the door. The blonde said she'd know what it meant."

A chill slithered down my back. "The door?" That was the message the raven had given me.

Gavin shrugged. "That's what she said. It didn't make

any sense to me, but she said that would be enough for the woman to give me the money."

"That woman is her mother and now she's missing and may be in real danger."

"I didn't know who any of those people are. I didn't do anything wrong."

"Where is this door?"

"I don't know. The woman offering the money should know. Find her and she can tell you."

I was done with Gavin. And irritated. Talking in riddles only complicated things.

"Do you know where to look for the door?" Tinkie asked him more gently.

"I don't. I would say if I knew. Really, I would."

I finally believed him.

He continued talking without prompting. "I tried to re-lay the information, but something went wrong."

"How so?"

"When I called the tip-line number, a man answered."

This was unexpected. Elisa had maids in her household staff, but I'd never seen a male. "What did he say?"

"Not to call back and try to extort Mrs. Redd. He wouldn't let me talk to her."

"Did he give you a name?"

"No. I asked but he hung up."

"And you're sure you dialed the correct number?" Tinkie asked.

A startled look came over Gavin's face. "I'm pretty sure."

He definitely wasn't the sharpest knife in the drawer. There was no time to grill him more and I didn't believe he knew anything. We had somewhere else to be.

30

We found Nettie in her backyard working in a greenhouse. "You should get a watchdog," I said as Tinkie and I approached her from different directions. She never looked up. She just kept loosening the soil around her plants.

"You lied to us, and now you need to make it right." Tinkie was really pissed. "I expected better from you, Nettie."

Nettie looked from Tinkie to me. If she was hoping for compassion from her social equal, she was doomed. Tinkie looked even more bloodthirsty than I felt.

"We've been running all over five counties, thanks to you," I said. "Your lying may have put Lydia's mother in danger. Elisa Redd is missing."

Nettie put her trowel down but remained silent.

I continued, "We believe Tope shot a state law officer,

not to mention murdering his fiancée, Vivian Dantzler. We're afraid he has Elisa. This is on your head."

Nettie slowly stood up. "I'm not going to let you blame me. I did what my friend asked me to do. And only that."

"You should have told us you knew Lydia was alive. I'm not working for Tope, we're working for Lydia's mother, who has been suffering for nearly seven years, wondering and worrying about her daughter."

Nettie calmly faced us. "Tinkie, I tried to convince Lydia to contact her mother. I did. I begged her to let me tell Elisa she was okay and nearby. She refused. She said Tope would kill her mother. She made me promise I'd never tell. She was truly terrified if Elisa knew anything, Tope would suspect it and hurt Elisa. Now, I suppose it doesn't matter what I tell you if he already has abducted Mrs. Redd."

"What was Lydia buying from you?" Tinkie asked.

Nettie looked down at the ground.

"You might as well tell us. We'll find out. And it could be a lead that helps us find Elisa Redd and maybe bring Lydia home."

Nettie sighed "She'd given me an order for a hundred of the best marijuana plants I could find."

"What?" Tinkie and I said together.

"Lydia was in trouble. She needed money. She didn't dare contact her mother or claim her inheritance, but she had a plan. She said she had the perfect setup to grow medical marijuana and someone to take the plants and process them once they matured. She could make a lot of money. I think she felt if she had money, she could take on Tope and win. She was desperate to have her mother back in her life, and she knew her inheritance was at risk."

This whole case had gone in another wacko direction.

Now Lydia wasn't in danger, she was a potential criminal. A drug supplier. Medical marijuana was legal in Mississippi, but growing it without the proper licensing would lead to nowhere but trouble. And what the hell? Lydia was heir to some of the richest soil in the world. Why wasn't she in Sunflower County planting medical marijuana?

"Are you lying about this?" Tinkie was obviously sharing my train of thought. It didn't make sense.

"Why would I lie?" Nettie asked. "I met them at Four Corners. I work with Mississippi State University on their organic, non-GMO trials for the marijuana crop. I had some seeds that had been discarded. I planted them and they sprouted. I sold her the sprouts. Nothing illegal there."

I wasn't so sure about that. Licensing was going to be a big issue, and I wasn't certain Mississippi was totally on board with medical marijuana.

"This sounds nuts," Tinkie said.

"You think?" Nettie said with more than a hint of sarcasm. "Just wait until they are growing it at Mississippi State Penitentiary at Parchman. That's twenty-two thousand acres of the richest soil in America. Parchman could revolutionize the production of medical marijuana."

Was Mississippi actually about to step into the twenty-first century? I found it hard to believe. "This sounds like a pipe dream, no pun intended."

"It will happen," Nettie said. "The marijuana plant has so many medical applications. Big Pharma has beaten it back for too long. The average citizen is demanding change."

I didn't say it, but the pharmaceutical machine that had for too long controlled the medical benefits of marijuana would nip this in the bud. Again, no pun intended.

Nettie had almost successfully sent us down a rabbit trail, but I pulled us back on course. "Where does Lydia live?"

Nettie shook her head. "She wouldn't tell me. She didn't want to put me in the line of fire from Tope. She's terrified of him. Even after nearly seven years, she still has nightmares."

Now, that I believed. Tope was that kind of creep.

"You have to know something about the soil where Lydia was going to plant her crop," Tinkie said. "Tell us. Maybe we can figure out where she is."

"She doesn't want to be found," Nettie emphasized.

"We need her." The constant protection of Lydia that Nettie showed was beginning to wear on me. Other people were at risk now. If we could get Lydia to talk to Tope, we might be able to trick him into giving up Elisa. Yes, I was willing to use Lydia as bait. In a limited way.

"If I see her, I'll tell her about her mother. She can contact you if she wants to." She held up a hand to forestall my protests. "I understand, Sarah Booth. I do. If it were me, I'd confront Tope to save my mother. But Lydia has given up her entire life. She's hidden away for over six years. That's a lot to demand a person put on the line. It has to be her choice. I gave my word."

Arguing would yield no results. "Tell us about the soil," Tinkie said. "If Elisa is injured or killed, do you really think Lydia will ever forgive you? No matter that you kept your word."

For a moment it was a standoff, then Nettie waved us into her home. She disappeared while we waited in the kitchen. When she returned, she had a soil analysis in her hand. I didn't understand the complexities of pH and other things, but Tinkie did. "Thanks," she said. "You made the right choice." She looked at me. "Let's go."

I didn't ask any questions until we were on the road. "How will that help us?" I asked her.

"For a woman who leases land for cotton production, I'm shocked you don't know more about soil analysis. We can match the soil to a specific location."

It made perfect sense. I just hadn't thought of it. "Billy handles all of that." Billy Watson leased my land. Sustainable farming was his ultimate goal, and I knew the Dahlia House acreage was in very good hands. All the same, Tinkie was correct. Farming was the lifeblood of Dahlia House and the entire Delta. I should educate myself.

"How are we going to figure this out?" I asked.

"By stopping in to see Calvin Ott, the county agent."

"How can he help?"

"Calvin knows the soil analysis for the different regions of the state. He can point us in a direction."

I actually put my thinking cap on and had something intelligent to say. "It's likely Natchez or Greenwood. That's where Lydia and Bethany have been spotted."

The county agent's office was in the courthouse on the second floor. We parked and rushed inside, glad to be in a warm place. The cold snap was holding for longer than I'd anticipated. A dome of high pressure had pushed the storm clouds west toward Shreveport. The Mississippi Delta was in a bubble of crisp cold and no moisture.

Calvin Ott had been a school chum, and he was happy to see us, especially Tinkie. I recalled that at one point he'd had a crush on her. Tinkie had never noticed. Calvin was shy and had let the opportunity slip through his fingers. He still thought fondly of her—I could see it in his eyes when he looked at her.

Tinkie laid out our dilemma.

"Let me take a look at the map," he said, pulling out a huge bundle of pages that showed the soil makeup of the entire state, county by county.

"Now fertilizer and lime can change all of this," he said, "but if you're wanting the basics of where to grow what, this is helpful. What do you want to grow?" he asked.

"Marijuana." Tinkie just blurted it out.

"What?" Calvin took his glasses off and cleaned them. "You're growing marijuana?"

Tinkie threw me a questioning look. I shrugged one shoulder. He was smitten with her, not me.

"It's hypothetical," Tinkie said. "If I were going to grow organic, non-GMO weed for medical use, where would that work best?"

"It isn't legal yet," he told her.

"I'm looking at future planting. Sarah Booth has some of the best land in Sunflower County, but we were thinking of places in Leflore or Adams County that might be a good, natural soil for this."

"Both are just a tad farther south, which could minimize winter damage of the crop," Calvin said, warming to the topic. He flipped the pages of his maps and pointed to a strip of land colored yellow in Adams County. "This is great soil for marijuana." He flipped more pages and showed us Leflore County. "Right here, south of Greenwood. You know the state of Mississippi is running trials of the different seeds and locations all over the state. You might be able to talk to someone at the university to get more exact information."

"That's a great idea," I said.

"We'll do that. Thanks, Calvin."

"If you decide to grow it, let me know. I can help with fertilizing and such. I know if it's organic you'll need . . ." He turned to me. "Horse manure."

"I've been composting it for a year," I told him. "Thank you."

When we were out of his office, I looked down the hall toward the sheriff's office. It would be a nice surprise to see Coleman, but we had to move along. "Where to now, Tink?"

"That land in Greenwood. I believe we're going to find Lydia and Bethany."

"And then we'll get Elisa back." We had to.

31

We headed back toward the Leflore County seat. When we passed Nettie's place, I looked hard but didn't see her. Normally she was in the yard working. It was possible she'd taken a runner to warn Lydia that we were closing in on her. If she did that, maybe Lydia would turn herself in to us so we could save her mother.

Tinkie called the sheriff's office and updated Budgie on where we were going and what we were doing so he could tell Coleman. It was a good safety step and a courtesy to the man I loved.

"Aren't you going to call Oscar?" I asked.

Tinkie bit her bottom lip in that gesture that made grown men drop to their knees. When it popped back out, and she still hadn't answered, I knew she was facing a dilemma.

"I can't tell him. He'll worry. Then he'll get mad. It's just better to wait and tell him after we're done."

"What if Coleman tells him?"

"It'll be okay. We'll be home before he sees Coleman. Right?"

"We'll do our best." I hoped I was good to my word. The thing about driving into the unknown was that neither of us could predict how this would end. If we found Lydia or Bethany, all the better. If we found someone or something else, then it could go in any direction.

Tammy's dreadful dream came at me hard. In my mind I saw the images of a heart beating beneath floorboards, shaking dust loose, pounding loud and steady. The vulture blue eye of a dead man stared through a window. "We don't have to do this now," I said. "Maybe we should call it a day. It'll be dark before long."

"We'll be perfectly fine. Lydia isn't going to harm us. Why would she?"

"Maybe it isn't Lydia." There, I said it.

"It's Lydia. We'll locate her and make her come home. When she realizes her mama is missing, she'll cooperate. I'm sure of it."

Tinkie had a big belief in human nature that I didn't always share. But calling up doubts and fears wouldn't help us, either.

We drove parallel to a bank of storm clouds that had popped out of nowhere. Tinkie checked the weather on her phone. Predictions were that it would move over Greenwood just after dark. The high atmospheric pressure was protecting Zinnia, but not the cities farther south. We entered Greenwood and drove on to the area we'd determined was good for growing a crop of marijuana.

I stopped at a crossroads and let the car idle while I tried to figure out how to find Lydia and Bethany if they were in the area. We didn't have a lot to go on. We'd left Zinnia on a hope and a prayer, but that wasn't going to get us very far. All we really knew was that they'd bought a lot of marijuana plants and needed to make big money.

"Call Nettie," I said to Tinkie. "Tell her if she doesn't help us, we'll press charges."

"What charges?" Tinkie asked.

"I don't know. Impeding an investigation. How about that?"

"We aren't cops."

"True, but maybe she doesn't know that doesn't apply to private investigators. It's worth a try."

"We're desperate."

I didn't disagree. "Desperation is the mother of invention. Aunt Loulane said that all the time."

"Heaven forbid that I disagree with the wisdom of the woman who managed to rear you for ten years." Tinkie dialed the phone and put it on speaker. "Nettie, tell us where Lydia and Bethany are. We know you were there. Someone saw you with them. You helped them set up their greenhouse."

Tinkie could embellish the truth with the best of them when she had to. She was taking a risk—what if they didn't have a greenhouse? But I approved of her attempt. We weren't squandering other leads because we didn't really have any, as this drive to Greenwood had proven. On a map, a search for Lydia had seemed reasonable. In reality, we could spend weeks driving along back roads and rutted driveways to find nothing useful.

"I can't tell you." Nettie wasn't even attempting to lie.

"You have to." Tinkie wasn't going to let her off the

hook. "I know you feel you're protecting Lydia, but you aren't. How is she going to feel if Tope kills her mama because we couldn't get her to help us?"

Nettie had begun to cry. The sting of regret at the strong-arm tactics we were using zapped me in the solar plexus, but we didn't have a choice.

"Nettie, Lydia may be able to save her mama. We're not going to give Lydia over to Tope. We won't do that, I swear. But we will give her the choice to decide what she wants to do to save Elisa."

"You swear you won't put her in harm's way?" Nettie snuffled.

"I swear that we will leave it up to Lydia to make her own choices. Is Bethany with her? She might be a valuable asset to us."

"She is. She's Lydia's protector. Listen to her. She's crazy smart."

"We will," Tinkie promised. "Now, where are they?"

A heavy weight lifted off my heart. Lydia and Bethany were alive. And they were close.

"They are renting the old Lincoln place. Lad Lincoln's farm on Cody Road."

"Is it off County Road 687?" I asked.

"Yes."

I knew where the farm was. It had been a big draw for teenagers on hot summer nights when I was in high school. Long abandoned, the farm hosted a number of legends about hauntings. Best of all, there were no adults anywhere nearby to keep an eye on us as we built bonfires or swam in the old stock pond. Never a fan of slimy-bottomed ponds, I'd still taken a few dares and jumped in. We'd sat up into the wee hours hoping for a glimpse of old Lad Lincoln or his wife, who was reputed to be crazy and a murderer of teenagers. The stories didn't contain a whit of truth, but on a starry summer night they were delicious fare for kids looking to be scared.

"I used to go there when I was dating Kent," Tinkie said. She smiled to herself at a memory. "We kids loved to scare each other, didn't we?" Tinkie brought up the great memories we'd shared. Nettie had been a little older, so she hadn't hung out with us.

"One of the joys of young adulthood." Like most teenagers, we'd loved to be a little scared.

"Please be careful." Nettie brought us back to the task at hand. "Lydia and Bethany have been staying at the farmhouse. It's primitive. They do have a well that works and power to the house. No heat or air-conditioning, though. It's rough living. They're determined to grow this crop, sell it, and cash out."

"Where are the owners of the property?"

"I don't know," Nettie said. "No one takes care of the property at all. It's been abandoned for years. Either they rented it or just moved in and occupied it."

That was smart. No paper trail to follow if anyone was onto them. "Thanks, Nettie."

"Don't let them get hurt," she begged. "They're good people caught in a bad situation."

"Did Lydia say why they needed the money?" I asked.

"To pay off Tope. Lydia was sure if she could offer him enough money, he'd agree to a divorce and let her go."

"Elisa Redd has money." The whole pot-for-profit idea seemed . . . illogical.

"Oh, but Tope thinks he already has that money loaded and waiting to jump in his pocket. Especially if he has Elisa

in his control. Don't you see? Tope views Lydia's inheritance as his own now. That's why he hasn't divorced Lydia
in absentia. He wants to inherit what is rightfully hers. If
she can't show up to claim her inheritance, it will go to
him. He has her over a barrel."

Now the scheme made a lot more sense. There were few
things a person in hiding could do to earn a lot of money,
but growing pot was one of them. Bank robbery, art theft,
and blackmail came to mind. But growing medical pot was
a victimless crime.

"Thanks, Nettie. We'll protect Lydia and we won't force
her to do anything she doesn't want to do," Tinkie assured
her friend.

"Ask her to please forgive me." She was crying now.

"Will do," Tinkie said. "When she realizes her mom is at
stake, she won't hold it against you."

The winding—and very rutted—driveway to the old Lincoln
farm wove through a plantation of poplar trees, a uniform
crop rather than a wild-growing forest. The trees, all the
same size and shape, creeped me out.

"It's a perversion of nature," Tinkie said.

I was once again struck by the way she knew what I was
thinking. "I'm getting the vibe of *Village of the Damned*. All
those identical little blond kids with evil on their brains."

"Humans harness the bounty of nature," Tinkie said,
but with an element of wistfulness in her voice. "This land
is the best anywhere. Let's hope people take care of it."

We cleared the poplar plantation and the land on either
side of the driveway opened up. The fields had been turned,
and the rich scent of the soil made me think of childhood.

This land smelled like money, as my folks always told me. It could grow anything.

We were moving slowly, in consideration of my antique car and our desire to scope out the terrain. I didn't expect Lydia to be overjoyed to see us, but I also didn't think she'd try to shoot us. Who knew, though.

As we turned a corner and cleared a stand of cedar trees, I saw the farmhouse. It was an unpainted structure, the cypress exterior a dark gray.

"Let me out here," Tinkie said.

We were still half a mile away. I checked Tinkie's feet. She was wearing hiking boots. "Why?"

"I want to slip up there first, if you don't mind. If I can just tell Lydia about her mom, I think she'll cooperate with us."

"Did you know her growing up?"

"Only a little. I served punch at her debutante ball. You know my mother lived for those things."

Tinkie did have an edge, and if she appeared in the doorway, it might give her the advantage. "Okay." I backed up so that the car was hidden in the cedars. No one would suspect I was there unless they came down the driveway.

"Be careful." I didn't like for Tinkie to go on her own, but I didn't say it. She was a grown, capable woman. Being a mother had only made her more strong willed.

She grinned as she closed the car door. "I have my gun." She patted her purse, and I felt a wave of relief. Better prepared than surprised. And while Lydia and Bethany might be glad to see us, we didn't know who else might be there. No cars were parked around the house, but they hadn't been dropped out of the air like aliens to land on this isolated farm.

I got out of the car with Tinkie and tucked myself into the copse of cedars to watch. Tinkie walked down the middle of the road. With open fields on either side, there wasn't a place for her to hide anyway. I held my breath as she neared the farm. The place looked deserted except for the flap of the greenhouse's plastic sheeting in an erratic breeze.

When she made it to the front door, she knocked. The door opened and I caught my first glimpse of Lydia Redd Maxwell. She was much thinner than I remembered, as if worry had eroded her down to the bone. She was joined by another blonde—Bethany, with her bleached hair. They stood side by side and listened to whatever Tinkie was saying. In a moment, Tinkie stepped inside and the door closed.

I was backing out of the trees when I felt a hand on my shoulder. I froze, my heart leaping painfully in my chest. I didn't turn around but I heard the jingle of a horse's bit and the snorting of an equine.

The clawlike grip on my shoulder tightened and I turned to find a tall, headless corpse standing behind me, a black steed pawing the ground behind him. When I looked closer, I saw the missing head resting in his right hand. He held it by the hair, and the sightless eyes stared directly at me.

"Get away from me." I was terrified. How was he standing and moving without a head? Where had he and the horse come from? Why hadn't I heard him approach? This simply wasn't possible.

I caught a whiff of Evening in Paris talcum powder. I knew it well because Aunt Loulane adored it. What headless concoction would wear such a feminine scent? My fear abated as I realized the only person it could be. Jitty!

A spectral voice came from the figure. "Where is my head? Give it back."

Even though I knew it was Jitty, I couldn't avoid being

repulsed. "You're holding it, you dweeb. Stay away from me!"

I heard a soft giggle and knew Jitty was enjoying this moment far more than she should have been.

"The headless horseman?" I asked. "Really? You show up in that long cloak with a black stallion just to scare the living daylights out of me." The horse shook his head and the bit jangled while his silky mane flew about.

"Ask no questions of the headless horseman!"

"And you brought a horse? He's very handsome, but if you want to ride, what's wrong with my horses?"

"Ask no more questions!" Jitty was getting annoyed.

The horse gave a snort and vanished. Jitty slowly morphed into her regular self, dressed in my riding gear. She had no qualms about helping herself to whatever she wanted from my closet.

"Are you trying to tell me this farmland is haunted?" I asked.

"Why, sure. There are spirits everywhere, Sarah Booth. Native Americans, settlers, farmers, talented women like your mama, children. Some are wicked, some good."

"Why don't these spirits leave?" This question nagged me at all hours of the day and night. Why did spirits linger? "If they're always around, why don't they help us? Why do they stay, lingering in solitude?"

"Some have work to finish. Some have justice to seek. Others just get lost. If they stay in this realm too long, they can become . . . dangerous."

"My parents aren't here, are they?" I had often beseeched my higher power to keep my family close to me, but not at the cost of losing their goodness.

"No, Sarah Booth. They crossed over long ago. That's why they use me as a messenger."

"Thank you." For all the cantankerous conduct of Jitty, she never failed in her mission to keep me connected with my family. I was humbled by her commitment to me and my family.

"Don't be all grateful. It makes it hard for me to devil you when you're sweet."

"You are rotten." I had to smile.

"I know."

"Do you have a message for me?"

"I do. What would you want someone to tell you if it meant you could help save your mama?"

"All they'd have to do is say her name."

Jitty's smile said it all. In a matter of seconds, she shifted into a tall, thin man. Lanky arms shot through his ill-fitting shirt cuffs. A beaked nose and green eyes were set in a narrow face. He turned toward the stand of trees and began to sing psalms. His clear voice made goose bumps dance on my arms.

"Stop it, Jitty. You're not Ichabod Crane, no matter how much you want to mess with me."

"'Blessed is the one who does not walk in step with the wicked or stand in the way that sinners take or sit in the company of mockers,'" Ichabod sang as he disappeared.

I checked my watch. The entire encounter had taken less than a minute. Creeping deeper into the cedars, I focused on the farmhouse, waiting for Tinkie to come back out. If she wasn't in the clear in fifteen minutes, I'd drive down there and get her out myself. Thinking of what Jitty had told me, I texted Tinkie—"Just say her name. Just say Elisa Redd."

In a matter of moments, the door opened and Tinkie

stepped onto the porch and waved me to come down. Sweet relief. I jumped in the car and bounced to the front yard.

Lydia Redd Maxwell came out the door, Bethany just behind her. All three women waited on the porch.

I assessed Lydia. She was older and worn. She dressed in a no-nonsense fashion: jeans, a flannel shirt, boots, and no makeup. Her hair centered her back in a long braid. Bethany wore the same type clothes, but her bleached hair was cut just above her shoulders. Both had weathered faces and hands. They'd worked outside in the sun.

"Who has my mother?" Lydia asked. "Tinkie says you know where she is?"

"I think Tope has her."

"No!" Lydia teared up and they spilled down her cheeks. "No! This can't happen. I've stayed far away to keep her safe."

Bethany had the opposite reaction. "I will kill him." She left no doubt that she meant it when she pulled a gun out from under her coat. "I will kill him if he harms Lydia's mother."

"It's okay. We're going to get Elisa back. But I'll need your help. Both of you. And we have to act fast. Tonight. If I can find you here, anyone can, and Tope won't be far behind us." A shudder ran down my spine as the sensation that I was being watched rushed over me. I looked all around and saw nothing out of place, but that didn't mean a thing. "Let's go inside."

32

The interior décor of the farmhouse consisted of unpainted walls and thick slabs. Durable. I imagined the beating heart from Tammy's dream, pounding beneath the house. The rough-hewn furniture was handmade. But there wasn't a speck of dust anywhere. Outside, a kitten cried to get in.

Lydia had once been a Delta princess who now looked like a woman who worked the land. The soft life was gone, but she'd found a tensile strength that gave her an internal glow of beauty.

"Have a seat," Bethany said. "I'll put on some coffee and let Clotilde in."

She returned a few minutes later with a beautiful smoke-gray kitten in her arms. She handed it to Lydia, who stroked the baby like her life depended on it. Clotilde was a comfort animal. The kitten curled into a ball in her lap, purring so loudly I could hear it across the room.

Tinkie and I exchanged looks, and I nodded.

"Lydia, I don't want to be mean about this, but if you've been around here all this time, why in the world didn't you let your mother know you were safe? She has worried and grieved and hunted. The last seven years have been hell for her."

Tinkie wasn't being unkind, just direct. And it was the question I most wanted answered.

Lydia nodded, the tears leaking from her eyes. "I know how horrible it's been for my mother, and for me. And Bethany's family, too. We only did what we had to do until I had the resources to get Tope off my back and his foot off my mother's neck."

"You couldn't have sent her a message, something to let her know you were alive and unharmed?"

"I couldn't. Tope watched Mother like a hawk. If she had shown any relief or joy, he would have harmed her to be sure the inheritance went to him. If she'd tried dating or having any kind of life, he would have killed her outright. He told me so."

"You've talked to him?" I asked.

"No, not in a conversation. I've . . . sent him some cryptic messages. I've staged reports that I was in Afghanistan. I've also encouraged folks to speculate that I was very much alive and coming for my inheritance. The only way to fight Tope is to keep him unbalanced. He will do anything to get what he wants. Including harming my mother. But if I could keep him unsure about what I was up to, he couldn't risk harming my mother. There would be no point to hurting her if I was alive. It's been hard and painful for everyone, but the goal was protection of my mother."

I hoped to goodness that a stupid game of one-upmanship wasn't at the bottom of Lydia's long absence. That would really annoy me.

"You put Gavin up to calling the tip line, didn't you?" I asked.

"Yes. I will give him some money. He was trying to help me."

"And you hit me in the head to get the ten grand, didn't you?" I normally didn't hold grudges, but I might begin to now.

"I'm sorry," Bethany said. "That was me. We had to have the money to buy the seedlings. I really didn't want to hurt you, but you were trying to trick us and catch us. That couldn't happen. Not until we get Tope out of our lives."

"You were going to steal from your mother what she would gladly give you?" Tinkie was still a bit huffy.

"I swear to you, I was only focused on her safety. Bethany and I talked about robbing a corner gas station, but we knew that would be stupid. We could have been killed or worse."

"For that I give you credit," I said. "But, damn, Lydia, you couldn't figure out a way to clue your mama in?"

"Not and keep her safe. As long as she was fighting Tope in court, he wouldn't be able to decide where I was and what I might do. The minute Tope realized I was within his reach, we were all in danger of getting killed. Tope will not let anything stand in his way. I know him too well. It was better to see Mother suffer and live than it was to ease her pain and put her in line for a bullet between the eyes."

Whatever I thought, Lydia and Bethany were certain

they'd done the best thing. But if protecting Elisa was their highest priority, it hadn't worked out exactly like they'd intended.

Bethany picked up the explanation. "Nettie helped us pick out the best plants. She's worked with Mississippi State University and she knows a whole bunch about what plants are in demand for prescription marijuana. All we had to do was stall Tope until the crop came in this fall."

"That's nine or ten months," Tinkie pointed out.

"A slice of time compared to living in hiding for nearly seven years," Lydia said. "You don't get it. We could see the light at the end of the tunnel. We could make a lot of money, give it to Tope, and he would allow me to come home, file for divorce, and spend the rest of my life taking care of Mother."

Elisa was still a vibrant, healthy woman, so they could have had a number of good years.

"Your parents are worried about you," I told Bethany. "Your dad is sorry he didn't support you. Your mother grieves for you every day. Could you not have gone to them?"

She shook her head. "No. Tope has spies in the bank, in the courts. It's only because Sheriff Peters is an honorable man that we even attempted this. We believed we could count on him for justice if we got caught growing these plants."

"You aren't in Sunflower County," Tinkie pointed out. "Coleman can't help you in Leflore County."

"Sheriff Peters has reach," Lydia said. "I've heard the local cops talk about him. About all of you. For private investigators, you have a pretty good reputation." Lydia smiled at last and the long, hard years fell away. For a brief moment, she was the beautiful young debutante again. So much had been robbed from her.

I had a far more difficult question to ask her. "Did you know Ernest and Florence Salter?"

I caught both women by surprise and from the shock on their faces, I knew the answer was yes.

"Why are you asking?" Bethany stammered.

"Because, somehow, they're tied up in all of this. Missing girls, herbal potions, folks disappearing. What did you have to do with them?"

"Everyone knew them," Lydia said, looking down at her lap.

Bethany picked up the explanation. "When a woman got pregnant, if she came to my self-defense studio and I knew she needed help, I'd send her to Florence. If it was too dangerous for her, Ernest would drive the woman to a clinic where she could be safely helped. Sometimes the herbs were enough; sometimes not."

"What happened to Florence and Ernest?" I asked.

"They disappeared," Bethany answered. "I went to their house one day and they'd moved out. I figured someone had threatened them, so they packed up and left."

"Who would threaten them and why?" Tinkie asked.

"Do you watch the news?" Bethany was annoyed. "Women's rights are constantly under attack. Constantly. It was only fifty years ago that a women couldn't establish credit or buy property without a husband or father cosigning. There are forces who want to see women back in that place. Barefoot and pregnant. The Salters were a threat to those people."

I'd followed the national political scene, but Bethany's words made me realize what a privileged life I'd had. She was right. Now those precious freedoms were sitting ducks to be taken out by men who wanted only power.

"There was a rumor that Ernest was hanged in that old cemetery. The hanging tree."

Bethany nodded. "Yeah, Lydia and I helped spread that rumor. Folks were starting to talk too much. There were threats against both of them. We figured the cleanest way out for them would be to die. If they disappeared, someone might come looking."

"So the rumors were all a subterfuge, an attempt to disappear?" I asked.

"Yes. We should have done a better job of making our deaths real."

"You buried an empty coffin in Florence's grave." Tinkie had put a lot of puzzle pieces in place.

"We had to make people believe she was dead," Bethany said. "And Ernest, too. We came up with the hanging and burning because it sounded so gruesome. We hoped that would keep the nosy parkers at bay. Otherwise, Ernest and Florence would have been hounded into the ground. Like I said, we should have made our disappearance look more like murder. Maybe Tope would have gone to jail."

"But then I could never go home, and I always hoped to get back to my mother." Lydia was crying silently. "I've watched over her, doing what I could to keep Tope at bay. Once he moved to have me declared dead, I knew she was in extreme danger. At least until she changed me as her heir. All this time she never wrote me out of her will."

"You're all she has left," I said.

"It's been hard for me, too," Lydia said.

"The whole Afghanistan teaching story was a ruse?" Tinkie changed directions and I was glad. I was feeling too sorry for Lydia. She'd done what she thought was best, even though her course had painful consequences.

"We had planned to go," Lydia said. "And, yes, our intention was to disappear as if we'd been killed. But there are so many issues with going into that country. And then the CIA came calling one day, wanting us to be spies or something. It was just too much for me."

"We'd heard the rumors about your spying."

"It wasn't anything Bethany or I wanted to do. We wanted to help educate women, not spy on the Afghan people. After that, we knew the CIA would contact us again if we went there, so we changed plans."

"And what have you been doing for nearly seven years?" I asked.

"We ran a free day-care center in Jackson for working mothers." She smiled at Bethany. "It was Bethany's idea, and we helped a lot of people. Young mothers who needed to work but couldn't afford care—we were there for as many as we could manage."

"Until?" Tinkie pressed.

"Until an employee from the state health department showed up. We knew her. She would have recognized me right off. It wasn't safe to continue with the day-care center."

"So you moved to Natchez?"

"Yes. We sold plants and crafts and kept a very low profile."

"It was a good life," Bethany said. "We were content, except for the deception of our families. As the weeks wore on, it became more and more intolerable. Last Christmas we hit on the idea of growing pot and paying Tope off to leave us alone."

"Have you contacted him?" I asked, wondering if Vivian's demise was triggered on the return of Lydia. Maybe Tope felt he had to get his new fiancée out of the way in a hurry. Maybe he had learned Lydia was alive and wanted to lure her back in—at least long enough to bump off Elisa and inherit everything if he killed Lydia. I had a very dark view of Tope Maxwell, and I believed it was deserved.

"I haven't contacted Tope, but someone did, on my behalf."

This was going to be the sticky wicket of this situation. "Then he knows you're alive?"

"Yes. Someone reported to him they'd seen me. The posters you put up in Greenwood were also helpful. Evidence that there was a search for me. But I needed more time. To bring the marijuana crop to market. I was afraid he'd get greedy and do exactly what he's done—harm my mother."

"Yes, the clock has run out. If Tope thinks you're nearby, you and Elisa are in real danger," Tinkie said.

"Unless we turn the tables on him," I said. A tiny little sprout of a plan was cooking in the back of my brain. Three dozen things about the case came crashing into my subconscious—Tammy's dreadful dreams, the creepy bedroom Tope had kept where Lydia had tried to hide from him, the wedding dress, the ghosts. There was plenty to work with if we could only get it all done. Coleman would have to buy into the plan and help us, but I thought he would. Tope had so far escaped being charged with Vivian's murder, and he was wanted for the attack on an MBI officer. If I could set a snare and get him, Coleman would be happy to help.

"You've hit on something," Tinkie said, seeing my expression change.

"Maybe. How much do you girls know about Poe's masterful short story, 'The Tell-Tale Heart'?"

33

By the time I summarized the short story for Lydia and
Bethany, they were on board with my plan. Tope had to be
brought to justice. We had to locate Elisa and make sure
she was safe. I thought there was a way to do this, but it
was also risky. I had to coordinate with Coleman, too.
Oscar was another matter, but Tinkie would have to handle him. I placed a call to Madame Tomeeka. She answered
on the first ring.

"I need a big, big favor."

"Uh-oh," she said. "This sounds like trouble."

"Good trouble," I said.

"Will it be dangerous?"

"It's Tope."

"Say no more. Whatever it is, I'll help. That man has to

be stopped and he has to pay for all the harm he's caused. But what about Elisa? You can't risk sending him over the edge if he has her held captive. He might hurt her."

"That's where you come in."

"How so?" Tammy was intrigued but cautious.

"I want you to host a séance for Tope. At his home."

"To what purpose?" Tammy asked.

"Make him believe that Lydia has met a terrible fate and that her ghost is there, ready to even the score."

"You really think Tope will believe in a ghost story?"

"I intend to make sure he does. I'll get Cece to print a story in the paper saying that Lydia is dead. We can make her up, take a photograph, and put it in the paper. Cece will help us, I'm sure. That's the first step."

Tammy's voice brightened. "I see what you're going to do. Genius!"

"Lydia? Are you in?" I asked. "You're going to have to make an appearance as a dead woman."

"Oh, I'm ready for this," she said. "I've been waiting a long time for such an opportunity."

"Tammy, I'll be in touch. I need to get with Cece to publish the article, and I have to clear this with Coleman."

"I'll do some research on Tope's house," Tinkie said. "We'll stage the body perfectly. He must believe she's dead."

Tinkie was clever at plotting schemes. I gave her a big hug. "I'll drop you at Hilltop and I'll get with Coleman. Lydia and Bethany, you need to come with us." I needed them in Sunflower County for my plan to work. "Tammy, get ready to send Tope some messages from the Great Beyond, talking about how Lydia's spirit is raging and only after revenge."

"I can do that. I'll work on some presentation."

"I'll give you a call when I'm in town. It's time to get on the road. We have a lot to complete before dark."

"I think a cotton field is the perfect place for my corpse," Lydia said. "I know just the spot. It will look familiar to Tope, but he won't be able to put his finger on exactly where it is."

"Good." I could see how that would work. "We need to make sure Tope is in the house and that he has Elisa where we can grab her if things go south."

"How are you going to do that?" Lydia asked.

I didn't have a ready answer, but I believed Coleman, DeWayne, and Budgie could help me. Once we had Lydia made up, arranged in the field, and photographed, our plan could not fail.

"Are you sure about this?" Bethany asked.

"I wish I saw another way. Once Lydia's body is found, I'll start leaving messages for Tope. Tammy can offer to hold a séance to bring her spirit to him."

"This is good," Lydia said. "He's desperate to get into my safety-deposit box in the bank. Oscar would never let him in until he had proof of my death." Lydia shot Tinkie a grateful look. "We can bait him with that. This will work. It has to. "

I wasn't nearly as certain as she sounded, but I knew that I couldn't allow doubt to creep in or this would fall apart. The only chance of success was if everyone sold their participation with everything they had. "Let's get on the road."

"We should water the plants," Bethany said.

"The plants can wait. Trust me. If this plan doesn't work, you won't be around to harvest your crop."

That killed further conversation and we headed out to

get in the Roadster. There were still a couple of hours of daylight. Time enough. I called Cece on the way to meet us with some stage makeup. She worked with a local theater group and she was terrific at creating bloody corpses. We had to do this just right.

I made it to Zinnia in record time and I let Lydia and Bethany out with Tinkie at her house. I went to Dahlia House to get the things I needed. And to tell Coleman my plan. He would not like it—that I knew. But I believed he would help.

He walked in the door shortly after I called him. When he stopped in the foyer and assessed me, I waited.

"Just hear me out," I said.

"Okay. Go."

I made a pot of coffee and told him everything.

"And you believe Tope will believe Lydia's dead when he sees the photo of her corpse?"

"Yes."

"And do what?"

"He'll want to contact her spirit to get into her safety-deposit box. I'm hoping Tammy can convince him to give up Elisa."

"If he doesn't, you're putting Elisa's life at risk."

"I know. Lydia knows, too. But since he escaped the house on the river, Tope's been running free and has taken Elisa. I don't have another plan."

"Nor do I," Coleman said. "This just seems more like drama and less like a solid plan."

He was correct, but I didn't have an alternative to offer. "I'll need you and the deputies to stand around the corpse in the cotton field. To make it look official. He has to believe Lydia is truly dead. She's the biggest hurdle to his money grab. If he believes Lydia is dead, he'll have to keep Elisa alive. It would greatly simplify his life if he could get Elisa to name him heir. Avoid all the rigmarole of probate. He will attempt to force her to do that."

"I'll follow you in the truck. Let's get this done."

34

Cece's artistry was exquisite. Lydia wore a white polo shirt and khakis so that the blood really showed up. Half of her head looked like it was bashed in. Brains and blood fell down the side of her face to her shoulders. Tinkie had a metal bat also covered in fake blood. The cotton field we'd settled on was only a few minutes from Tinkie's house. I could shoot the picture so there was no way to locate the actual scene.

Dusk was falling and the nip of a chilly day had become a bite of bitter cold. We drove to the location and in the fading light, Lydia was stretched out on the ground, vacant eyes staring up at the sky, the bat at her side. It looked too real, and for a moment I wondered if this was a good idea. What if I were tempting this vision to become reality?

"Hurry up, she's freezing," Tinkie said, prompting me to finish taking the photos. Coleman even knelt beside the pretend corpse and placed a sheet over Lydia. He gave a statement to run in the press.

When I was finished, I sent the statement and the photos to Cece at the newspaper. She would take it from there. And now we'd wait for Tope to make his move.

Because we had to keep Lydia and Bethany concealed, and we couldn't leave them alone in Leflore County on a potentially illegal pot farm, I took them with me to Dahlia House. Coleman agreed it was the best plan—to have them close.

Despite the craziness of the concept, the plan was coming together.

Tinkie joined us at Dahlia House with Pauline and Maylin. Madame Tomeeka slipped in the front door, and Millie arrived with fabulous dinners for all of us. I'd worked up an appetite, and there was nothing better than field peas, okra, and Millie's corn bread on a dank winter night.

Cece and Jaytee showed up later, and Cece had the digital front page of the *Zinnia Dispatch* for show-and-tell. The picture of "dead" Lydia, in all her gruesome glory, was center of the front page, above the fold. Tope wouldn't be able to ignore it. Just as I was getting worried again, Oscar and Coleman showed up with Lydia's wedding dress.

"Where did you find it?" Lydia asked.

"In your room at Tope's," I said. "Tinkie and I saw it when we were investigating. I saw the wedding photos. I thought it would be the perfect dress for a ghostly visitation."

"You are wicked bad," Lydia said with a big grin. "This will scare the snot out of Tope. He's a big coward anyway."

"How is this going to work?" Bethany asked. She looked at the wedding gown with distrust, and I didn't blame her. Lydia's decision to marry Tope had drastically changed her life for the worse.

"Madame Tomeeka is going to put it out there that she is being visited by Lydia's ghost, who has a secret to share. Cece and Millie will write a special 'The Truth Is Out There' column for the website in the morning. Tammy will request that all of Lydia's people contact her for a séance."

"But there's only Tope," Bethany said. "Elisa has been taken."

"Yes, that's correct. So it will be only Madame Tomeeka and Tope at the house for the séance." I grinned. "And the rest of us in hiding, waiting to spring the trap."

Bethany's face came alive with anticipation. "And how will this get him arrested?"

"Lydia is going to get him to confess. She will say she signed a will, leaving everything to him, and she'll tell him where it is if he returns Elisa and admits his wrongdoing."

"Tope is smart." Lydia was worried.

"And also greedy. I'm counting on the fact that greed will win out over cunning."

"And if it doesn't?" Lydia asked.

"Then it's up to you to scare him into an early grave." I was only half kidding.

"You think this will all be in place by tomorrow night?" Tinkie asked.

"I do." Madame Tomeeka nodded, and Coleman agreed. When the Zinnia gang got busy, they could achieve miracles.

"It has to be now," Coleman said. "Every hour Elisa is missing bodes badly for her. We'll force Tope to tell us where she is. That's more important than any confession. I'll send DeWayne and Budgie to rescue her. Tope will eventually confess—to everything."

Coleman never used force against a prisoner, but Tope was a murderer and an abuser. Coleman didn't have a lot of tolerance for those activities.

"Now, let's write that column," I said to Cece, Millie, and Tammy. "We have to do this perfectly or he'll smell a rat."

Coleman took up the role of bartender and kept the crowd supplied with libations while Tinkie showed off Maylin's tricks. She could smile and coo. And if it wasn't Nobel Peace Prize material, it was adorable.

At the end of an hour, we'd hammered out a basic story involving Lydia's ghost and her desire to make amends with her husband so she could cross over. Tammy, in her role as séance conductor, would also demand that Lydia get to speak with Elisa so she could say her goodbyes and depart in peace—leaving the road clear for Tope to get the money. I had to bury a smidge of guilt for using my friends, but Cece, Millie, and Tammy were all over it. I wasn't the only one who had serious issues with men who abused women. In setting up the fake website story, Millie had even worked in a reference to Elvis and how he'd played "Are You Lonesome Tonight?" as Lydia's ghost drifted about the mansion.

We'd done all we could, including making sure Tammy's cell phone number was in the article. If Tope was going to bite, he would. If he didn't, we'd have to cook up something else.

I poured two drinks and led Tinkie to the porch, where it was cold and quiet. "You sure you're good with this?"

"It's Lydia who's taking the big risk," she pointed out.

"And Bethany." She chuckled softly. "I'm a little worried that if Bethany gets Tope in that house and there's no one to stop her, she'll take justice into her own hands."

"She'll want to, but we can't let her. What good would it do to end up with Bethany in jail? That would break Lydia's heart."

"Do you think they're a couple?" Tinkie asked.

I shrugged. "I honestly don't know, and I don't care. Platonic, romantic, permanent, fleeting—love is the only thing in this life worth having. I just know that it should be nurtured, whatever form it takes."

"Wow, you got wise somewhere along the line. I agree." She got back to business. "So we're set. Oscar and I need to take Pauline and Maylin home. They're out cold on your sofa."

"See you in the morning. And pray that Madame Tomeeka gets a call."

Tinkie hesitated. "We aren't putting our friends in danger, are we?"

"Yes, but they're aware."

Tinkie nodded. "Then we'll take care of them and, ultimately, Tope, too."

Her voice was laced with worry, but I gave her a nod. "We've got this covered."

"At least we aren't lying to Coleman and Oscar," she said, and then laughed. "I can't believe they went along with this."

"It's about the only chance we have of finding Elisa. It's a risk. Everyone agrees with that. There aren't any better options, though."

Tinkie linked her arm through mine. "Let's go back inside. You need to throw everyone out and have some time with your guy. He is such a champion for you, Sarah Booth. You should see the way he looks at you when you aren't aware. I almost expect a choir of angels to come sing your praises."

"It's definitely time for you to go. You're delirious."

We laughed together as we went back inside and sent our friends home to prepare for what could be a very eventful day.

35

The eastern horizon was a dull gray when I went out to feed the horses. The sun was on the way, but it was taking its time. Coleman left for work, and I paced the front porch while I finished a cup of coffee. My head felt like it might explode from all the thoughts and anxieties whirling around inside.

After the horses finished cleaning up their grain, they blasted out of the barn like Satan was swinging on their tails. I went to the fence and stood for a long moment, watching them race over the pasture like dancers in a perfectly choreographed show. The horses eased my troubled heart. As did the vista.

I was about to go inside when a large black bird flew up

and landed on the fence beside me. He tilted his head back and forth, his bright eyes examining me.

"'Nevermore,'" I said.

The raven only nodded.

"Did Jitty send you?"

"Beware," the raven said.

I reached out a hand, unafraid of the bird. He had such intelligence that I trusted that he wouldn't hurt me. I offered my finger and he hopped on it, then moved up to my arm. He was a heavy bird.

"Who are you?" I asked.

"'Nevermore,'" he answered.

Before I could ask anything else, he flew into the branches of a crepe myrtle that was in the paddock area. "I can't believe you followed me here."

I should have been creeped out, but I wasn't. The bird seemed . . . to be a friend. It was hard to explain, but I felt he had my best interests at heart.

"Beware," he called out before he flew behind the barn. That was when I noticed Pluto angling down the fence rail toward where the bird had been. The cat had one thing on his mind. Raven pie.

"Pluto. I don't think that tough old bird would taste very good at all."

Pluto declined to answer.

I scooped him into my arms and hurried inside to shower and head to town.

I gave up pretending to be too chill to fret. I was nervous as a crook at a sheriffs' conference. I paced Dahlia House until I exhausted myself. Finally, I took Sweetie and Pluto to

Millie's. We slipped in the back door and went to her office where the critters could eat breakfast without disturbing the customers. Millie had sworn she was going to institute a policy of allowing well-behaved pets in the restaurant, but I suspected Mississippi health code laws would prevent it no matter how sly she was about it. Pluto and Sweetie Pie were happier in the office. They could eat and snooze without worrying that some yahoo would step on them.

One by one, my friends joined us. We all looked as if we'd stayed up all night. Anxiety, nerves, and worry had been our companions. Today was our chance to end all of the struggle.

We lingered at Millie's as long as we could without hogging table space from other customers. At last, Tinkie and I decided to go to the park for a walk with Maylin. Chablis was in the office, too, and I was glad to see the little dust mop. Tinkie and Oscar loved her as much as ever, but Maylin had stolen the spotlight and I wanted to be sure Chablis got her quota of praise and adoration.

Tammy had a client and went home to give a psychic reading. Cece went to the newspaper. Her online article about Lydia and how people had seen the dead woman wandering about the cotton fields near Tope's big mansion had stirred up a lot of interest and comments.

"Do you think Tope will take the bait?" Tinkie asked.

"I wish I knew."

"He will." Tinkie found certainty and clung to it like a drowning man on a raft.

"We can only hope." I checked my watch. It was only nine, but since I hadn't slept well I felt like it should be late afternoon. The pale gold morning sunlight painted everything anew.

"That was a great article Millie and Cece wrote. They honed it perfectly. Just the right amount of graphic detail about the body and then the reports of Lydia sightings near Tope's place. That should at least flush him out."

"I hope so."

The day was lovely. Children played on the swing sets and slide. Mothers sat on benches, talking as their pre-schoolers played. In the afternoons, the park filled with an older set of kids, but the mornings belonged to the babies.

Sweetie Pie and Chablis were sniffing everything they came across, investigating the delicious smells of strange humans and dogs. If Roscoe, Harold's evil little dog, had been with us, he would have peed on everything. He was neutered, but that didn't stop him from marking his territory. Everywhere he went was his territory.

Pluto walked directly in front of Maylin's stroller, his beautiful black tail plumed out and held straight in the air, ignoring everything as if he were the King of Sheba.

As we passed two mothers talking, we heard the babble of another baby. Maylin heard it, too, and answered with her own baby talk. The other baby seemed to reply.

Tinkie lifted Maylin out of the stroller and held her so she could see the other child. I could have sworn an instant bond formed. Maylin reached for the other little girl, and the mothers invited us to sit for a moment.

We weren't clocking any miles, so we did. The babies were adorable and we both needed to see something good and hopeful. After a few moments we moved on, swinging through the wooded area where the sunshine was espe-cially welcome.

The caw of the raven told me he was back. I wasn't

surprised when Tinkie pointed at him. "That's the same bird, isn't it?"

"I think so. Yeah, it is." No point pretending otherwise.

"Is it following you?"

"Why would it be tracking me and not you?" Tinkie had instantly assumed it was my bird.

"I've never had a wild bird take up with me. That bird likes you. See how it stares at you." She was making me paranoid.

"Ravens are messengers from the spirit world. Maybe your mama sent it," Tinkie said, giving me a dazzling smile.

"Maybe she did." I liked that idea, and suddenly the bird was no longer tainted with shadows but was a welcome presence.

We kept walking, making the circuit that would take us back to where we'd parked the car. As we took the final turn that was in the thickest part of the woods, the bird flapped down from a tree limb and clutched the handle of the baby stroller. Caught by surprise, Tinkie stepped back.

"Hey!" She was going to take a swing at the bird, but I stopped her.

"He won't hurt you or Maylin," I said.

"How can you know that?"

An honest question I couldn't answer. I just knew it. "He has a message."

"Beware," the bird said, looking directly at me.

"That's great." Tinkie shifted her weight from foot to foot. Any minute she was going to grab the stroller and run. The raven was too close to Maylin for her comfort.

Before she could do anything rash, my cell phone rang. "It's Tammy," I said. Was this the call we'd been waiting for?

"'Nevermore,'" the raven said before he flew back into the woods.

"Answer it," Tinkie said. She was all but jumping up and down.

"Hey, Tammy, did he call?" I put the phone on speaker and Tinkie crowded close.

"Oh, he called. He made threats and said if I didn't stay out of his business he would sue me until I ended up cleaning toilets to buy food."

"Lovely man."

"Did he want a reading?" Tinkie asked. She was more impatient than I'd ever seen her.

Tammy's laugh said it all. "Oh, he wants a reading. He was mean and dismissive, but he wants to make contact with Lydia's spirit. I told him that Lydia had information for him and that she needed to see her mother so she could cross over. We're set for a séance tonight at his place, midnight."

"Did he mention where Elisa was?" I asked.

"No. He pretended he didn't know anything about her. I'm sorry."

"Don't be sorry. You're doing everything you can to help us. Thank you, Tammy. I know you are putting yourself at risk, but—"

"Hush up, Sarah Booth. I'm doing this because I want to. Elisa is a client of mine. I happen to have deep feelings for her. And, as a child, Lydia was a sweet girl. No one deserves to have to assume a new identity to prevent her husband from killing her. This is a blow for the greater good."

I wasn't surprised by her answer, but I wondered how many times my friends had acted for the greater good, not because they would be rewarded, but because it was the right thing to do. Tinkie and I often took a case because of the money, but we didn't work so doggedly only for financial reward. We cared about our clients.

"Okay," I said. "Tinkie and I are going shopping to get the things we'll need for tonight."

"We'll talk later," Tammy said. "Another client is here. I've had a million calls this morning from the column Cece and Millie wrote. People want to know if I can bring Elvis across for them." She laughed, but I heard the tension crackling beneath her jovial front.

"If anyone can, it's you. Later, gator." I closed the phone and whistled up the pets. At last we had things we needed to do and no time to lose.

36

Our "shopping" spree began at Tope's house. We needed to photograph the rooms of the house so we could properly prepare for the séance.

When we pulled up to the gate, I recognized one of Coleman's emergency deputies standing guard. Because the sheriff's office was so critically underfunded, as was true of many rural departments, Coleman occasionally called on young men who'd gone through academy training on their own dime. Some hoped for a full-time job eventually and others needed supplemental income and were happy to work crowd containment, stakeouts, etc. Ricky Rodgers was a young man Coleman often praised.

"Hi, Ricky."

"Coleman said you'd be by."

"Yeah, we need some photos. We won't be there long at all. Have you seen anything?"

"I walk up to the house every thirty minutes and check around. Tope may know some trail through the property and try to sneak in. It's been quiet, though." He was disappointed at the lack of action.

"Be careful what you wish for," I teased him. "We'll be back soon."

He opened the gate and let us through. I heard it clank behind us. Coleman would pull the guard off tonight to give Tope the space necessary to get into the property. Like Ricky, I suspected that Tope had plenty of routes in and out of the estate.

I pulled up to the front door, noting how empty the house seemed. For a new structure, it had seen a lot of drama and suffering. Vivian, beautiful and fragile, was a lingering presence. I shook the feeling off and went with Tinkie to the front door. I was surprised to find it open. And happy. It would save time.

We rushed upstairs, Tinkie leading the way. We'd found the secret bedroom on an earlier search, and that was our destination. Again, the bizarre décor of the bedroom stopped us at the door.

"It's good Coleman got the wedding dress," Tinkie said as she went to the big closet looking for shoes.

"Probably more than that." For good measure I grabbed the nightgown and slippers, too. Just in case. After we sprang our trap tonight, I didn't want to come back in this room or this house ever again.

"What else did we need?" Tinkie asked. She had several boxes of shoes tucked under her arms.

"This is it. Let's set up the game table in the foyer for

Madame Tomeeka. It will be interesting to see how Tope will react to walk in and find it ready. Madame can tell him the spirits are eager to help."

We set up the sound system that had a series of spooky noises, like chains rattling and ghostly moans. The entire scheme depended on timing and Lydia's skill at pretending to be a ghost.

In laying out our plans, we'd chosen the foyer so Tope would have a clear view of the stairs from which Lydia would descend.

The game table was in the library. Tinkie and I carefully moved it, along with two chairs. Then we found all the candelabras in the house and moved them into the foyer so it would take a minimum of time to light them.

We grabbed the shoes and nightgown and left the big house. Our next location was the barn. Luckily, no animals depended on Tope for care or kindness, but the huge interior was unnerving. Creaks and groans from the fully stocked hayloft gave me the willies. We both scooted out of there as fast as we could. I found exactly what I needed in the spacious equipment shed. A golf cart, charged and ready to go. "Look, Tinkie! Our ticket to hauling everything we're going to need. It was so generous of Tope to have left this for us."

Tinkie hopped on the seat with me. "I'm sure he'd have shot out the tires if he knew he was helping us."

"True. Let's find a way onto this property that doesn't require us to go by the guard at the gate. I'm worried that Lydia might need an escape plan if Tope gets aggressive."

"Sarah Booth, do you really think that Tope will believe she's a spirit?"

"A lot depends on how Tammy and Lydia sell it."

"You staked your future on acting," she said. "Did you ever doubt yourself?"

I didn't answer immediately, because I had to really think. "I always doubted myself. But the desire to try was stronger than the fear of failing."

"Do you ever think that now, after the things we've lived through, that you might be able to take Broadway by storm?"

The idea of it flattered me, and I laughed. "You're a tonic, Tinkie. You make me feel special. The truth is, maybe I'd be a better actress now. Less wounded and afraid. More confident or more generous or more of whatever I needed. But that desire to be an actress is gone." I hadn't even acknowledged this to myself, but I found the truth as I talked. "Sometimes we do outgrow our dreams. After these years at Dahlia House with you as my partner, Coleman as my man, and all of my fabulous friends I've come to love and need, I don't want to go to New York. I'm exactly where I belong."

She reached across the cart and captured my hand. "That's good, because I don't want you to go. I wouldn't begrudge you, of course. I'd do everything I could to make your dreams happen. But I want you here, in Zinnia, to help me raise Maylin."

"An assignment I'm happy to take on." I squeezed her hand and then took a sharp right turn into a trail. She grabbed the golf cart frame and squealed.

Most of the Delta was wide open fields, each foot of soil precious in its power to grow crops. The wise farmers, though, had kept strips and sections of woodlands to prevent erosion and also provide some area for the abundant wildlife. I wasn't shocked when I found a deer stand. Tope would have one of those. I stopped the golf cart and went to look at the stand. It had been recently used, whether by Tope or a guest, I couldn't tell. When I had more time, once Lydia was returned to her family land, I would ask her if I could have the joy of dismantling the stand.

"What's that over there?" Tinkie asked. She pointed west.

I drove the cart over and looked up at a tiny little shack with a tin roof. And electricity. I couldn't believe it. This was exactly what we needed.

I opened the front door and stepped into a camp cabin, complete with a bed covered in quilts, a fireplace, an electric heater, and canned goods. I flipped the light switch and the power came right on.

Tinkie had followed me over. "This is excellent. Cece can put the makeup on here, and then ride them over in the golf cart. It's electric and silent; no one will hear."

I had to agree. Now all we had to do was find a trail to a road so that Cece could leave her car for a quick getaway. We hopped back in the cart and took off. Fifteen minutes later, I stopped the cart on the verge of Country Road 339. I got out and took a stick to mark the place so that we could find it later.

"Here, use this." Tinkie took off her beautiful scarf and handed it to me. "Just drop it on the ground where we can see it."

"Those are some expensive bread crumbs," I said, knowing the scarf was designer.

"Not as valuable as our friends."

She had a good point and a big heart. We headed back to the main house. We would drive out together, and then I'd double back to bring the golf cart to the edge of the woods so it would be there for Cece, Lydia, and Bethany.

"I'm hungry," Tinkie said.

"Me, too."

"Pauline was making chicken gumbo. Let's run by Hilltop and grab a bite."

I knew she really wanted to see Maylin—and so did I. "That's a plan."

The hours of the afternoon wore slowly by. Tinkie and I paced and checked our phones every five seconds. We'd talked with Tammy, Cece, Millie, Coleman, Budgie, and DeWayne. Everyone knew their roles and was ready to go.

At two o'clock, Cece ran another installment of "The Ghost of Lydia Redd Maxwell" in the newspaper and earned herself a call from the Maxwell legal firm in Memphis with the threat of a libel suit. She was overjoyed. "If they come out threatening a lawsuit, you know I'm pinching their toes," she said. "And we all know you can't libel the dead."

It was a relief she was so deeply engaged in our farce, but I didn't want my friend to suffer consequences for helping us.

"Fiddle-dee-dee," Cece said. "The Maxwell family has more lawyers than common sense. They can't touch me for what I wrote. Go on with the plan and forget about it. I may have to add another installment just for good measure."

I could only hope that Tope was reading along with the rest of his clan.

I called Coleman. "Any word about Tope?"

"Not a word. He's either found a great hiding spot or he's left the country."

"Do you think he'll show up tonight?" I couldn't help asking. I needed some reassurance.

"Oh, if he's still in this area, he will," Coleman said. "I've spread the word that me and my deputies will be attending a seminar in Jackson. Tope will think the road is wide open to him."

"Thank you, Coleman. It means a lot that you have my back."

"We have to get our hands on Tope and put him behind bars," Coleman said. "I support you, but I have a job to do also."

"And one I highly approve of."

"Hey," Tinkie said. "Quit making lovey-dovey on the phone. Coleman, come by Hilltop for some chicken gumbo. Perfect for a cold day like today."

"It's really good," I threw in. "Pauline is a superb nanny and a good Cajun cook."

"I'm on the way. Shall I invite DeWayne and Budgie?"

"Absolutely," Tinkie said. "Now hang up."

"I live to obey," I said loud enough so that Coleman could hear me before I hung up the phone.

At last dark began to settle over the Delta. The peach sunset gave way to lavender, blue, indigo, and finally, navy. The first star appeared in the sky, and I made a simple wish, to complete my case with safety for all.

I left Tinkie at Hilltop to spend an hour or so with her baby, and I went home to feed the horses and get Sweetie Pie and Pluto. They would go with us. I needed Sweetie for sound effects, and Pluto was excellent at hopping out of places and scaring the bejesus out of people. The critters had their talents, and I was ready to put them to work. Tinkie would join me at ten.

As I poured the pelleted food into the horses' feeders and crammed flakes of hay into sacks to hang in the stalls, I enjoyed the feeling of brisk work on a cold night. I was nervous and upset. Working with the horses always calmed me. Life was so uncertain at the best of times, but my three magnificent steeds anchored me to the long sweep of Father Time's clock hands. For this instant, life was secure and safe. The sound of the horses eating lulled my jitters. When they finished their grain and turned to the hay sacks, I opened the stall doors. They were already blanketed, and I'd always been taught to let them move around to stay warm. They were grazing animals and, as such, needed to move and chew what grass they could find. That was their nature, and my job was to honor it.

Soon the new spring grass would come in, and the world and considerations of a farm girl would change with the seasons. My horses were family. I never intended to sell them or try to make money, but I was well aware of the daily gambles farmers made to produce grains or cotton. Half science and half luck. That was farming.

"Pensive, are we?"

The female voice came from behind me. Jitty had arrived.

"What's up?" I asked, turning slowly to find my haint in a long, dull dress from the mid-to-late 1800s. Tall, straight, and unsmiling, she was no Scarlett O'Hara.

"I shouldn't be here." She looked around at the stars brightening the sky. "It's lovely here, but this isn't my time or place."

"Who are you?"

"Charlotte Perkins Gilman. I'm a writer and lecturer." She took in my jeans, boots, and generally "masculine" attire. "I see women have made some progress, though."

I knew her work, especially "The Yellow Wallpaper," a terrifying story of a young woman driven to insanity by the rigid expectations of her role in society. Perkins had experienced a mental breakdown. She'd divorced a husband and, when he remarried, sent their daughter to live with her ex-husband and stepmother. Charlotte had determined that two roles she didn't want to play were traditional wife and mother. And, sadly, she'd been a racist.

"We have a long fight ahead of us," I told her. "We need more women like you. Except maybe without the prejudice." I was a little surprised Jitty had selected a woman with such a past.

She shook her head. "Societal expectations broke me. I regret many things that I once believed."

"But you didn't give up."

"Yet here I am, coming to you as a writer of Gothic fiction. A category I may not fit in."

"I'm sorry you never found your place."

She shrugged. "Do you consider my writing Gothic?"

I was a far cry from a literary critic, and I'd seen her lumped with other feminist writers with a dark worldview. "Maybe. But I don't see it as a bad thing."

For the first time, she smiled. "Your point is taken."

"I love the Gothic writers," I told her. "Poe was one of my first literary loves."

"He had his share of woe, too. And his share of mistakes and bad behavior."

There were a million things I wanted to discuss with her. The role of the artist in bringing about social change, the image that had been painted of her as a physically pampered, bigoted wife who was starved emotionally, the choices she'd made—to give up her child and to commit suicide when she found her cancer was untreatable. Selfish, or the epitome of selflessness? I wondered if she knew the answers.

"I read your story when I was in college," I told her. "It gave me the courage to reach for my own dreams."

"Did you succeed?" she asked.

"Not in the way I anticipated." I decided to press. "Do you have a message for me?"

"I don't have to tell you, you know."

"But tell me anyway." I felt suddenly very alone in life. "I don't want to be searching the wallpaper for answers."

She laughed, and I caught a glimpse of her softer side, a side she often hid. "Your parents love you. Aunt Loulane tells you to never put off until tomorrow what you can do today." She smiled. "And Great-Uncle Crabtree wants you to tell the big lies every chance you get."

"A rogue's gallery of bad advice." I had asked for it, after all.

Charlotte's features softened, plumped, and shaded in a light coffee swirl. Jitty walked amongst us, wearing my favorite pajamas and slippers. "You could have just asked me," she said. "You think literary stars have better advice for you?"

"I did ask you." She wasn't getting one by me like that. "And, no, I think you have good advice sometimes, too. Thank you, Jitty."

"You have an active imagination, Sarah Booth. You conjured up all these dead writers. You can't blame that on me!"

"Oh, I blame you for plenty."

"Harrumph!" Wearing my favorite pair of pink fuzzy slippers, Jitty stepped right into a pile of horse apples.

"Jitty!" I was shocked.

She let out a cackle and gave a twirl. A cascade of alphabet confetti scattered all around her and she disappeared on a blast of cold air. That haint would be the death of me yet.

My cell phone rang, and I answered as I walked hurriedly to the back door. The night was cold. It was time to get into my boots and winter gear. "Hello."

"Is Lydia really dead?"

Elisa Redd's voice stopped me in my tracks. I found myself without a ready response. If I told her yes, it would break her heart. If I told her no and Tope was listening, I would blow our entire plan to catch him.

"I'm so sorry, Elisa. I can only tell you that the future looks better for all of us."

Her sob tore at me. "Where did you find her?"

"She was found and photographed in a cotton field. But remember Persephone." I was fairly certain Elisa would catch the reference of the goddess who returned to life every spring. Death could not defeat her. It was the best I could do without giving it away to Tope that she was alive. "Where are you, Elisa? I can come get you; just tell me where you are."

"I don't care about me anymore."

Those words could well be her death sentence. The one thing I hadn't calculated on was that Elisa would make it easy for Tope to kill her, too. She was the only thing standing between him and a ton of money.

"Buck up, Elisa. Think what Lydia would want. She'd want you to fight. Hear me. Don't give up. You didn't raise a quitter. Hold tight to that."

I couldn't say more but I hoped it was enough. "Where are you?"

"You can't save me. It's too dangerous. I never should have gone to Tope's place to confront him."

Was she at the mansion? Was that the clue she was giving me? "Just hold on. Midnight will tell the tale. Remember Poe and the ever-beating heart. The power of that heartbeat, steady and strong. Lydia wants you to be strong. For the future."

"Sarah Booth—"

The line went dead.

37

My first reaction was to call Tinkie and tell her. My heart pounded as I dialed. Elisa had sounded so defeated. Would she harm herself before we had a chance to spring our trap and catch Tope? Before I could let her know her daughter was alive and safe?

"Damn, damn, damn," I whispered to myself as I waited for Tinkie to answer. When she finally did, I blurted out my fears and worries.

"You did the right thing, not explicitly telling her. You gave her plenty of hints," Tinkie reassured me. "You couldn't say more. You know damn good and well Tope was listening to everything you said. That was the only reason he allowed Elisa to call you. He wanted to see what we were up to."

"What if she harms herself?" I paced, clinging to my phone for dear life.

"What if we rescue her and Lydia and put Tope in jail?" Tinkie countered. "We work for the outcome we want. We'll deal with whatever happens."

She was so calm and wise.

"Now let's get over to Millie's and make sure things are on track there."

"We can't keep eating every twenty minutes," I told her. "My pants are already tight."

"We'll burn those extra calories tonight," Tinkie said. "Now get on the road. I'll meet you there."

By the time we finished an order of fried dill pickles, catfish strips, and hush puppies, I was about to pop. But we'd hammered out the last details. Coleman and the deputies had been alerted. It was time to put the plan into action.

We stopped by Madame Tomeeka's to pick up gauzy material to drape over the lamps and the tools of her trade. It was after nine o'clock when we headed to Tope's place. We had three hours to prepare the scene. My gut churned with anxiety, but I kept my worries to myself. Tinkie was busy making lists to be sure everything was finished on time. We had to get this done and hide away.

A huge oak tree centered the front of the house and was perfect for our schemes. A large picture window gave a view of the oak, which was ablaze with fairy lights. I climbed the tree and hung the blood-soaked nightgown that Cece had decorated with fake blood. A simple rig with a bag of sand for a weight would "float" the bloody nightgown slowly by the picture window. Since we'd arranged the table in the foyer by the window, Tope would be looking directly out into the night as Tammy called forth Lydia's spirit.

We were finishing up as Bethany and Lydia arrived. They'd found the golf cart and come into the property that way. Not five minutes later, Cece and Millie arrived. We sent them all in the golf cart to the little cabin so they could prepare. Everyone had to be in their places by the time Tope arrived. Budgie was hiding at the gate, and he would call the house as soon as Tope turned in to the property.

I turned Pluto loose in the house. He had a battery-operated catnip mouse that I intended to turn on while Tammy was conducting the séance. Pluto growled and yowled as he chased the mouse. It was one of his favorite games. Sweetie Pie cozied into a plush wing chair in the front parlor. I had taught her to howl on command. Arthur Conan Doyle's *The Hound of the Baskervilles* had scared me into near paralysis as a young reader, so a dog howling would be perfect.

I checked the weather on my phone. The storm that had been hovering on the horizon had finally started to move. It had threatened us for several days. Predictions were for freezing rain, sleet, and hail. It was perfect for a creepy séance evening. I just hoped we could get the ball on the special effects rolling before the rain came and washed the nightgown free of blood.

My cell phone buzzed, and I answered Cece's call.

"Lydia and Bethany are ready," she said. "Shall I bring them over so they can take their places?"

"Yes. This isn't complicated, but everything really hinges on Lydia. And Bethany hiding upstairs is our security if things go wrong. Any word from Madame Tomeeka?"

"She said she'd be here," Cece said. "She'll check the setup so she knows how everything is supposed to go, and then she'll leave to come back once Tope is here. She doesn't want to be here waiting for him."

"Good thinking." My friends had lots of smarts.

Even though I knew the plan, I was unprepared for the gruesome horror of Lydia dressed in her former wedding gown with blood, dirt, and effluvium from the grave all over her. Cece had done an exquisite job. Lydia's eyes were sunken in, her skull evident in places where her hair had fallen out. She was slowly rotting. Exactly as a dead body would.

If Lydia was nervous at seeing her abusive husband, she didn't show it. "I don't care what I have to do," she said, "as long as my mother is safe and Tope is put behind bars."

"That's what we're all hoping," I reminded her. "Now hustle up to your old bedroom and get ready to rattle some chains and ring some bells."

She lifted the edge of her wedding dress and ran up the stairs. At the top, she turned back to me. "I never thought I'd be in this house again, not while Tope was alive. But this is my family's land and my house. I paid for it, and Tope merely took it over. Things are changing. Right now. I'm taking back what's mine, including my mother."

Lydia had finally hit the wall. She was ready for a toe-to-toe with Tope, and, looking at her, I had no doubt she would win.

The minutes ticked by. The elements for the séance were in place, but even though we hustled, time dragged on. Knowing we had this one chance—and that if we blew it, we might not have another—had me coiled like a big spring.

As the hall clock chimed 11:30, everyone began to settle in their places. Madame Tomeeka would arrive at the stroke of midnight. Tope, if he was going to show, would arrive any minute.

I was upstairs helping Lydia settle into a chair by an open window of her bedroom. I couldn't guarantee what Tope would do, so it was best for her to be somewhere she could startle him if necessary. Bethany was in the adjoining bathroom, ready to do her part. Cece and Millie were at the cabin, waiting for midnight before they showed up. I wasn't exactly sure where Coleman and his deputies were but knew they weren't far away. They would be here in a flash if they were called.

I was standing at the sidelight of the front door when Tope pulled up in his Mercedes. I hurried to my location and hid. Tope came in the front door, using his key. He stopped at the table and chairs in the foyer, the candles waiting to be lit.

"What the hell?" he said under his breath.

I tensed, but he walked past the table and into the front parlor, then continued touring the first floor of the house, looking for other changes. The doorbell rang and he answered it.

"I'm Madame Tomeeka," Tammy said. "If you're ready, let's get down to business."

Tope stepped back and ushered her inside. "Excellent," she said. "I hope you don't mind, but I asked your household staff to prepare for the séance. They did an excellent job."

"How did you know who to contact?" Tope was wary.

"I wouldn't be a very good psychic medium if I couldn't ascertain a few basic bits of information, would I?"

Her smile seemed to catch him by surprise, but then he smiled back at her. His words, though, were chilling. "I hope you aren't trying to pull something over on me. I agreed to this because Lydia needs to tell me where some things are."

"I told you on the phone, I can't guarantee anything. The spirits either come or they don't. They talk or they don't. They answer questions or they don't."

"They'd better be cooperative tonight." Tope was menacing.

"You'll learn the hard way that threatening the spirits is a waste of time and breath. And sometimes dangerous."

"What? A ghost is going to crack me in the head or shoot me?"

Tammy walked past him, ignoring the question. She walked to the table and pointed to a chair for Tope where he had a view of the staircase. She opened her purse and pulled out a deck of tarot cards and a long butane lighter designed for grills or fireplaces, then lit the candles, a task that took several minutes. Tope began to twitch.

"None of that is necessary. Let's get on with it. This is all bullshit anyway. Come across with the information I need or you'll regret it."

"Have you ever brought a spirit across the divide?" she asked.

He frowned. "No."

"Then shut up and let me do my work," she said. She hid her anger well, but I clearly saw it. Tammy didn't take herself seriously, but she did take her bond with the spirits seriously. Tope mocked her and all she believed. It got under her skin. "I'd like my pay in advance," she said. "You look like a man who might skip out on his obligations."

I thought for a minute Tope would smack her, but he didn't. Scowling, he reached inside his coat and drew forth an envelope. "Cash, as you requested."

Tammy took it, counted it, then put it in her purse. She took her time. She was doing everything in her power to agitate him, and it was working.

"Mrs. Tomeeka," Tope said, his tone frosty, "can we just get this over with? If you can't do it, give me my money back and let's get on with the evening."

"I can summon the spirits," Tammy said, "but I can't make them respond."

"Get Lydia here and I'll make her answer my questions. She knows full well what I'm capable of."

Tammy inhaled deeply. "There's a spirit here. A young woman. Beautiful. Vivid." She hesitated. "Not vivid. Vital . . . no. Vivian."

"Shut up!" Tope reached across the table for her, but she leaned back.

"Vivian has a message."

"Shut up. Vivian is nothing to me. Shut up now or I'll shut you up."

"Vivian says your day is coming. She's so beautiful, and smiling. She seems so happy."

Tope rose to his feet. "I've had enough of this foolishness. You're a fraud and I'm done. Give me my money."

"Sit down and hold my hands." Tammy's voice was an iron command. "The midnight hour is here. The veil between the living and dead has thinned to the point of transparency. I'm here at the request of Tope Maxwell to speak to his departed wife, Lydia. Are there any spirits with us?" she asked. "If you are here, make your presence known."

The candles guttered as the front door opened and a cold

wind blew into the room. I'd left the door unlatched and Cece was outside, fulfilling her role. Tope almost stood, but Tammy held his hands. "Don't move," she said. "You'll send them away."

Tope settled back down, but his body was coiled like a snake. It wasn't hard to imagine him leaping across the table and into Tammy's face. To stay still, I pressed my hands against the wall in the alcove where I was hiding. My fist itched to smack into his face.

"Spirits, if you are here, give me a sign." Madame Tomeeka drew a card from the tarot deck. She held it up to show Tope. "It is the card of Death."

"You're full of it. I'm not going to die," Tope said angrily.

"No, it isn't about your death. It's about change. Some things must die for new things to grow. You're in a position of change. You will lose someone you care about very soon."

A cold winter wind sent dead leaves fluttering into the foyer through the open door. The storm—the one thing I couldn't control—was about to break bad with fury. Goose bumps marched along my arms and back.

When Tope started to get up to shut the door, Tammy stopped him. "Leave it," she said.

"It's freezing outside," Tope protested. "We need to close the door."

"I'll close it." Tammy pointed at the door, and it swung shut and latched. Outside, Tinkie had a fishing line on the knob. Our setup was so simple and basic, but so effective. I wanted to clap at the theatrics we'd managed to create. "Someone is here with us, Mr. Maxwell. Someone wants to communicate with you."

Tope started to say something but stopped. He looked at Tammy with respect now.

Tammy gazed into a far corner of the room, and in the candlelight it seemed her eyes had gone white and blank. Even though I knew it was an illusion, it gave me the heebie-jeebies.

"Oh, spirit, who has bravely crossed the divide between worlds. Who are you? Why are you here?" Tammy began to moan softly and rock gently. "Oh, spirit, we are here to listen to your words of wisdom."

The curtains in the parlor began to twist and bunch, as if something were in them, tangling and pushing to get free. I knew exactly who was in them. I recognized the toe of a very shiny black shoe. DeWayne was helping us out. I wanted to kiss him!

Once again, Tope started to rise from the table, but Tammy held his hands. "You wanted to speak with Lydia. Give her a chance to come through."

Tope's gaze was riveted on the thrashing curtains. "What if that isn't Lydia?"

"Then someone else on the other side has business with you. The door has been opened. You can't avoid this confrontation, Mr. Maxwell. The spirits are here. They will be heard. Sometimes your past deeds come back to find you."

"Bring Lydia to me," Tope ordered. "I have no business with anyone else."

"Divine spirits who have honored us with your presence, will you tell me if Lydia Redd is with you?"

"Lydia Maxwell," Tope corrected her. "She's my wife."

"Not in the Great Beyond," Tammy said bluntly. "The spirits tell me she is Lydia Redd. She disavows her marriage. The spirits say she was coming for retribution when she died in that cotton field. If you wish to speak with her, you must call her by her name."

Tammy was laying a heavy trip on Tope, and I was enjoying every second of it.

"Whatever. Just get Lydia Redd here. I need to know where the key to her safety-deposit box is. When she left, she took some things I need back, and she sure doesn't need them where she is."

The front door crashed open with an unexpected force. This wasn't one of the special effects I'd engineered, and a thrill of fear grabbed me hard. Apparently, Tinkie hadn't closed the door completely and the wind had joined our team to unnerve Tope. The wild night cooperated with us. A bolt of lightning struck near a pine tree a hundred yards from the house. The storm that had been brewing for several days had finally moved in. Judging by the wind and lashing trees, it was right over us. I hadn't counted on this, but, if possible, I'd use it.

"Lydia Redd, are you here with us?" Tammy called out.

Another gust of wind blew through the open front door and doused the candles. One candelabra blew over and fell to the hard tile floor, clattering. It almost covered the sound of rattling chains. Bethany was at work with the sound system upstairs. A low, throaty, "Tope" echoed down the staircase. Lydia was now playing her role.

38

The sound was electric. So soft I couldn't tell where it originated from. It seemed to float on the air, coming from everywhere. "Tope, I'm here."

"Lydia!" Tope leaned forward. "Is that Lydia?" he demanded of Tammy. "Tell her to show herself."

Any doubts that Tope might have had about the séance appeared to have been erased. He believed he'd made contact with Lydia from the grave. He also didn't appear to care at all that she was dead.

From somewhere outside the house, the baleful howl of a dog sent additional goose bumps over me, even though I knew it was Sweetie Pie. She was chipping in to devil Tope, following the cues that Coleman was giving her. The parlor mirror offered me an excellent view of Tope as he leaned toward Tammy, tensed for action. At that moment, Pluto darted across the foyer. Tope caught the movement too late. He knew something was moving but he hadn't seen what. Superb job, Pluto! As wild and crazy as my plan was, the elements were coming together to create the impact I'd hoped for.

"Is that Lydia?" Tope was ready to rush up the stairs, but Tammy checked him with a word.

"Beware! We don't know who that is. It could be Lydia or someone else. Someone with a very different agenda. Many of the spirits trapped between life and death are angry, scared, lost. Be still and let me find out who this is."

Tammy lifted her face up just as a bolt of lightning flashed outside the window, followed by a boom of rolling thunder. Hail struck the roof with a sharp impact. Even I was chilled by how well the weather was cooperating.

"Lydia?" Tammy said. "Are you here with us?"

Outside the front window, Lydia's nightgown, which we'd rigged up on a fishing line, floated up to the front window. Hail pummeled it, and the fake blood began to run in rivulets. Tope gasped and went white.

The nightgown danced in the wind, flattening against the window and then retreating. I knew the mechanism that controlled it, and it still terrified me. The nightgown seemed to be filled with living flesh.

"Lydia!" Tope called out.

"Murderer!" The voice rippled down the stairs, accompanied by moaning and the sound of someone walking, one foot dragging behind. Bethany and Lydia had gone whole hog on the sound effects, and they were working. Tope had begun to fidget. His gaze swept from the front windows and doors up the staircase.

"Stop it, Lydia." Tope's voice cracked. "You're making a fool of yourself."

"I thought you wanted her help," Tammy said.

Tope glared at her. "She'll help me. If she ever wants to see her mother alive again. Elisa's fate is in my hands. I can set her free or let her die where she is."

There it was. A confession. Thank goodness I'd put the nanny cam in a porcelain shepherdess beside a bouquet of Stargazer lilies. The little table where the figurine sat was only four feet from Tope. Tope's confession of taking Elisa was on the record now. When we found out where Elisa was, we could end this charade and Coleman could rush in and arrest Tope. Tinkie always bought high-end products and it was going to pay off in aces this night. We'd have Tope convicting himself of abducting Elisa.

"What is it you want to know, Mr. Maxwell?" Tammy kept her cool. "The spirits are here. I believe Lydia is in the house. I feel her presence, but she is reluctant to come forward. Ask her nicely what you'd like to know and maybe she'll answer."

"Nicely?" Tope laughed. "Sure. I'll ask nicely. Lydia, darling, where is your will and the safety-deposit box with your jewels? I'm asking nicely. But don't stress me or something tragic will happen to your meddling mother."

A low, mournful moan came from the top of the stairs. "I'm here, Tope."

Tope looked at Tammy and chuckled. "I'm not afraid of the dead," he said in a low voice. He looked up the stairs and spoke louder. "Come visit with me, darling," he said. "We have a lot to catch up on." He had more backbone than I'd been willing to believe. If he didn't buy into the ghost of Lydia, my plan was doomed.

"You killed me, Tope. I came home to see my mother and you killed me. You bludgeoned me in that cotton field."

"I didn't harm a hair on your head. At least not this year. Remember, just because you're dead doesn't mean you can escape me. I'll follow you straight to hell if I have to."

Tammy slapped the table so hard her deck of tarot cards jumped up and scattered on the table. One card flipped over. Watching it in the mirror, I knew she'd concocted this by marking the cards in some manner.

Tammy picked up the card and held it for Tope to see. "Death."

"Whose death?" Tope asked. His voice was edgy but still in control.

"Why don't you ask Lydia?" Tammy suggested.

The sad, mournful voice came again. "You killed Vivian. You choked her and then pushed her over the balcony rail."

"That's none of your business, darling. She wasn't nearly the challenge you were to break."

"Confess," Lydia said softly. "Confess your sins to seek my forgiveness."

"Not in this lifetime," Tope said. "I don't need your absolution. You're dead. Your mother will soon be dead. Everything will go to me, and I won't even have to file paperwork since you so conveniently got yourself offed in a Sunflower County cotton field. Yes, Sheriff Peters will file the paperwork and I'll be a rich, rich man."

"Look at me, Tope." There was the sound of breaking glass at the top of the stairs. Lydia stood there, bloody and beaten, the gore soaked into her wedding dress. "You'll never live to enjoy my inheritance."

Tope gasped. At last, the effect of seeing Lydia's "ghost" had touched him.

"I came for you," Lydia said, taking one step down the stairs. "I came to get you. You killed me when you beat me and broke my spirit, and now I'm going to drag you straight to hell with me. Your words are inspirational." Lydia took another step down the staircase. She reached out and pointed at Tope. Her hollow eyes in her battered face almost burned with a fevered light. "You are evil, Tope Maxwell. I have judged you."

"You think you can scare me?" Tope jumped to his feet. "I'll beat you like you've never been beaten." He stepped around the table. He was going after Lydia. I had not counted on this reaction.

Tope started up the stairs at a mad dash. He was halfway up before I could get into the room from my hiding place. Lydia backed up a step. Then two.

"You are going to be so sorry for this foolishness, Lydia. You should have remembered you can't con a con." He reached for her with both hands.

A huge book came flying out of nowhere and struck Tope full in the face. Another book struck him and then another. He reeled, fighting for balance for a moment, and then he toppled backward down the stairs and landed at Tammy's feet in the foyer. Beside him were the first three volumes of Marcel Proust's work of involuntary memory, *Remembrance of Things Past*. Amazingly fitting.

"Mr. Maxwell!" Tammy knelt beside him. Tope wasn't unconscious, but he'd been knocked loopy. I had to get Lydia and Bethany out of there before he came to his senses.

I sprinted up the stairs and caught Lydia by the arm. "You've got to go!" Tope wasn't going to passively let them escape. "Come on! There are back stairs. Let's go."

She shook free of me. "I'm not going anywhere, Sarah

Booth. I appreciate what you're trying to do, but I'm sick of running. I'm here and I'm going to face Tope. He can't hurt me. There are witnesses."

"That's right," Bethany said, stepping to the top of the steps. She held two more volumes of Proust's masterpiece. "Just give me a reason."

39

"What will this gain?" I tried to tug Lydia toward the back staircase, but she balked. "We have his confession to taking Elisa and threatening to hurt her. That's kidnapping at the very least. It's enough to put him behind bars. Let it go!"

She pulled her arm free. "We're going to finish this. Now." She rushed down the stairs to stand over the addled Tope.

Bethany joined us on the foyer's beautiful tile floor. "I should just kill him," she said. "I could do it with my bare hands."

"No! He knows where Elisa is." Killing Tope was a bad idea for a lot of reasons, but I found the one I hoped would appeal to Bethany and Lydia.

"She's right," Lydia said, disappointment clear in her voice. "We can't kill him. Yet."

"You can't kill him ever." I wasn't going to back down. "I came to help you, but I can't be part of a murder."

"We wouldn't really kill him," Lydia said, but I didn't believe a syllable of it.

"Maybe we could just make him wish he was dead," Bethany added.

I could go along with that, but I wasn't going to say it out loud. Lydia and Bethany didn't need any encouragement to be bloody. I believed they'd truly kill Tope if they thought they could get away with it. And I didn't blame them. But vengeful actions weren't going to help us find Elisa.

"Tope," Tammy was kneeling beside Tope's body. He began to groan and slowly attempt to roll over.

"He's coming to," I said. "You have to leave. It isn't safe here." I didn't want to call Coleman to come get them, but I would if I had to. I pulled out my phone only to discover that the storm had knocked out cell service. "Damn."

"Let's finish this," Lydia said. "I want to scare him into a heart attack."

"If he comes after you, he may kill you. When he finds out you're not really dead, he's going to be furious." Why didn't she see the danger? Why didn't Bethany convince her to be safe?

"He'll never lay a finger on me again," Lydia vowed. "If he tries, I have every right to defend myself."

"We're going to end this," Bethany said. "Tonight. And we'll get Elisa back, too."

Those were bold statements. I could do only one thing— continue as we'd planned. Tope gained his knees with Tammy's help. She was worried that he'd seriously injured himself. I couldn't hear what she was murmuring, but Tope was white with fury. This time he'd bitten off more than he might be able to chew.

"Lydia!" Tope stumbled to his feet. "I'm coming for you. Ghost or dead woman, I don't care. You are going to regret this."

"You need to go to the emergency room," Tammy said, trying to hold on to Tope's arm to keep him from falling again.

Tope quickly spun around, caught Tammy under her jaw, and began to squeeze. "You're trying to put something over on me, and I don't like it."

"You're hurting me, Tope," Tammy said, gasping for air. "Are you sure you want to do that?"

"What? Are the spirits going to come get me and punish me? Come on, Lydia. Bring it on. I beat you into submission when you were alive, and I can do it again if you're dead."

"Let me go," Tammy said.

"Not a chance. You're trying to trick me, and now you're going to pay. You women, you think you can get away with anything because you're never held to account. I don't put up with it. You play, you pay. And now you're going to pay."

I drew my gun and cocked it, but Lydia pushed past me.

"Tope, let her go," she said. "You want to know where my safety-deposit box is, I'll tell you."

"Not so ghostly now," he said. "Come here and I'll let her go."

Lydia cast a glance at me. "Where is my mother? Tell me and I'll tell you whatever you want. Release Madame Tomeeka. She has nothing to do with you or the money."

"She was engineering a scam. You thought you could scare me into giving up Elisa and running away?" He laughed. "You always thought a lot more of yourself than was deserved."

Even now, years after she'd left him, he wanted only to break Lydia down. He was a brute. I couldn't shoot him until we knew where Elisa was—and he knew it.

"I'm not afraid of you, Tope. Not anymore. I'm coming." Lydia took one step closer to him. "Where's my mother?"

"Elisa is safe. Did you ever consider that your mother wanted to get rid of you?"

That was the cruelest thing I'd ever heard a man say. Instead of denying it or crying, Lydia took another step toward her furious husband. "Let Madame Tomeeka go."

"First you tell me what I want to know."

"I don't think so. Where's my mother?" She went closer.

The game she played was terrifying. Tope could push Tammy aside and rush to grab Lydia and I wouldn't have a clear shot.

"Elisa is here. In the hayloft. She's perfectly safe. Maybe a little uncomfortable, but safe."

Would Lydia believe him? I sure didn't. He'd given up the information too easily.

"Let Madame Tomeeka go," Lydia insisted. "She has nothing to do with this."

"Except, like your little friends Ernest and Florence Salter, she wanted to trick me. You know what happened to the Salters. They're dead. Their farm is abandoned. I'm surprised you'd risk another woman's life on this quest to screw me over."

I could only hope that the nanny cam was recording the confession Tope was so eager to give. I hoped Lydia would ask for more detail about the Salters.

"Tope, walk with me to make sure my mother is okay. Once I see that she's alive and well, I'll tell you what you want to know. You can have the money. The property. The stocks. I don't care anymore."

"What about that fine crop of marijuana you're cultivating?"

"How did you know about that?" Lydia was truly shocked.

"The county agent in Leflore County has a big mouth, Lydia. Several years back I helped him find his home and then made him a rich man by developing the property he wanted to sell. When Sarah Booth and Tinkie Richmond went asking nosy questions about growing weed, I knew your mother had hired them and I hoped it might lead me to you, Lydia. I just had to bide my time."

Lydia had recovered her composure. "The seedlings are planted. You can have them, too. I'll turn it all over to you. I just want my mother safely returned and a divorce."

"You've hidden out all this time trying to hang on to your family inheritance. Why are you giving up?"

Lydia sighed. "I know what's really important in life. Being free to live how I choose is all that matters. Money hasn't ever brought you happiness or joy. Look at you. You destroy everything you touch. You can have all of this because it won't serve you. Not even for an hour. You're hollow inside. There's not enough money in the world to fill that hole."

"You're not getting out of this scot-free."

"Free? I'm buying my freedom with my inheritance, you buffoon." Lydia had reached the end of her patience.

She gathered herself. I saw it and I reached out for her. She meant to leap onto Tope and knock him off Tammy, who he still held with his arm around her throat. Tope let Tammy go and reached into his coat and came out with a gun.

Before I could do anything, Sweetie Pie appeared in the foyer with a full head of steam. She covered the ground like the Baskerville hound. The scene appeared to unfold in slo-mo as her mouth opened and her teeth closed around Tope's wrist. I heard the crunch of bone and his scream. Before I could do anything, Bethany rushed Tope. She'd had a baseball bat concealed at her side and she brought it out and gave a home run slug to Tope's knees. I didn't even get a chance to shoot him. Bethany was on him like a duck on a june bug.

Sweetie had his wrist in her mouth and Lydia drew back and kicked him in the groin as hard as she could.

"I'm going to kill you," he screamed at her.

"You can try." Bethany kicked him again. Unlike Lydia, who was barefoot, Bethany wore heavy boots.

Tope collapsed on his side, heaving and retching. The fight had been kicked out of him.

I pulled out my phone, relieved to see I finally had a signal, and called Coleman, who was at the front door in record time. He quickly put Tope in handcuffs and read him his rights. In the distance I could hear the sirens.

Tope had finally regained his breath, and as DeWayne and Budgie led him out of the house, he struggled to turn back to Lydia. "You think you're so smart. You don't have a clue."

I wanted to slug him in the mouth with the butt of my gun, but I didn't. It would only reflect badly on Coleman. Besides, I needed to check the hayloft. When I'd been in there earlier with Tinkie, I'd heard something moving about. I'd assumed it was mice, but now I wasn't so sure.

40

Coleman sent Tope to the county jail with Budgie and De-Wayne, then headed to the barn with me and my gang. We had to find Elisa if she was there. Jogging toward the barn, I was filled with hope and dread. If she wasn't there, we might never convince Tope to give her up. I had terrible visions of "The Cask of Amontillado." This whole case had begun with Tammy's dream of a beating heart beneath the floorboards. And Jitty was flirting with dead Gothic writers. No wonder my brain turned to the darkness.

Lydia and Bethany ran with us. Lydia's fake blood-soaked wedding gown dragged in the mud, a fitting end to what had been a horrible marriage.

"Do you think she's really there? In the barn?" Lydia asked.

"I hope so." I opened the big barn door and we all rushed in. The lights were out, thanks to the storm. We used our phones as flashlights and spread out, searching each stall, the tack room, the feed room. And last, the hayloft.

"Mama!" Lydia called. "I'm here. Where are you?" Her voice broke.

We all listened, but there was no answer.

"Elisa!" Tinkie and I called.

Cece and Millie found the ladder to the loft, but they let me go up alone. If something awful was up there, I didn't want Lydia to see it. Tinkie moved into position to block the ladder. As I began to climb, I looked down at Coleman. He gave me a thumbs-up. If Elisa was alive and there, he was giving me the chance to recover her. I appreciated that.

The hayloft was dark, and the bales of hay were stacked tightly together. Even with light it would be dangerous, but in the dark it was a gauntlet of possible tragedy.

I stopped to listen for any indication of life. There were creaks and groans, the sound of a barn settling on a stormy night. Nothing that would indicate a woman was alive somewhere in the hay.

I tried to think like Tope. Where would he have put her? A million hiding places came to mind. It was a vast area, the size of the entire lower barn. "Elisa?" I called softly.

"You okay?" Coleman called up to me.

"I'm fine. It's just hard to see up here. The hay bales are stacked really tall and the paths between them are hard to find." When I squeezed down one aisle, I felt growing anxiety. The haystacks were tall and musty. Old hay. And if they tumbled, I would be crushed and suffocated. Tope couldn't have picked a more dangerous hiding place.

"Hold on. I've got a Q-Beam in the patrol car. I'll be right back," Coleman offered.

That would help a lot. Until Coleman brought up the flashlight, I'd listen. My ears were far more useful than my eyes right now.

A soft scuttling in the center of the hay caught my attention. Mouse or missing mother? I couldn't be certain. "Elisa?" I called.

Two thuds were the response.

"Get the flashlight. Hurry!" I called down. "I think she's up here. I heard something."

Coleman cleared the loft and flicked on the light. He offered it to me, but I waved him on. He was taller and stronger and could see over some of the stacks. I fell in behind him.

"Elisa?"

Again the two thuds answered him.

"Sounds like it's coming from the center of the hay," he said. Worry laced his voice. "If the hay falls, she could suffocate."

"I know." Stacking hay was an art, and not everyone knew how to do it. I had to wonder why the barn was filled with hay and there were no horses. It didn't make a lot of sense, unless Tope was hoping for a barn fire as an insurance write-off. I didn't put anything past him.

"Elisa?" I called to her. "Make a noise. We're looking for you."

The two thuds came again, closer. We were making progress. I felt a hand on my shoulder. Lydia had joined us.

"Mama," she called out. "It's me, Lydia. Tope is in jail. Are you here?"

This time the thuds were emphatic. Elisa was in the hay

somewhere. We just had to be very careful to find her without starting a hay avalanche. Knowing Tope, he'd booby-trapped her.

"Be still, Elisa," Coleman warned her. "Just stay calm. We'll find you."

We moved through the stacks. The path we followed was a maze. I'd lost all sense of direction, but I was following Lydia, who had fallen in behind Coleman.

"Mama?" Lydia called out.

The thuds were close, just to my left. Coleman held up a hand. "Stay here. I don't want to risk the hay crushing her."

Lydia wanted to rebel, but I put a hand on her shoulder. "He's the tallest and the strongest. Let him do this."

I held her arm as Coleman stepped down a narrow path and disappeared. I held my breath as long as I could, hoping to hear something. But the barn was now silent. It was as if Coleman had stepped into a dark void and disappeared.

"Let's go." Lydia was tired of waiting.

"Wait. Give him a chance. If we rush in and stumble, we could hurt both of them and ourselves."

"Lydia." Coleman's voice was quiet. "Your mom is here. She's alive. Just wait there and I'll bring her out."

"I'm okay, Lydia," Elisa called out. "The sheriff took the tape off my mouth. He's cutting me free. Just wait there. I'm coming."

Lydia fell to her knees, sobbing. I did what I could to comfort her, but the only person who could really soothe her was coming our way. I saw the flashlight beam. In a moment, Lydia was enveloped in her mother's arms. Coleman pulled me to his chest and held me close.

"You did it," he said.

"We did it. All of us." Everyone had pitched in to make

this happen. Tope was in jail, but I couldn't be certain he would stay. Then again, Elisa was alive and could testify against him. That should put the nail in his coffin. No telling how many people Tope had killed. Vivian, maybe the Salters, maybe more. Coleman would drag it out of him.

"You guys okay?" Bethany called up.

"Better than okay," Lydia said, sniffling. "Mom is fine. We're coming down."

I hung back with Coleman and let Lydia and Elisa move to the ladder first. As they descended, loud clapping erupted from my friends. Catcalls, cheers, and whistles made a joyful noise. I inhaled, finally able to draw a full breath. I'd been so nervous I hadn't been able to breathe.

"We're free of Tope forever," Bethany announced. She was jumping the gun a little, but I wasn't going to steal her thunder. Coleman still had a lot of work to do to build a case that would send Tope Maxwell to the state pen.

"All is good," Coleman said. "We still have a lot of loose ends, but today is a good day."

"Yes, it is." I kissed him soundly before I started down the loft ladder.

Millie took the golf cart, along with Cece, Tinkie, and Bethany, so they could retrieve their cars. I had a ride with Coleman. When I opened the truck door, the critters flew inside, jumping into the middle of the seat. Pluto and Sweetie Pie were more than ready to go home. It was almost two a.m. I turned on the heat for the animals, but Coleman and I needed to walk through the house to be sure we hadn't left anything dangerous on if the power returned.

The worst of the storm had passed, but it was still bitter cold and wet. DeWayne and Budgie had returned from depositing Tope in jail, and they drove Elisa and Lydia to the courthouse, where we'd all agreed to meet to clear up the final details of the case.

With Bethany's permission, I called her parents to tell them she was alive and waiting for them at the sheriff's office. I teared up listening to Mrs. Carter's happy sobs. "We're on our way," she said. "Not another hour will pass before I hold my daughter in my arms. Her daddy feels the same way."

That was one worry off my plate. I'd been concerned that the Carters might have some hard feelings, but it looked like they'd turned the corner on whatever judgment they'd held against Bethany. Life was too short to miss a moment with a child or loved one.

Coleman and I took one last tour of the house, making sure everything was turned off and safe. I didn't want the place to catch fire and burn down before Lydia could have the pleasure of moving in or selling it, depending on her future plans.

"What about Vivian Dantzler?" I asked as Coleman slammed the truck door.

He turned the heater down before he answered. "I don't have the physical evidence to charge Tope with murder. I hope to find it. But if I don't, we still have him on kidnapping and shooting a state law officer. The time he'll serve for those will keep him behind bars for decades."

"Will Lydia ever be free of him?" Wondering and waiting for him to eventually be released would be a hard pill to swallow after all the years she'd suffered.

"There's always the chance he'll use his arrogance against the wrong person in prison."

I didn't say it, but that wouldn't be a bad thing. Karma was real and sometimes paid off quickly.

"Let's finish up at the office," Coleman said. "I have a lot of reports to file."

The paperwork of law enforcement was a big hurdle to clear. Coleman and the deputies would be working until daybreak. My car was hidden down one of the woodland trails. "Drive me to my car, please."

"Absolutely. Or you can leave it until tomorrow and I'll bring you back for it."

I would have to clear out the props we'd staged to try to scare Tope. "That sounds like a great plan." I slumped against the passenger door as the heat seeped over me like a warm blanket. I could finally feel my toes again.

The last vestiges of the storm had blown through, and a full moon scudded behind a few lingering clouds. It was a magical night. Justice for Lydia and Elisa hadn't been swift, but it had arrived at last. Lydia and her mother were together, and nothing and no one could come between them again. The victory was bittersweet for me. What I wouldn't give to be in my mother's arms, even for a brief moment.

"Are you okay?" Coleman asked when we were halfway to the courthouse.

"I am. I'm . . . replete."

He laughed. "Not the word I would have chosen."

"I know. But these women will finally be reunited with their families after all this time." I had another thought. "What will Lydia do with her pot farm?"

"That's not a question I can even answer. I'll have to notify the state about it. If she doesn't have the proper certification, it could get messy."

"Maybe Nettie Adams can help with that."

"You mean like get the Lincoln property set up with a state agency as a test plot?"

"Exactly," I said, visualizing for a moment how that could work to everyone's advantage.

"Don't get their hopes up. Let's just see what we can work out with Nettie's help," Coleman said.

"You're a wise, wise man. My lips are zipped."

"That won't last long," Coleman said under his breath, but he gave me a warm smile. "I'll bet I can make you talk."

"I dare you to try."

"As soon as we get home," he promised.

41

The sheriff's office was filled with people when we walked in. Elisa and Lydia were in one corner with the deputies taking their statements. Tinkie, Cece, and Millie were writing their own. The Carters, Bethany's parents, arrived in a whirlwind of tears and proclamations of love. I watched the joyful reunion of another family.

When they were finished writing, Millie and Cece slipped out of the office. Cece had to be at work in a few hours, and Millie said she was heading to the café to get a head start on the morning biscuits. We all agreed to meet for breakfast there. Lydia and Elisa said they'd be there, too.

When the level of noise in the office decreased a little, I could hear someone in the jail hollering and having a conniption fit. Tope was not a happy camper. "Can you stop that noise?" I asked Coleman.

"Not worth the effort," he said. "We're leaving in a few minutes. Let Tope wear himself out."

"He's demanding a phone call," I said.

"Funny, I didn't hear that," Coleman said. "In fact, I didn't hear anything. Did you?" He looked at the deputies.

They shook their heads. "Nope. Quiet as a church tonight. It's time to hit the sack unless you have anything else we need to do."

Coleman shook their hands and waved them out of the sheriff's office. Sweetie Pie and Pluto were curled up next to an electric heater, but the minute Coleman jangled his truck keys, they were on their feet, ready for action.

When I heard Elisa laugh, I realized that Lydia and her mother were still in the sheriff's office. Bethany had gone home with her parents. Lydia and Elisa were tucked into an alcove by the supply closet.

"Hey, time to head for a warm bed," I said to them.

"Not yet," Lydia said. She checked her watch. "There's someone I want you to meet."

"Who would that be?" Coleman asked.

"Give me five more minutes." Lydia's secretive smile hooked me. "You'll be glad."

Coleman took my hand and led me into his office and closed the door. "If this is a prank, I'm going to have to arrest Lydia."

"She has something up her sleeve, but it isn't a prank. I just don't know who could be coming here in the wee hours of the morning that we would want to meet."

"We should know any minute."

Before I could even respond, I heard a cry of joy and I opened the door and stepped out. The first person I saw was the older man from Natchez who'd loaned Lydia and Bethany his truck. I'd suspected all along that he played a bigger role than he'd led me to believe.

"What are you doing here?" I asked him, realizing that a slender woman stood behind him. When she stepped forward, I knew her. "Florence Salter?"

She nodded. "Yes, I am Florence. And this is Ernest, my husband."

"Well, I'll be damned," Coleman said. "You aren't dead."

"Not even a little," Florence said. "But we had to pretend to be. Tope was bird-dogging us and waiting for an opportunity to catch us with some of our clients."

"We did what we had to do to protect Lydia, Bethany, and ourselves," Ernest said. "We didn't want to deceive you or anyone, but lives were at stake."

"You've been helping Lydia all along," I guessed.

"We've tried. If Lydia had heeded my advice, she would have moved to the West Coast, but she didn't want to be too far from her mother. Even if she had to live a rougher life. One in hiding."

I wasn't certain I agreed with Lydia about hiding her presence from her mother, but I had to give her credit for doing everything in her power to keep Elisa safe. Based on Tope's behavior in the last week, I could see where Lydia would feel he was capable of any cruelty or harm. Now, hopefully, he would be safely held in prison for a long time.

"Several families in the area have worried and wondered about you," I said to Ernest. "People you helped in the past. When you disappeared, they didn't know what to think."

Ernest nodded. "I'm glad to be done with hiding and pretending to be someone I'm not. But Lydia and Bethany needed all the help they could get. Me and Florence continued to help folks, as best we could. Florence made potions and effusions and sold them at Four Corners. I'm surprised no one noticed them, but people are in such a hurry, they don't see what's right in front of them."

"Yes, I had a good supply of herbs and roots. I made my tinctures. I helped the sick when I could without giving away who I really was. Natchez is another world from the Delta. It's a river town more connected to New Orleans than Sunflower County. I found work teaching classes in New Orleans on potions and cures. I'd go down on the riverboat to New Orleans to sell my medicines to a little shop in the French Quarter and come back two days later." Florence went to Lydia and put a hand on her shoulder. "I did my best to look out for this one."

"Thank you," Elisa said. "Thank you, Florence and Ernest."

I wasn't upset, but I was still a little flummoxed. "Mr. Salter, you lied to me and Tinkie. Why didn't you tell us the truth?"

"I didn't know if you could be trusted. I knew your folks, Sarah Booth. Good people. But you went off to college and then up north and I didn't know who you might have turned into."

"I told you what I was doing."

"And people lie all the time. What if you'd been hired by Tope Maxwell and I'd told you where to find Lydia? Do you think she'd still be alive?"

He had a point.

"Folks around here thought you were dead," Coleman said. "There's a grave for you, Florence, and stories of Ernest being hanged and burned."

"I know." Ernest was contrite. "Bethany and Lydia started those rumors. Then we left clues to make sure folks believed we were dead and no threat to anyone."

"What about your farm?" I asked.

"We still own it. Been paying the taxes every year."

I wanted to slap my forehead. I should have looked at the tax records. Someone had to pay them, or the county would've taken the property and sold it. I hadn't had my thinking cap on.

"What are you going to do now, Lydia?" Ernest asked her. "Will you sell that house or reclaim it as your own?"

"I'm moving into my house," Lydia said. "I designed it and paid for it, and I'm going to live there and enjoy it. I'm going to build a place for you and Florence. If you want to sell the farm, you can bank the money. I have plenty of good land you can farm. If that's what you want."

It was a generous offer, but Florence and Ernest had some issues to settle. Like, what about some of the women who were listed as missing? I looked at Coleman.

"Have you ever helped young women leave the state?" Coleman asked.

"On occasion," Ernest said. "When there was no other choice. When there was abuse or violence and no chance of protecting them. We'd give them money to relocate and start over."

"The girls who took your help to leave, do you ever hear from them?" Coleman asked. "If they're listed as missing persons, we need to clear it up."

"We did when we lived in Sunflower County, but when

we decided we had to die, we lost touch with everyone except Lydia and Bethany. We worked together to help as many people as we could. But I have a list of all the women who pretended to disappear. I'd love to help find them and reconnect them with their old lives. Times have changed now."

Ernest looked hard at Coleman. "What's going to happen to Lydia and Bethany about the marijuana production?"

"They're working to get a cooperative deal with one of the universities to grow organic medical marijuana. If that comes through, no one will have a problem. If it doesn't, we'll have to figure it out at that time."

Ernest nodded. "Thank you."

"Medical marijuana can help people," Coleman said. "I don't have any issues with it."

"Maybe the world is changing," Ernest said. "Wouldn't that be a good thing?"

"Yes." I knew the answer. "Now I'm about to fall over. I need to go home and get some rest. Sweetie Pie and Pluto are starving." I checked my watch. It was almost six in the morning. Millie's Café would be open in another few minutes. "Let's go to Millie's and have that breakfast we talked about."

"An excellent idea," Elisa said. "I'm starving, too."

There were plenty of things to do—cleaning up Lydia's house being at the top of my list—but after Coleman tanked down a pot of coffee and left for work, the critters and I settled on the front porch of Dahlia House. The blue, blue sky stretched to the horizon. The fallow fields rested, waiting for seed and fertilizer. Growing things was what the Delta was all about.

I'd fed the horses breakfast, but lethargy tugged at my limbs. Tinkie was on her way to pick me up to drive me to Lydia's house. We had to retrieve our props and put things to order. Retrieving my car was also on the list. But the warm winter sunshine felt so wonderful that I stretched my legs out and let the rays soak into me through my jeans. I'd almost nodded off when a flurry of motion made me open my eyes and sit up.

The raven was on the edge of the porch. It gave a "croak-croak," watching me with bright black eyes. He was a big fellow, with an impressive beak—not as refined as the crows I saw every day. I wondered if he'd escaped. Maybe he'd been a pet and needed help.

"What's your name?" I asked, earning a disgusted huff from Sweetie Pie. She wasn't impressed with the bird.

"Poe."

Now I was wide awake. "As in Edgar Allan?"

"Poe." He made a whistling sound that was almost a song. "'Nevermore.'"

I got up and walked over to sit beside him. The bird had no fear of me at all. He had to have been someone's pet. I offered him an arm for a perch, and he hopped right on it. "Poe?"

"'Nevermore.'"

It wasn't exactly a conversation, but the bird was able to express a lot with his limited vocabulary. He'd obviously belonged to a big reader of Poe. "'Annabel Lee.'"

"'Lenore.'"

"'Sepulcher.'"

"'By the sea.'"

"'Lenore.'"

"'Nevermore.'"

"Do you want to live here?" I asked. I could see the bird living at Dahlia House. He could come inside with us or live in the barn where he'd be protected from bad weather. I'd have to talk with my veterinarian about diet and care, but it wouldn't be a hardship for me.

"The door."

He'd said that earlier, but it hadn't panned out to be a clue that I could use.

"The door," he insisted.

I frowned and turned around to look at the front door of Dahlia House. I gasped and stood up. A man was standing in the doorway. He was mostly a shadow but was somehow familiar.

Edgar Allan Poe stepped out into the sunshine.

"You never appear as the same person twice," I said to Jitty. "What gives?"

She lifted her hand, and the bird flew over and settled on it, then hopped to her shoulder. It was a perfect image of Poe and the raven. If only I had my phone. Then it occurred to me that neither might show up in the photo. Poe was my haint, and the bird? Was he from the spirit world? Had I been talking to a ghost raven all along?

"Jitty, why are you here as Poe again?"

"Answer the phone. You'll understand."

Right on cue, the phone rang.

I answered to find Madame Tomeeka on the other end. "I had that terrible dream again. The beating heart, the blue vulture eye at the window."

I didn't understand. I thought we'd resolved the whole issue of "The Tell-Tale Heart." Lydia had been found. It was over. And, happily, I might add, it was going to end with Tope being tried and convicted.

"I just talked to Doc Sawyer," Tammy said. "I wanted you to be the first to know. He has forensic evidence to prove that Tope killed Vivian. Tope will be on death row."

The whole time I was talking to Tammy I was watching Jitty and the bird. I observed that a raven could look extremely satisfied. Not to mention Mr. Poe/Jitty.

"Justice will be served, Tammy. And it's all due to you. You put the ball in motion."

"I'm just glad we found Elisa and Lydia alive and safe."

"Me, too."

"Elisa wrote me a check for ten thousand dollars." Tammy sounded a little flustered at this turn of events.

"You earned it. That performance last night. It was perfection."

"I'm going to put a down payment on a house in Zinnia for Dahlia."

"I love this," I told her. Her daughter, named for my home, would always have a place in the Delta where her husband drew inspiration for his music.

"He got a job with the band at Playin' the Bones. Scott hired him."

Tammy was just full of good news. It was a tonic to my slacking body. It was time to move, to finish up this case. I had a sudden yen to cook something for Coleman and the deputies. I owed everyone a lot.

"I'm thrilled for all of you, Tammy."

"Gotta go. A client is coming in."

The line went dead, and I was left staring at Poe and the raven. "Did you engineer that?" I asked.

Poe shrugged. "'I became insane, with long intervals of horrible sanity.'"

"'Quoth the raven, "Nevermore,"'" I added.

"'Nevermore,'" the bird said. He flew from Jitty's shoulder to mine just as a clock somewhere struck the tones of midnight and Poe disappeared and returned as Jitty. She was wearing my favorite sweatsuit and sneakers.

"Another case resolved, Sarah Booth. You done big."

"I had a little help from my friends."

"Let's go inside and play some of those old Beatles albums your mama loved so much. We all need a little help from our friends at times."

It was a perfect solution to pass the time until Tinkie arrived to whisk me away to work. The raven remained on my shoulder as I went inside the house, Sweetie Pie and Pluto following me. We'd just added a new family member, and one that promised lots of antics.

Acknowledgments

There are so many people involved in the creation of a book, and all are due thanks. My editor, Hannah O'Grady, and copyeditor, Lisa Davis, are top of the line at what they do. My books are always better for the work they give them.

Kudos to my agent, Marian Young. And special thanks to my niece, Jennifer Haines Welch, who is my first-round editor before I turn the book in.

Many thanks to the art department for the fun and colorful covers, the interior design, and the fact that my book becomes a physical entity on bookstore shelves. Thanks to the booksellers and librarians who recommend my books, too.

And a million thanks to the readers who have come to

care about Sarah Booth and the Zinnia gang as much as I do. Writing is my love, something I am so incredibly lucky to be able to do for a living. Caring for the stray animals is my mission; how remarkable that I've been able to build a life where one feeds the other.